Previously published by Doug Lalli
PETER AND BETH

"A fast-paced novel, *Peter and Beth* immediately draws you in and holds your interest, from Peter's first meeting with his unconventional psychotherapist to the very end."
—*TCM Reviews*

"Doug Lalli [has written] this novel with great sensitivity and insight . . . Nothing should deter you from opening this book and reading through to its surprising conclusion. A wonderful first novel!"
—*Curled Up With A Good Book*

"Lalli's first novel is relatively short, but it does not short-change readers. It's easy to get caught up in Peter's quest."
—*Pioneer Press*

"Intriguing . . . a MUST READ!"
—*Bette Corbin Tucker, IP Book Reviewer*

"An introspective and illuminating novel with a voice and style all its own."
—*John Mella, author of* Transformations

"A spare but powerful novel . . . deeply affecting."
—*Michael James, author of* Cloud Gazing

Swimming Across the Hudson

Doug Lalli (signature)

DouglalliJazz@gmail.com

Swimming Across the Hudson

Published by Wheatmark®
2030 East Speedway Boulevard, Suite 106
Tucson, Arizona 85719 USA
www.wheatmark.com

ISBN: 979-8-88747-205-8 (paperback)
LCCN: 2024908688

Bulk ordering discounts are available through Wheatmark, Inc.
For more information, email orders@wheatmark.com
or call 1-888-934-0888.

AUTHOR'S NOTE

In 2006, Hats Off Books published my first novel, *Peter and Beth*. A few years later I completed its sequel, *Dying or Going to Europe*. Before long it occurred to me to combine the two novels into a single novel. I started by changing the names Peter to Alan and Beth to Brooke. Then I reenvisioned the story, making substantial changes which included eliminating a subplot from each of the two novels. The result is *Swimming Across the Hudson*, a literary novel of just over 77,000 words.

Doug Lalli, 2024

To Wendy and Jeff and Lily
And, of course, to Kevin

Swimming Across the Hudson

a novel

Doug Lalli

In anguish or madness or power and glory,
we each get to live out our singular story.

Part I

1

It's surprising to see snow on the streets of Manhattan in early November. "Surprising," though, is not "shocking." Shocking is when you look up and suddenly there's someone you haven't seen in years and a flood of emotions comes rushing in. He glances at his watch. No time to dwell on this, he says to himself, and he rushes down Seventy-ninth Street.

A minute later, still reeling from what he saw, he enters the building and walks into the lobby. The elevator is staring him in the face but he decides to take the stairs, hoping the two flights will give him time to pull himself together. Some seconds later, slightly winded but no less disoriented, he rings the buzzer to 2-G. After an extended silence he reaches into his back pocket to check the apartment number, but then there are footsteps. In the next moment the door opens to reveal a statuesque black woman, early forties probably.

"I'm Alan Agnalini," he says. "I have a seven-thirty appointment with Dr. Millstein."

"Come in," the woman says. "I'm Dr. Millstein."

In response to his surprise, which evidently he wasn't quick enough on his feet to hide, she adds, "I know. I don't look Jewish."

She leads Alan down a hall into a fairly large room. Considering that the woman is impeccably dressed, he's surprised to see that her office has an almost slapdash quality to it.

"Sit down," she says, pointing to one of the two black leather armchairs that sit opposite each other toward the back of the room.

He looks around, trying to get his bearings. "You mean you don't want me to lie on the couch?" he says, eyeing an oversize sofa that monopolizes one wall.

"Couches are for psychoanalysis. I don't do psychoanalysis. What I do here is quite different, but you'll learn that."

Alan waits for her to sit, not only so that he can do the same but also because he always feels awkward standing across from a woman who has a couple of inches on him.

"Please," she says, indicating his chair and sinking into her own.

They're eyeball to eyeball now, squared off in identical armchairs, but he tells himself that she's the one with all the power.

"By the way," she says, "you can call me Rhonda. All my patients do."

She wants him to call her by her first name?

"Don't worry," she adds as if she's read his mind, "you'll get used to it. Now, tell me. What brings you here?"

Alan has prepared a whole speech, but now he draws a blank.

"I don't know where to begin," he says finally.

"Begin with what you're feeling right now."

She wants to know what he's feeling? And all this time he thought therapy was supposed to be about rehashing your miserable childhood and bitching and moaning about all the people who screwed you over. He remains silent, and feels for a moment like a three-year-old, controlling the world with a simple refusal to comply.

"Does this make you uncomfortable?" she asks.

"No," Alan is quick to answer. "I'm just not in the habit of thinking about how I feel."

"And you resent my request."

"Resent? I don't think resent—"

"Then what? What word describes how you feel right now?"

"Put upon?" he says.

"Angry?" she says.

He looks down at his lap, for lack of anywhere else to look, and becomes aware that he's tapping his hand on his knee. "I don't know about angry," he says, "but agitated seems right."

"Angry, good. You're starting to own your feelings."

When Alan says nothing, Dr. Millstein—that is, Rhonda—continues. "Let me explain something. Therapy, contrary to what you may have thought, is more than the exploration of past hurts and grievances. That approach belongs to the old school. I sense you're upset about something, and my guess is that it has in part to do with your expectations."

"Expectations?"

"Let me ask you something, Alan. If I said, 'Okay, tell me about your childhood,' how would that make you feel?"

"Better."

"Because you had a rotten childhood and you came here prepared to tell me all about it."

He feels almost vindicated.

"Don't worry, you'll get your chance," she says. "Therapy is a process, and it's not haphazard. Before we can explore your past and how it may be relevant to your present, we need to establish a rapport, you and I. You need to trust me."

Trust her? He doesn't trust anybody.

"It requires a leap of faith," she says.

"I don't follow."

"You give the person the benefit of the doubt. You assume that the person isn't out to get you. That he or she is, in fact, a friend."

Here's an alien concept.

"But how can you trust people," he says, "when you don't trust people?"

"It can be difficult, especially when you've been hurt repeatedly, as you obviously have been. But the therapeutic setting is the perfect place to start."

She leans forward slightly, and to Alan's surprise he doesn't feel himself drawing back from her.

"You should know, Alan, that there are no right or wrong answers here. You're free to say whatever comes to mind at any time, and I won't judge you. My job, part of my job, is to provide a safe haven for you, so to speak. To be a sounding board."

"And everything is confidential," he says, although he doesn't really care about confidentiality.

"One hundred percent confidential. You're free to open up in a way, I'm guessing, that you never have with another person."

Alan looks down at his watch without registering the numbers. Is it true he never opened up to another person? There was Burt, back in high school, but that was a while ago.

He glances at his watch again. It seems as if he's been sitting here for two hours, when in fact they're not all that far into the session. Now he looks up and meets the woman's eyes, then quickly looks away. He waits for her to say something but apparently she's shifted into some kind of cat-and-mouse game.

"Let me clarify something," she says at length. "Just as there are no right or wrong answers here, there are no right or wrong responses of any kind. Short of violence, of course. By that I mean, if you need to fidget or tap your fingers or look at your watch—whatever you need, it's acceptable here. It's part of the process, and it yields information."

"Information?"

"Information. About you. We're more than our words, Alan. I'm certain you're aware of that."

Now he really feels naked. She's picking apart every move he makes. He has an impulse to run out of the room, to run back on the street—and then he thinks of Brooke.

"What was *that?*" Rhonda says.

"What was what?"

"I don't know, you gave a start, a movement. As if a thought had occurred to you."

"It's nothing," he says. "I was just thinking of something that happened before I came here."

"Why don't you tell me about it."

"There's nothing much to tell," Alan says. "I saw this woman out on the street that I haven't seen in . . . I'd say, about five years. And I guess it surprised me."

"And you talked to her?"

"No, she was getting on a crosstown bus. I saw her from a distance."

"And you're sure it was the woman you're thinking of? It's dark out, maybe you were mistaken."

"There's a streetlight where the bus pulled up," he says. "It was definitely her, but that's the thing—she looked really different."

"And that's what surprised you, more than just seeing her out of the blue?"

"I suppose . . . No, it was probably a combination of the two things."

He waits for Rhonda to say something else, but she seems puzzled.

"It's not my place to pry," she says finally, "but I sense there's a significance to all this. What's the significance?"

"Isn't it your job to tell me?"

He's aware that his remark probably sounded hostile, but then he remembers what she said. That there are no right or wrong responses.

She smiles. "My job is multifaceted. But in this case, no, it's not my job to interpret the situation. The situation, remember, has meaning for *you*, Alan. It's important that you be the one to interpret it."

He thinks about this. Why did seeing Brooke unnerve him so?

"I think it was the way she looked," he says.

"Yes?" Rhonda says, as in *Go on . . .*

"This woman—Brooke, by the way, is her name—well, she used to be kind of . . . I guess you could say, unkempt. She's pretty tall—not as tall as you but kind of tall for a woman—and she used to slouch and she never washed her hair, it seemed. She was just kind of . . . Not slovenly exactly, just unkempt. But she was very sweet."

"And now?"

"You mean, what does she look like now? She looks really different. Good."

"Attractive."

"Very. I mean, compared to what she was. I guess for

some reason she finally decided that making the most of her appearance is worth the effort."

Again Rhonda leans toward him. She seems to be intensely interested in what Alan is saying, and in a way, it's a heady experience for him.

"Let me ask you something," she says now. "Or let me speculate. This woman, Brooke—she wasn't a casual acquaintance."

"No, we were friends."

"Just friends, or more than that?"

"No, just friends, pretty much?"

"Pretty much?"

Alan instinctively recoils from the cross-examination but finds himself answering the question. "We'd become good friends," he says, "but then we made the mistake of sleeping together."

"I see," she says, jotting something down in her notebook. "Multiple times?"

"No, one did the trick."

"You mean, one time was all it took to undermine your friendship in some way?"

"Undermine?" he says. "Destroy, is more like it."

He watches her write something else in her notebook. Then she looks up. "No reconciliation of any sort?"

"No, I'm afraid it ended pretty badly."

Rhonda says nothing, choosing instead to observe Alan as if he's some kind of specimen in a biology lab. For his part, he prefers her scrutiny to any further questions she might have about Brooke.

"I'm not going to grill you about the particulars," she says finally. "That's your business. My concern is that this woman, this Brooke . . . You say you haven't seen her in five years?"

"Actually, it's more like five and a half. This was back in college—1969, my senior year."

"And there's been no contact since then?"

"None."

"Yet she still gets to you."

"She does?"

"Doesn't she?"

Now he actually gets to his feet but quickly pushes himself back down into his chair.

"It's best not to move around, Alan. It distracts you from what you're feeling. And remember. What you're feeling is what will ultimately make you better."

He's confused. "But I thought you said it's okay to fidget?"

"You're right, I said that, but I need to qualify my statement. Physical movement is acceptable, but within limits. Gross physical movement—like getting up and pacing the room, for instance—that's counterproductive."

"Actually, I was thinking of bolting altogether."

"Even more counterproductive."

They laugh in tandem—just a joint chuckle, but it scares the shit out of him.

Now it's her turn to look at her watch, a gesture that has the effect of deflating him somehow. Then she says, "Whatever it is, Alan—it doesn't have to come out today. Or ever.

If it's truly insignificant, then I apologize for wasting your time."

Alan looks up at her and, for the first time, he's able to discern a professional distance. This woman is not his mother, and she's not about to lose sleep if he withholds his secret from her for another week.

"You're not wasting my time," he says. "The fact is, I might have gotten Brooke pregnant. For all I know, I could be the father of quintuplets."

2

"What are you working on, Alan?"

He looks across his desk at Rick, who's looking across his desk at him. They spend half their lives looking at each other.

"*Advances in Electron Microscopy*," Alan says. "Bruno Koenigsmann, PhD."

"Bruno's a PhD now? Last time I saw him he was selling hashish out of the back of his '57 Chevy Bel-Air."

Rick and Alan are opposites in many ways—for instance, Rick is tall and Nordic while Alan is short and decidedly un-Nordic—but he's one of the few reasons Alan has been able to keep his sanity at Spaniel. He's been working at Spaniel Publishing for nearly two years now and, in that time, has gone from a direct-mail writer making eleven thousand dollars a year to a direct-mail writer making slightly more than that. He keeps telling himself that his real interest lies elsewhere. He just doesn't know *where* elsewhere.

His phone rings.

"Maybe that's Bruno himself," Rick says.

"I'll give him your regards," Alan says, then into the phone: "Alan Agnalini." He listens for a few seconds. "Okay, I'll be right in."

"Who was that?" Rick asks when Alan hangs up.

"Jim. He wants to see me in his office."

Rick considers this. "Been screwing up lately?"

"Not that I know of," Alan says, wondering if his profound boredom has begun to have an adverse effect on his work.

He walks down the hall and half-knocks on Jim's half-open door.

"Come in, Alan."

Jim Tate, ruddy and slightly overweight, is sitting behind his desk. "Sit down," he says, indicating the underling's chair across the desk from him.

He stands now and steps across the room to the door. The sound of it closing is like the clank of a jail-cell door, yet Alan hasn't done anything wrong, has he?

Jim eases himself back into his chair, in no apparent hurry to talk. Finally he says, "You know I'm leaving Spaniel in a month, right?"

"I hadn't heard that," Alan says.

"The commute got to be too much for me. Just getting to the train in Westport takes me twenty-five minutes, and then it's another hour to Grand Central. But I got lucky. I found something ten minutes from the house. It'll give me a lot more time with the kids."

Alan wants to say *Mazel tov*, but figures Jim wouldn't know whether he's been blessed or cursed. He merely nods.

"That's where you come in," Jim says.

"Me?"

"I've been very impressed with your work, Alan. You're a bright guy. I know direct-mail writing isn't the most glamorous profession in the world, but you're good at it."

He pauses here, perhaps waiting for a thank you, but just as Alan is about to comply Jim adds, "If you're interested I'd like to groom you to take over for me."

What!?

"As marketing manager?" Alan says.

"Why not?" Jim leans back in his chair. "You have the basic tools for the job. You're organized, intelligent . . . To tell you the truth, that's about all it takes. And it's a career opportunity."

It's like being wooed by your best friend's little sister; the idea of it is flattering but the reality merely annoying.

"I never really thought of myself as a sales kind of person," Alan says.

"There's no sales, not in the way you mean. You just have to stay on top of things and play with the numbers."

"I'm not very mathematical."

Jim leans back again and appears to scrutinize Alan. "You've always been a tough one to read, Alan. I can't tell if you're just not interested in the job or if you think maybe you couldn't handle it."

"To be honest, this comes as a complete surprise. It's not anything I've thought about."

"No biggie."

Alan watches as Jim gets to his feet and takes a step from his desk to the window behind it, then peers down at Bryant Park. Things could be worse, certainly, than to have a job where you get to look out your window at the comings and goings in Bryant Park. Especially at lunchtime, when all the women are out. But the idea of becoming a middle management flunky—it's the kind of thing Alan would do only at gunpoint. And then only if the pay was good.

"Take a few days to think it over," Jim says, turning back to him. "Don't get me wrong, I'm not trying to force you into anything. I just thought you might be interested in the opportunity."

"Oh, I am," Alan says, somehow convinced that he's doing Jim a favor by postponing his refusal. "I just need some time to think about it."

They're walking to the door now, and it seems to Alan that if Jim could, he would retract his offer on the spot.

"The prodigal son returns," Rick says as Alan walks back into the office and sits down.

Rick has talked repeatedly about how he has designs on Jim's job. *I'm not going to be a copywriter forever*, he's been saying. *Sitting in a big office running the show is more like it. And then when the time's right I'll move on to greener pastures, like Macmillan or Random House.*

And now Alan has been offered the job Rick covets. He has zero interest in it, but, irrationally, he feels like a thief.

"So I take it you haven't been canned," Rick says.

"No, I'm still in one piece."

He opens his folder on the Koenigsmann book, hoping Rick will do the same with whatever he's working on.

"So what did he want?"

"Who, Jim?"

"No—his brother-in-law."

"Nothing really. He just wanted to compliment me on that space ad I did last month in the *Journal of Molecular Biology*. You know, he has to keep morale up."

"It's about time he started doing some of that stuff. Jim knows his job, but he doesn't know how to handle people. If I had his job—*when* I have his job—I'm going to let everyone leave at four o'clock on Friday. If you cut people a little slack they work harder for you and they don't even realize it."

Alan needs to steer Rick onto another topic and he knows just how to do it, although he's aware there'll be a price to pay. "How's Sally?" he says.

"Sally's great," Rick chirps. "She's always great."

"And Emily? Doesn't she have a birthday coming up?"

"Next month. She'll be four."

"Four, that's amazing," Alan says. "I remember when she was just learning to talk. It seems like two weeks ago."

"No, she'll be four next month."

Rick is smiling to himself now—basking in the joys of fatherhood, the joys of a happy family life. And *that*—the happy-family-life speech—is the price Alan knows he'll begin to pay momentarily.

Hoping that something, perhaps another phone call, might distract Rick, Alan makes a show of getting back to work.

> Dr. Koenigsmann [he reads] was a Fellow at the University of Bonn from 1951 to 1953, during which time he published extensively in journals both in Germany and—

"You know, Alan"—here it comes—"you're not getting any younger. You should think about settling down, finding a woman who can make you happy."

Rick has been spewing variations of this speech for the last three weeks. Almost from the moment Alan handed his apartment key back to Claire. He takes a breath now and launches into his standard defense.

"Rick, give me a break, man. I haven't even been separated a month and you've already got me married."

"I'm not trying to get you married," Rick says. "I'm just saying you're not getting any younger. Before you know it you'll be thirty."

"Not for another few years. Besides, what's the big deal about thirty?"

Rick looks at Alan as if the answer is self-evident. "What's the big deal? When you turn thirty, Alan, you're not a kid anymore. *That's* the big deal. Remember last year when *I* turned thirty? I was depressed about it for days."

"Yes, I remember that. You actually got some work done for a change."

"Very funny," Rick says. "But all I'm saying is, it's never too soon to look. You never know who's out there unless you keep your eyes open. And a good-looking guy like you? Shouldn't be a problem. Chicks dig those dark, Mediterranean types, you know."

"You sound like one of my aunts."

"Which one?"

"All of them."

Rick is undaunted by the comparison. "Your aunts have your best interest at heart. You're not the kind of person who should be alone, Alan. I'm serious. I know you didn't have an easy time of it with Claire, it's never a good thing when a marriage doesn't work out. But you've got a second chance now. You don't want to blow it."

"I just need some time to get my head screwed back on," Alan says, feeling somehow like a liar.

Rick turns back to his typewriter but for only a moment. "You know what your problem is?" he says. "You read too much poetry."

"I don't read poetry."

"Well, you think like a person who reads poetry. You're a romantic. It's your tragic flaw."

"You mean I have only one?" Alan says.

Rick ignores this remark and turns to one of his folders. "It's not my life," he says under his breath, and he actually seems a little pissed. (His passion about married life—his passion in general—is one of the reasons Alan likes him.)

"We'll see what happens in a couple of weeks," Rick adds, looking up from the folder.

"What's in a couple of weeks?"

"The Christmas party."

"Oh, right," Alan says.

Rick undoubtedly has more to say on this score, but now the door opens and Grace Maiser, the gadfly of the copy department, if not of the entire company, flits into the room.

"You two boys getting any work done?" she says.

"Something like that," Rick mumbles.

"Alan, could we have a little chat?" Grace says.

"Sure."

He waits for her to begin but she says nothing. Then she glances over at Rick as if waiting for him to vacate the room so that she and Alan can have their little chat. Rick, who's clearly aware of her agenda, doesn't budge.

"Why don't we go out in the hall?" Alan says to Grace.

Out in the hall (the big one, by the elevators) Grace flashes him a cheesy smile. "I have a favor to ask you, Alan. I have to do this copy test for this job I'm interviewing for, and I wanted to know if you would write it for me."

Write it for her? Is she serious?

"You're such a good writer," she continues, "that I'd be sure to get the job if you could just write it for me."

Alan scrambles for a tactful way to tell her to go fuck herself. Then it occurs to him that if she were good-looking—and significantly less obnoxious—he would jump at the chance. What kind of hypocrite does that make him?

"I don't know," he says. "Ethically I would have a problem with that."

"Oh, I don't care about ethics. I just want the job."

"Actually, it's *my* ethics I was thinking about."

"No problem," she says, slipping into defense mode. "Just thought I'd ask." She begins to turn away.

"I'll tell you what," Alan says. "You write the first draft and I'll edit it for you."

Her face falls another centimeter in response to this suggestion. "Sure Alan, thanks. I might take you up on that."

This is turning out to be an interesting day. First Alan is singled out by the boss, then he's solicited by the company pest. He supposes he should be grateful his work is getting some recognition, but it makes him feel even worse than usual; being a star among a bunch of benchwarmers is not what he had in mind for himself.

"What did that one want?" Rick says when Alan gets back to the office.

"She has to do a copy test for some job interview. She wanted me to write it for her."

"To write it for her? For free?"

"No mention of any money."

"Where does she get off!?"

"Not at *my* stop," Alan says.

"Fuck her."

"I don't want to fuck her, you fuck her."

"I don't want to fuck her," Rick says, "but I've got this *really horny* cousin who'd probably consider it."

Rick leaves at the dot of five—a strange practice considering he's bucking for a promotion. Alan stays behind a few minutes to finish the bio he's working on. And then? . . . Chinese takeout again?

3

It's Saturday now—four days since Alan's session with Rhonda. He's standing in front of Gus's International Coffee Shop in downtown Fort Lee, New Jersey, waiting for Mike. They were supposed to meet at noon, but it's going on twenty after. Maybe Mike is having trouble finding a parking space big enough for his new Olds Cutlass. Or maybe he's just driving around the streets of Fort Lee so that people can ogle at it.

Alan is getting cold and considers going inside to wait. Then he notices an attractive woman coming out of a dress shop on the other side of Lemoine Avenue. Since she's not only attractive but tall as well, he immediately thinks of Brooke. In fact, he's been thinking of Brooke on and off ever since he saw her on the street a few days ago. In the last five years he'd pretty much put to rest the idea that she may have had his child, but now the idea is back. He doesn't know what to make of it and has been trying not to think about it. Then he'll see some tall woman, or someone who otherwise looks something like Brooke, and there it is again: the idea, staring him down.

"Alan!"

There's no mistaking that bellow. Alan looks up and spots Mike walking toward him. For a sixty-three-year-old man who's survived two heart attacks and a bout with prostate cancer, he looks remarkably robust.

"Sorry I was late," Mike says. "There was an accident on Route 4. The traffic was backed up it seemed like half a mile."

"You're looking good, Dad," Alan says, happy to see Mike in spite of himself.

Inside they find a booth and settle in.

"I'll take you for a spin around the block after lunch," Mike says. "It rides like a dream, the Olds."

They each pick up their menu and for a minute use it as a shield against the awkwardness of having nothing much to say to each other.

"What're you having," Mike says finally.

Alan gives his menu another glance. "I think I'll have an omelet," he says. "Western."

"Have anything you want. Have a steak sangwich if you're hungry, they make good steak sangwiches here."

"No, I think an omelet would be about right."

"I think I'll have the roast beef *au jus.*"

He's pronounced the French words with a certain disdain, as if to imply that the French are impostors who developed a language of their own just to torment people like him.

A waiter comes by and takes their orders.

"So how you been doing?" Mike says now.

"I've been pretty busy."

"The job keeps you on your toes, right?"

The job bores the shit out of me, Alan would like to say.

"You know how it is," he says. "Writing junk mail isn't the most challenging thing in the world, but I guess I'm surviving."

Mike takes a sip of water. "I never understood how come you gave up the job at the college. You woulda been a professor by now, no?"

They've been over this same ground many times, but two years of fielding Mike's questions haven't stopped them from coming.

"No," Alan says, "it would've been a while before I became a full professor."

"Still, it seems like you gave up a good thing."

"You're right, I did. In some ways it was good, but in other ways it wasn't."

"But anyways, at least you got that friend at your job— what's his name, Nick?"

"Rick."

"Rick. At least you got him to talk to. Makes the day go by, right?"

"I guess," Alan says, but Mike is right; even though Rick can be a bit long-winded at times, having him sitting across the desk does make the day go a little faster.

"By the way, Alan, I meant to tell you. I was in town the other day and I ran into Mr. . . . . I forget his last name, the father of that boy from the neighborhood that got killed in Vietnam."

"Ken Machelot."

"His name was Ken, that boy? I thought it was Ben. Anyways, I didn't know what to say to the father. Having your son go over there and get blown to bits . . . That ain't something you can put behind you."

"It was rough on all of us, when we found out."

"But you was lucky, Alan. First the student deferment and then the high lottery number. That other kid wasn't so lucky."

The waiter appears with a basket of dinner rolls and Mike grabs one and takes a bite. "Yeah, that was sad," he says now. "But I was wondering about your friend from work. Rick. I remember one time you said he's Swedish, right?"

"Right," Alan says, not surprised that Mike has remembered this little detail.

"You remember, Alan, we had that Swedish family around the corner from us? What was their name? Nelson, was it?"

"Nilsson," Alan says.

"Right, that sounds familiar. I used to talk to the father once in a while—Lars his name was, I think. But they're okay, the Swedish, I guess. But they musta felt outa place in our neighborhood, don't you think? We was all Italian and Irish but mostly Italian, and then they come along—"

"So Dad, you like the new job?"

Mike seems taken aback by Alan's attempt to steer the conversation in a different direction.

"The job?" Mike says. "Couldn't be happier. And it's only fifteen minutes from the house. I used to have that long commute before, this makes my life a lot easier."

"That's good," Alan says before an extended silence overtakes them.

Finally Mike says, "So you getting used to living alone again?"

"We were alone even when we were together," Alan says, surprised that he's disclosed to Mike what he normally would reserve for Rick. Or for no one.

"It's a shame," Mike says. "She wasn't a bad girl, Claire. She had her good points. Though you gotta admit the two a you rushed into it. It never seemed right to me, the two a you. I bet you never woulda married her if youda known her longer."

"What can I say, we were young and in love."

"I know how that can be. But at least you had the sense not to have any kids."

"We were too busy fighting."

Mike gnaws on his roll for a second. Then he says, "But that's water under the bridge. You did the right thing, splitting up."

After another minute the waiter arrives with their orders.

"This is delicious," Mike says, making kind of a mess with the *jus*. "You wanna try some, Alan?"

"No, this is fine."

For a few moments Mike focuses on his sandwich. Then he says, "You still parking your car out here near Grandma's?"

"I was, until a couple of weeks ago. It's next to impossible finding a parking space in Manhattan, but it's even more of a hassle going all the way out to Fort Lee every time I need the car."

"Yeah, I suppose," Mike says. "But if you lived in Jersey you wouldn't have that problem. You can always find a parking spot in Jersey. And Weehawken, where Ralph used to live? Five minutes on the bus to New York. Hoboken the same. And if you wanted to move down to Jersey City—"

"Dad," Alan says. "I'm fine. I like living in Manhattan, it's exciting."

"Exciting, sure. But is it safe?"

"That's what you said when Claire and I moved near Lincoln Center. Most neighborhoods in Manhattan are safe. My neighborhood is okay. There's nothing to worry about."

"Well," Mike says, "you're a big boy. You can take care a yourself."

Alan can tell from the expression on Mike's face that he isn't entirely convinced of this. Or maybe he' just having a hard time accepting the idea that his son is no longer a little boy—not to mention the concomitant idea that he himself is getting to be an old man.

"Where'd you say you live? West Eighty-third Street?"

"*East* Eighty-third," Alan says. "About a block and a half from the East River."

"The East River, I don't know that area. . . . Anyways, it's none a my business. You're a big boy, like I said. You know what's best for your life."

Alan watches now as Mike returns to his meal, a slightly

smaller man than the one who tried, a minute ago, to assert some parental clout. "Good," he says a few times, indicating the food that's vanishing before him.

They eat in silence for a while and then Mike says, "I guess you're wondering why I asked you here, huh?"

Alan looks across at him. It's scary, sometimes, how much alike they look. But for Mike's leathery features and graying hair and the beginning of jowls, they could be mistaken for twins. Sometimes it's hard for Alan to look into Mike's eyes (they have that same doe-like innocence as his own) and remember that for years he despised the man. Not that Mike has atoned for his sins. Just that Alan is too old for hate. He doesn't know what he feels for Mike now, but it isn't hate.

"You don't need an excuse to take me out to lunch," Alan says now, although he does wonder what's up with Mike.

"No, I don't need an excuse, but there's something I wanted to ask you. About Dolly."

"What about her?"

Mike hesitates and seems embarrassed, which is not typical of him. Then he says, "I been thinking a asking her to marry me."

Alan smiles, though he isn't sure why, considering how much he loathes Dolly. Or more to the point, how much she loathes him. "Really?" he says. "I didn't know you were that serious, but that's great! Congratulations!"

"Except I'm not gonna ask her unless I have your permission."

His permission?

"You don't need my permission," Alan says.

"But I want it."

"Okay," the son says, feeling a little silly. "You have my permission."

"Good, cause I think she'll make me a good wife. She's a good woman in her way. She's got her faults—who don't—but she'll do right by me, I know it."

"That's great, Dad," Alan says, starting to get into the swing of this sudden role reversal.

Mike takes the remaining bite of his sandwich. "She'll never replace your mother, of course." He winces—doubtless at the image of his wife he evoked in his mind's eye—and then gamely, Alan would say, seems to shake off the pain.

"Your mother was one of a kind," Mike continues, "but the past is past. You can't live in the past, so I'm moving on."

"Good," Alan says again, not knowing what else to say.

"And I'd like for you to be my best man."

Mike has tossed off these words with his eyes plastered somewhere on the wall in back of his son.

"Sure," Alan says. "I'd be honored to. But what about Ralph?"

If he'd stopped for a moment to consider the question, he never would have asked it. Regardless of what went down in the past, he couldn't expect that Mike would insult his own son by asking Ralph Passacantando to be best man.

"Ralph?" Mike says. "He don't come around no more. He's got his own life, he don't need me. He's lucky if he calls his mother once a month."

"I guess he's too busy conquering the world," Alan says, unable to resist an opportunity to get a shot in at Ralph.

The waiter has sidled up to their table. "Everything it's okay over here?" he says. "I can get you anything else?"

"You want dessert?" Mike says to Alan.

"Sure."

"Have whatever you want," he adds, still slave to the old-world conviction that food is the surest way to convey love.

They each order apple pie—Mike's with coffee, Alan's *a la mode.*

"You know that joke Danny Thomas tells about the apple pie and coffee?"

"Yeah," Alan says, "I know that one."

"That's a funny joke. You remember on the show his uncle, Uncle Tonoose? He come over from the old country?"

"Yeah, I remember him."

Mike glances over his shoulder. "That guy reminds me a him."

"Who?"

"That waiter, see him? That tall guy with the big mustache?"

"You think he looks like Uncle Tonoose?"

"Don't you think so, Alan. And I bet he's a Greek, that guy. You can tell—"

"So when are you going to propose?" Alan says in another attempt to short-circuit one of Mike's ethnicity rants.

"When am I gonna propose? I thought Christmas Eve."

"In front of everybody?" Alan says, attempting some humor.

"Not in front of everybody. I'll take her off to the side, in private."

"You're sure she'll say yes?" This was a more blatant attempt at humor—in fact a pretty lame one—but again Mike takes it as an actual question.

"Are you kidding me? A girl like her, been alone all these years? She'll jump at the chance."

"Actually, I *was* just kidding. And you're right, she's lucky to have you." Alan doesn't really think this, of course—that she's lucky to have Mike—but as best man he'll need to play the role of loyal son, so why not get in a little practice?

"When's that pie coming," Mike says now. As if on cue the waiter appears with their pie, and Mike takes a bite the moment his piece is set down in front of him.

Alan takes a bite of his own and then he remembers Vera. "So Dad, tell me. Is Vera going to live with you?"

"With me and Dolly? In *our* house? No way. She's gonna stay across the street at her mother's for a while but then she's gonna have to move, we could use the extra money from selling that house. When we get a buyer she'll just have to find an apartment somewheres."

"And you think her mother will be okay with that?"

Mike pauses—a telltale pause, it seems to Alan. "Dolly?" he says. "She might balk at first, but she'll see the light, she's no dumbbell."

Alan can see the issue of Vera's living situation as the

first in a long line of disagreements Mike and Dolly are likely to have, but he isn't about to rain on Mike's parade. "You're right," he says. "Living on her own would be good for Vera. And who knows, maybe some guy will come along and sweep her off her feet."

"That'll be the day," Mike says. He takes a sip of coffee and glances at his watch. "But she's a nice girl, Vera. Very good-hearted. . . . She loves her mother, that's for sure."

Suddenly, like a blow between the eyes, Alan realizes that Vera La Forgia is going to be his stepsister. It was bad enough having her across the street while he was growing up—skulking around, making goo-goo eyes at him. Now she's going to claim him as family. He can just hear her: *How you doin', bro? Oh, it's so good to have a brother, I never had one. I feel like I'm part of a big happy family.* And she'll probably start calling Mike "Dad." *And how you doing, Dad? You been taking your heart medicine I hope? And your blood pressure medicine—you been taking that, Dad?* Ingratiating bitch!

"More coffee you want here?"

"No, just the check," Mike says. "Unless you want something else, Alan."

"I couldn't eat another thing."

The waiter disappears and Mike turns to his son. "Speaking a that," he says, "you been eating enough since you're separated?"

"Yeah, I'm okay. I eat out a lot."

"Gets expensive. You should find a nice girl what'll cook for you."

"I'm fine, Dad, really."

"A nice *Italian* girl. I never said nothing, but I think the Jewish ones don't cook so good. I heard this one time. She wasn't a good cook, Claire, right?"

"She wasn't bad," Alan says, caught up short by the realization that he actually defended Claire.

The waiter brings the check and Mike pays.

Out on the street he says, "So you wanna go for a spin before you have to get back to New York? The Olds drives like a dream, like I was telling you."

"I don't know, I have a lot of stuff to catch up on this afternoon."

It was the wrong answer and Alan knew it the moment it hit his lips. Five long years after Mike's tool and die business closed its doors for good, he finally landed a decent-paying job—witness the new car—and it's obvious he wants to share his good fortune with his son.

"Come to think of it," Alan says with a feigned glance at his watch, "I have some time."

"Good, we'll go for a little spin, you'll see what I mean. It handles like a baby, the Olds."

4

Mike Agnalini was born in New York City's Little Italy in 1911, the second-born son of Guiseppina and Luigi Agnalini. When he was six the family moved to Edgewater, one of those tiny New Jersey towns that line the Hudson River from the George Washington Bridge on the north to the Holland Tunnel on the south.

The Agnalini family—Mama, Papa, the four girls and two boys—were, from all accounts, close-knit and happy, though quite poor. According to Mike, he already had his own newsstand by the time he was eight, and he continued to supplement the family's meager income throughout grammar school and high school. After high school he entered technical school but had to quit after only a few weeks; his father had suffered a stroke that left him unable to work, and it fell to Mike to assume the role of breadwinner—a role he took on, he always said, with no resentment toward his older brother, Vini, who was somewhat of a playboy and had never been counted on to contribute to the family income on a regular basis.

How many times had Alan seen that photograph of Mike, with his slicked-back chestnut hair and broad shoulders? Yes, there was no denying he was a handsome young man, but he was the opposite of Vini when it came to women. Quite simply, he was too busy supporting his family—holding down two and sometimes three jobs at once—to have the time or energy for much dating. Then he met Agnes Cardarelli and suddenly he began to pay attention to the old line about all work and no play. Agnes, a dark-eyed beauty from the neighboring town of Fort Lee, had never wanted for suitors, as legend had it, but in the end it was Mike who won out. On a balmy summer evening in 1941—on the Ferris wheel at Palisades Park—he slipped the engagement ring on her finger. They were married soon after.

Perfect for each other—that's what the newlyweds' friends might have said about them. *And isn't it about time,* they might have added, *that Mike had a little happiness in his life considering all he's sacrificed for his family?* And then, just a month after the wedding, those same friends undoubtedly said *It's awful, just awful, about his parents—killed like that, the car came out of nowhere, they never had a chance.*

People of Mike and Agnes's background knew that bad things come in threes. The shocking death of Mike's parents had been the first thing, and now he and Agnes waited apprehensively for what might befall them next. While they were waiting, a real estate opportunity presented itself to them. Mike's sister Fiona and her husband, Sal, owned half of a small duplex in Morehead, New Jersey, a tiny town a few miles northwest of Paterson (itself about fifteen miles west of the George Washington Bridge). Less than a month after the tragedy, Mike and Agnes learned that the other half of the duplex was for sale and that the owner had to sell in a hurry. The couple scraped together all the money they could find for a down payment and then made a ridiculously low offer. To their surprise the offer was accepted.

They were homeowners, things were looking up. And their good fortune extended to the physical as well: because of a congenital heart murmur, Mike was exempted from the draft. This meant he was free to concentrate on preparing for fatherhood. His dream of a cozy little family proved to be short-lived, however. In December, right around the time the Japanese attacked Pearl Harbor, Agnes suffered an attack of her own.

A fatal car crash and now a miscarriage, their friends must have said. *What could be next?* What came next touched Mike and Agnes only indirectly but it changed their lives profoundly. Fiona's husband died after a brief bout with cirrhosis, leaving behind a two-year-old son, Ralph. Suddenly a double vacuum had been created in the modest duplex in that small New Jersey town: an expectant father had lost his unborn child, and now a little boy had lost his father. No one was surprised when Mike rushed in to fill the vacuum. Even before Sal was laid to rest, Alan's mother used to tell him, Mike began campaign-

ing to become Ralph's "surrogate" father. He pointed out
to his sister Fiona that Ralph was going to need a strong
father figure and a strong sense of right and wrong. And he
swore to her that he would treat Ralph as he would his own
child. When it became clear to him that Fiona would go
along with the idea, he told her he wanted to be free to discipline the boy if he was misbehaving, even to spank him if
that was necessary to instill discipline in him and a proper
respect for authority. There was little doubt that Fiona had
some misgivings, especially about the spankings, but ultimately she acquiesced.

Mike threw himself into his new role as a father. The
fact that his "son" was not his son at all but his nephew did
not dampen his enthusiasm for his parental responsibili-
ties. Although he never insisted on being called "Dad," he
established a strong bond with his nephew-son which grew
stronger still as the boy grew older. From as far back as Alan
could recall, Mike and Ralph seemed inseparable. He could
remember standing in the front yard as Mike taught Ralph
to hit a baseball or the correct way to hold a football. And
Alan remembered some spankings he was secretly pleased
to watch his cousin get.

But back before Alan was born it was just the four of
them in the little Agnalini-Passacantando duplex, and their
relationships must have created an interesting dynamic.
Mike, to start with, served multiple roles: he was his wife's
husband, his sister's brother, and was both de facto father
to his sister's son and uncle to his nephew, who, of course,
were one in the same person. Then there was Agnes, who,

Alan had always imagined, was ambivalent about Mike's relationship with Ralph. One the one hand, she had to have been proud of her husband for taking on part of the responsibility for Ralph's upbringing, and there's no doubt she was happy that he now had an opportunity to be the father she knew he'd yearned to be. But she couldn't have been entirely pleased that he spent so much time with Ralph, not just because the time he spent with Ralph was time he didn't spend with her but perhaps more so because seeing Mike in his role as father was a painful reminder of the child she'd lost. As for Agnes's feelings for Fiona, Alan's guess had always been that his mother resented, or at least envied, her sister-in-law. After all, Fiona may have spent the best years of her life taking care of a drunken husband whom she then had to find a way to bury with some kind of dignity, but at least she had a little boy who was alive and well. And as for Fiona, despite any misgivings she might have had about Mike's new role in her son's life, she was no doubt grateful for his interest in the boy; there was no question that Ralph was better off with this new arrange-ment than he would have been with no father at all, and probably better off than he'd been when Sal was alive.

As if this family dynamic was not complex enough, it soon grew more so. In 1947 a baby boy was born to Agnes and Mike Agnalini. Enter Alan.

Good for Mike! Fiona might have said. *He finally has a child a his own. It's funny, though,* she might have added a few months later. *He still spends all a his time with Ralph.* For it seems that Alan's arrival had done nothing to change the nature of Mike's relationship with Ralph. Alan had no actual memory of this period of his life, needless to say, but given his later memories and given what he'd been able to piece together from various members of his extended family, it was logical for him to conclude that from the outset he received far less attention and—ostensibly, at least—far less love from Mike than Ralph did.

As Alan grew into a little boy and then a schoolboy he began to show obvious signs of being affected by Mike's cavalier treatment of him. He was a shy child—overly dependent on his mother and easily intimidated by adults, especially male adults. A psychiatrist might have spotted in him a good deal of latent anger toward Mike, but as far as Alan was concerned his father was God, Buddha, and Eisenhower rolled into one compact, Italian package. And he did everything he could think of to please the man. As he grew a little older his anger toward his father began to surface but he expressed it in veiled, ineffectual ways. For instance, when he was about eleven he began to refer to his father as "Mike," but only in his mind; he never would have expressed to another person what he saw as an act of disrespect.

In the meantime he was developing an interesting relationship with his cousin Ralph. From the time of Alan's infancy, Mike and Fiona had demanded that Ralph think of him as his baby brother, and as Alan passed through babyhood into little boyhood he became grateful for their demand. He liked having someone to look up to and to emulate, someone who would protect him from bullies and teach him things and answer his questions. As he grew older, however, it became increasingly clear to him that Ralph had been merely tolerating the arrangement. He'd never objected to the role that had been thrust upon him, as far as Alan knew, but he'd never fully embraced it either— not because Alan wasn't his actual brother (this, at any rate, was unlikely) but because it simply wasn't in Ralph's nature to concern himself, to any significant degree, with the wants and needs of others. What satisfaction he took in the role of big brother seemed confined to those moments when he was called upon to defend Alan against one bully or another. Then he would swing into action, using either his superior verbal skills or the threat of his superior physical strength (he was a few years older than most of Alan's tormentors) to intimidate the bully. But by the time he'd reached his mid-teens Ralph clearly no longer enjoyed this activity. What's more, he began to resent—and to rebel against—the role that had been assigned to him. Since Ralph was only a couple of years away from leaving home for college, Mike and Fiona didn't press the issue. And so, at about the age of nine or ten—and after having lost his father by default even before he was born—Alan lost what had passed for his big brother.

But big brother-cousin wasn't the problem. Young as he was, Alan understood on some level that his relationship with Ralph wasn't essential to his emotional well-being. His relationship with Mike, however, was essential in the extreme. Alan's need for Mike's approval was all-encompassing, and with the naïve optimism that only a child can entertain in the face of evidence to the contrary, he was certain he could win that approval once and for all if only he could come up with the right plan. Finally, after weeks of thought, he hit upon the answer: he would find a way to make money and he would save all the money he made. What better way to reach Mike, he reasoned, than to display the same ambition and self-discipline the man himself had always displayed? Alan began to consider various ways a ten-year-old boy could earn money. At first he thought of doing odd jobs around the neighborhood—mowing lawns, washing cars, and so on—but decided he did enough of that kind of work for Mike around the house. Then one day he rode his bike to the local supermarket and got permission from the manager to spend his Saturdays helping customers load their groceries into their cars. Later that same week his mother arranged for him to be assigned a paper route with the *Paterson Evening News*.

Suddenly he was making money and, according to plan, he began to save every penny of it. When Alan had accumulated about fifty dollars, Mike took him downtown and they opened a savings account for him. Every Monday morning he would give his mother whatever cash he'd earned the previous week, and she would take the short bus ride into town to deposit the money into his account. By the time he was thirteen Alan had saved nearly two-thousand dollars—a small fortune for a boy his age.

But something else had taken place by the time Alan was thirteen: he'd come to realize that nothing—not even working hard and saving his money—could win him

Mike's approval. A knee-jerk reaction to this realization might have been to quit his jobs and just go outside and play like the other kids. But if anything his new understanding of the limits of his relationship with Mike inspired him to work harder than ever. He had a new goal now, a new reason to save his money—namely, to spite Mike. And the mechanism he would use to do this was simple: when the time came he would provide for his own college education. *No thanks, Dad,* he would say on that glorious day. *I have my own money and I can go to college wherever I want. Maybe even California.* Yes, by the time he was thirteen Alan was quite a different person from the one he'd been at ten. His innocence was gone and in its place were the seeds of a seething resentment toward the man he'd formerly thought of as "my dad."

Late one Saturday afternoon in the spring of 1960 he returned home from his job at the supermarket. Mike had recently decided that his son was old enough to have his own key, and now Alan took it out and entered the house. He didn't know if anyone was home but then he heard Mike in the kitchen.

"Sure, Ray, give Ernie Bisconti a call. He averages almost one-fifty, we can get by with him for a week."

He was on the phone with Ray Testa, the captain of his Thursday night bowling team.

"Right. . . . Nothing to worry about, Ray. Ernie'll do a good job. . . . Okay. . . . Sure, see you next week."

Alan took a step toward the kitchen and then he heard his mother's voice.

"Was that *Amelia* Bisconti's Ernie you was talking about?"

"Right," Mike said. "Ernie Bisconti."

"I never liked that girl. She's snooty if you ask me."

Alan was about to call out to them, but something—maybe some kind of adolescent precognition—stopped him. Then he heard his mother say, "By the way, Mike. Today when I was over in Paterson doing some shopping I ran into your sister Jeanette. She said that last week when you was down her place fixing her television you were bragging about Alan, saying what a hard worker he is."

Alan waited for Mike to confirm this but the man allowed a few beats to go by. Finally he said, "Yeah, I was bragging about him. What of it?"

"I don't know," Alan's mother said. "Maybe you should tell Alan to his face once in a while that you're proud a him."

By this time Alan had inched closer to the kitchen and was now officially eavesdropping.

"Who says I'm proud a him?" Mike said.

"Whata you mean? You told Jeanette—"

"I know what I said, Agnes. . . . Look, a father's gotta make like he's proud a his son, right? And I ain't saying I'm not proud a him, exactly. But you know as well as me that the boy's got problems."

"Here we go again."

"Look Agnes, maybe you don't wanna hear it but we gotta face facts. You can't tell me you don't lie awake nights worrying about that boy—worrying what's gonna happen when he grows up and has to go out on his own."

"But Alan's a smart boy. He's a little shy but he'll get over that in time."

There was a pause, and in the silence of the house Alan could hear the click of Mike's cigarette lighter. Then Mike said, "Just like that he's gonna change? Wouldn't it be nice if Alan could just snap his fingers and he'd be different. But he's growing up now, it's time we face facts. Alan ain't gonna have an easy time of it making his way in the world. He just don't have what it takes."

Alan became aware that he was holding his breath. He'd finally heard Mike say it in so many words: *Alan doesn't have what it takes. He's not good enough.*

"You been saying the same thing for how many years now, Mike, and I still don't understand what you want from the boy. He's got two jobs, he's saving all his money. . . ."

"Here we go with them jobs again," Mike said. "You wanna know why he's got them jobs? Cause he wants to impress me, that's why. He wants me to make a big deal about how ambitious he is, how he's a chip off the old block."

"Well, can you blame him?" Alan's mother shot back. "The way you're always going on about Ralph, who *wouldn't* try to get his father's approval once in a while? He used to idolize you, Mike, and he still would I bet, if you gave him half a chance."

There was another pause, probably Mike taking an extended drag on his cigarette. Then he said, "I try, Agnes, you *know* I try. But he's just not . . . Talking to him's like talking to the wall. You don't get nothing back."

"But he's still your son anyways you look at it. So what if he ain't the life a the party. He's still your son and he needs his father. Ralph don't need you no more, he's in college now and he's got his plans for the future. But Alan's just a boy. Why can't you spend more time with him, why can't you try to understand him a little?"

"There's the problem right there, Agnes. I understand him too good. It ain't just that he's quiet that's the problem. My Uncle Louie was quiet, but he had self-confidence. With Alan, it's like he don't know who he is. He's always trying to please everybody. He does what he thinks everybody *else* wants him to do, not what *he* wants to do. I hate to say this, Agnes, but whatever that boy amounts to in life, it ain't gonna happen cause he wanted something and went after it. It's gonna happen cause he settles for what comes his way. He don't have the gumption to go after what he wants in life, and you know this as well as me."

Again there was silence. Was it true? Alan wondered. Did he lack the gumption to go after what he wanted? *Wasn't* it true?

"But he's just a boy," he heard his mother say, her voice taking on the timbre of desperation. "Give him time, he'll learn how to stand up for himself."

"Is that a fact. You think that's all he needs is time? Lemme ask you something, Agnes. Can a leopard change his spots? No, and Alan can't change the way he is either, I don't care *how* much time you give him. This is how he's gonna stay and we gotta accept it."

Alan waited for his mother to say something else—to

defend him, maybe by pointing out that some leopards had been known to change their spots, despite the odds. But she said nothing. Soon he heard the clatter of pots and pans, which indicated she was starting to make dinner. The discussion was over. She'd come out on the short end and so had her son.

He quietly slipped upstairs to his room and sat down on the bed. He felt numb, probably in the way a physical trauma victim feels numb until his body can begin to mount an attack against whatever has violated it. But it was days before he began to mount any attack. And then it was only to abruptly quit both his jobs—an act, he knew, which would rob Mike of the one thing about his son that reflected well on him. This meant, of course, that Alan had to give up the idea of putting himself through college to spite Mike, but now he didn't have to wait the five years until he'd graduated high school; Mike's remarks, devastating as they'd been for him to hear, had led him to the realization that quitting his jobs was the perfect way to get back at the man. And he needed to feel he was getting back at Mike, that he was making him pay in some degree for the shoddy way he'd treated his son his whole life. It was a way of saving face. Unfortunately, it wasn't enough to save Alan. For the real upshot of this incident was that, as the days and weeks went by, he began to feel himself shutting down—retreating further and further from what, to that point, had been a largely ineffective but at least a legitimate attempt to engage the world. But what was the use in trying to engage the world if there was something fundamentally wrong with him? Why put up with the pain in trying to find the right thing to say when he had no *idea* what to say? Mike was right. Alan just didn't have what it takes and there was no use pretending otherwise. And so, within a couple of months of listening in on his parents' conversation, he'd become a new Alan—identical to the old one but only more so. His withdrawn personality, in other words, had reached full fruition, leaving him afraid to look people in the eyes, likely to cross the street when he saw an acquaintance walking toward him, afraid, as he grew older, to ask girls to dance or on a date, and all the while subconsciously expecting other people to fill his needs because he'd forgotten how to fill his own. In short, he'd become the kind of person who might have to wait until he's nineteen before he has his first girlfriend or twenty-two before he finally loses his virginity. The kind of person who, if he marries, might do so more out of desperation than for any other reason. And the kind of person who might wake one day to find that his inability to deal with a new problem in his life has undermined what was already a shaky sense of well-being.

5

Alan was undecided about returning for a second session with Rhonda, but the moment he enters the lobby of her building he knows he's where he needs to be.

"So, Alan," Rhonda says as they sit down. "Tell me about your week. Was it eventful? Boring? Painful? What?"

"You want me to describe it in one word?"

"Not necessarily. Just tell me about it."

"It was strange," he says, a single word seeming to be all that was required after all.

"Strange how?"

When the word "strange" popped into his head, Alan was thinking about Mike's pending engagement to Dolly. This was unexpected and, therefore, strange. But now he realizes that what's really strange is the whole thing with Brooke. Brooke Hadley has reappeared in his life much in the way a corpse might suddenly sit up in its coffin. Try keeping your equilibrium next time you see a corpse sit up in its coffin.

"Alan?"

"I'm sorry, what did you say?"

"I said, 'Strange how?' In what way was your week strange?"

He adjusts himself in his chair as if for fortification. "Do you remember last week," he begins, "when I told you about the woman I think I may have gotten pregnant?"

"I don't forget these things, Alan. Although from the way you described the incident I wouldn't jump to any conclusions if I were you."

"Right," he says. "But just the possibility . . . I don't know, I can't get it out of my mind. I can't get *Brooke* out of my mind."

"And this upsets you."

Wouldn't it upset *you?* he thinks to himself. But then he remembers that Rhonda is a paragon of emotional stability. Or, at least, that he presumes her to be one.

"Yes," he says now, "it really bothers me. I just want it to go away."

"Wouldn't it be nice if life were that simple."

Alan doesn't know what to say next, and Rhonda seems in no hurry to help him out. Finally he says, "I don't know what to do about it."

"But you seem to know that you should do *something* about it. That's good. It's a healthy response."

He mulls over the words "healthy response," feeling

they've been misdirected at him. Then he hears her say, "So what precisely *are* you going to do about it?"

Now she really has him confused. Didn't he just tell her that he doesn't know what to do about it?

"I know," Rhonda says, "you didn't expect that question. But I'm making a point here, which is that—like it or not—you need to take responsibility for the problem and decide how you're going to handle it. You can't get her out of your mind and you're not happy about that, so you must do something about it. The problem isn't going to take care of itself."

Alan has no response to this, since he already knows that problems don't take care of themselves (although he's spent much of his life waiting for that one exception).

"And I should say," she adds, "that I see the problem—at least, the immediate problem—not as the possibility that you may be a father, but as your emotional upset over that possibility. Do you get the distinction?"

"Yes . . ." he says, and he lets the word hang in the air in anticipation of a *but* that refuses to materialize.

"Now, what are some of the ways you could deal with this problem?"

"Meaning, my emotional upset."

"Exactly," she says. "What are the things you could do to eliminate your emotional distress?"

Alan chews on this for a second. "Well," he says, "I could do nothing and hope that in time it doesn't bother me so much."

"I thought we ruled that one out."

"Actually, I was making kind of a joke."

"Yes, humor can be an effective defense mechanism. But I'll take your answer at face value. How effective would such an approach be? To sit back and wait for time to take care of the problem?"

"Not very," he says. "But there's one thing I don't understand. I've known about this possibility for years and I never really dwelled on it. Now all of a sudden it's important to me. I don't get it."

Rhonda tilts her head slightly as if to perceive Alan from a different angle. "Let me ask you something, Alan. Are you the same person you were five years ago? Or four years ago? Or even last week?"

"I'm not?"

"No, Alan, you're not. Your experiences have changed you. The passage of time, in and of itself, has changed you. Wouldn't it be illogical, then, to expect that you would respond to something in the present exactly the way you responded to it in the past?"

"I never thought of it that way," he says.

"It's clear to me, Alan, that you've grown to the point where this situation is no longer something you can sweep under the rug."

"Thanks," he says. "I think."

"It wasn't a compliment. Growing up isn't something we should be rewarded for. It's our job."

This takes him down a notch.

"But let me get back to the question I asked you. What could you do . . ." Rhonda glances at her watch. "Let me rephrase that. What do you suppose would be the most effective thing you could do to help you overcome your emotional distress over this situation?"

This is one question Alan knows the answer to. "Actually," he says, "I've been thinking along those lines in the last few days. I need to find her and confront her and put an end to the speculation."

Rhonda throws her hands in the air—not so high that you would expect a *hallelujah* to accompany them, but high enough to indicate that she's pleased he finally sees the obvious. "Excellent," she says. "Do you think you'd have trouble finding her?"

"No, I don't think so. She had her oboe case with her when I saw her last week, so I assume she wasn't just visiting New York."

"A musician, is she? Maybe she was here for an audition."

"Maybe," he says. "But I have a feeling she lives here. In fact, she may live not too far from me. There's a B. Hadley on First Avenue—in the Sixties, from what I can tell from the address."

"So are you planning to call that number? Maybe it's not Brooke, but it's a start."

"Yes," he says, "a start. But . . . I don't know. I know I said I need to put an end to the speculation, but I'm not sure I'm ready to try to track her down."

Rhonda gives the slightest shrug. "You might not feel ready, but you have to ask yourself what you would gain by putting this off."

"But it's only been a few days."

"You're right, Alan. It's only been a few days. But I'm going to assume that if this were merely a matter of curiosity on your part you would have begun your attempt to locate her by now."

He considers this. "I guess you could assume that," he says.

"But my guess is that you're quite emotionally involved in the outcome—in finding out whether or not you're a father."

He looks away, involuntarily seeking shelter from the intensity of Rhonda's gaze. "I suppose so," he says.

"Then that's the *core* question, isn't it. What do you want the outcome to be? To learn that you're a father or that you're not?"

This is a question Alan hasn't dared ask himself, and now that it's been served up his only response is silence.

After an extended moment Rhonda says, "I understand. This isn't easy for you. But it's a question you have to ask yourself. How would you want this to turn out?"

"I don't know," Alan says. "The whole thing seems too complicated. I can't even think clearly about it. How can I tell what I want?"

"And this is understandable," she says. "But not knowing what you want shouldn't stop you from finding out what's what. And whatever you find out, you deal with. If there's no child, if there's a child and you're the father, if there's a child and you're not the father . . . Whatever the outcome, that's what you deal with. The point is, knowing is always preferable to not knowing. It's only been a week since you saw this woman and already you're showing the negative effects of being in limbo."

"I am?"

"You appear tired, Alan. Stressed. Have you been sleeping well?"

"Not as well as usual," he says.

"And there you are. The situation needs a resolution, and you're the only one who can begin to make that resolution happen. If I seem to be pressuring you, it's because this is something you need to do."

He glances at the old standby, his watch, but this time because he wants to make sure there's enough time left in the session for him to get an answer to his next question. "But what if I find her and she admits to having a child the age *our* child would be, but she denies it's mine. How do I know she's telling the truth?"

"You don't," Rhonda says. "And that's one of the risks you have to take. If you think she's lying, then you do whatever seems to be the next logical thing to do. I don't know—hire a detective. But that's supposition. There's no point in thinking about it?"

"And what if there's a child and the child hates me for abandoning it? *Then* what do I do?"

"It's the same question, Alan, and the same answer. You deal with the future in the future."

He sits back in his chair and tries not to think about the future. Then a thought enters his head which he recognizes as being both new to him and in some way critical to his confusion about the whole issue.

"What if..." he begins, but he pulls back.

"What if what, Alan?"

Now he leans forward in his chair—not intentionally, but as if impelled to do so. "I hate to say this, but what if there's a child—my child—and it has a severe handicap, maybe cerebral palsy, maybe to the point of being a vegetable. Or it's severely retarded or has some kind of horrendous birth defect, like arms where there are supposed to be legs and legs where there are supposed to be arms? Then what?"

"Then you love your child."

It's at this moment that Alan sees Rhonda for the first time. Up until this point she's been little more than a person sitting across from him, and he's been able to keep her at bay with his usual mechanisms of distancing himself from others. But now, in the wake of her simple statement, he sees her as another side of himself, as if they've both been placed in this point in space at this moment in time so that they can share something—something bigger than the particular matter they've been discussing. He quickly looks away.

"When you have a child," Rhonda continues, *"your* child—whether yours biologically or simply because you take responsibility for it—you love that child. It's not something you choose to do. It's something that happens to you—that you have no control over. And in loving your child, you love it in spite of the problems it may present and in spite of the heartache it may bring you to witness those problems day after day, year after year."

She pauses here, and it seems to Alan that she's had an epiphany of some kind. He waits for her to share it but she remains silent.

"Weren't you about to say something important?" he ventures. "Maybe I'm wrong, but it seemed like you just came to some kind of conclusion about something."

A hint of surprise crosses Rhonda's face. "You're very perceptive, Alan. Yes, I did just have an insight. I now see exactly what it is that keeps you from taking action where Brooke is concerned."

"You do?"

"Yes, Alan, I do. But I would be doing you a disservice if I revealed it to you. Insights are far more productive if the patient can come to them on his own."

It's nearing ten o'clock. Alan has spent the last hour-and-a-half walking slowly up and down Broadway—from Seventy-second Street to Eighty-sixth Street—trying to sort out all the feelings Rhonda has stirred up in him. Is it all about being scared shitless that he might fall in love with a little child and that his life as he's known it would be over? Or is he afraid he might be one of the exceptions—one of the ones who *can't* love unconditionally, who are too shallow to love unconditionally? Has he changed sufficiently from the selfish, irresponsible college senior he was to something better than that, something a child could look up to? Then again, maybe he's just afraid of the unknown, as he's been afraid of it his whole life. And what if it turned out there's no child—not *his* child? What would that particular sense of loss be like? And is it worth the risk to find out? And what about Rhonda's claim that she discovered the precise cause of his failure to act? If he can find the answer to *that* riddle, would the other answers fall in place? And who, finally, would answer these questions? Not Rhonda, that isn't her job. Not his dead mother. And not the Alan he's been. Only the one he's becoming. And *there's* a thought: he's becoming a new Alan, in spite of himself.

6

Rick and Alan have been office mates for nearly two years now, and they've become pretty good friends. So it's no surprise that Alan finds himself at Rick's apartment on the Saturday night between Christmas and New Year's.

"Why don't you do a cartwheel, Em?" he hears Rick say.

"I don't know," Sally says to Rick. "There's not enough room."

Rick stands and moves the coffee table and a standing lamp out of the way. "Okay, Mommy?" he says to his wife.

"Can I, Mommy?" the little girl says to her mother.

"Okay," Sally says, "but just one, to show Uncle Alan."

Uncle Alan is sitting in an armchair across from his friends, and after all the family-holiday-togetherness bullshit he's been through in the last few weeks, he's happy to be here. At the same time, he's feeling a little awkward. At some point during dinner he realized that this is the first time he's been to Rick and Sally's without Claire. It's ironic; he's genuinely pleased—beside himself with pleasure, really—that he and Claire split up, but he's having a hard time dealing with the reality of being unattached after years of being part of a couple.

"Uncle Alan! Watch!"

He looks up at the sound of Emily's little voice and watches as she does not one but three cartwheels and finally has to be whisked up into her father's arms. As Rick holds his daughter and stipples her cheek with kisses, Sally and Alan applaud, though he's too self-conscious to match her *yay* with one of his own.

"That was wonderful, sweetie," Sally says as Rick sets the little girl back down to ground level.

"Can I do a handstand, Mommy? Can I, I wanna show Uncle Alan."

Sally gets off the couch and corrals her little daughter. "No," she says playfully, kissing Emily on both cheeks and then on the nose. "You have to get ready for bed now, it's past your bedtime."

Emily breaks into tears, clearly in response to the word "bed."

"Listen to your mother," Rick says, too delighted with his little daughter to do much in the way of effecting an authoritative tone of voice.

"Emi*lee*," Sally says, and the little girl, clearly in response to the inflection in her mother's voice, stops crying as abruptly as she started. "And then after you've washed up," the mother continues, "Daddy or I will come in and read you a story."

"I want Uncle Alan," the little girl says, choosing, for some reason, to jump up and down in time with each syllable.

Rick and Sally each look at him in surprise.

He doesn't know what to say, but Sally speaks for him.

"Okay, sweetie," she says, taking her little daughter by the hand. "When you're all done washing up and brushing your teeth, Uncle Alan will come in and read you a story."

Uncle Alan merely smiles, though somewhat sheepishly.

Now he tries to direct his eyes to Rick, sitting across from him on the couch, but he can't help sneaking a glance at Sally and her little daughter as they disappear down the hall. It's remarkable how much alike mother and daughter look—each with that blond Dutch-boy haircut and Ivory-girl complexion. He wonders if Emily will grow up to have her mother's hour-glass figure.

"Are you ready for your moment in the sun?"

Rick's question jolts Alan back to the here and now.

"It's been a while since I've read to little children," he says.

"You used to read to your niece and nephews?"

"Actually, they're my second cousins, but who's counting? No, I used to be a camp counselor."

Rick takes a sip of beer. "You were a camp counselor?

I didn't know that. But I'm not surprised, you're great with Emily."

"She's delightful."

"She is, but she can be a handful. All kids that age are handfuls, but it's worth it."

Alan figures another lecture on the joys of family life is coming, but he's too tired to try to circumvent it. Rick surprises him when he falls silent. Finally he says, "Want another beer, Alan?"

"No, two's my limit."

"Mr. Teetotaler," Rick says. "But you're better off, you don't want to be getting a gut." He looks down at his slightly swelling stomach. "I'll be starting to get a paunch on me if I don't watch it."

Alan looks away from Rick's stomach as if something in the room has attracted his attention. The fact is, in an oblique way, Rick's reference to his stomach has reminded Alan of his third-wheel status *vis a vis* Rick and Sally. He needs something to distract him from this particular negative self-perception, and reading to Emily might do the trick—though in truth he's a bit apprehensive about the prospect.

"So Alan, what do you think about Jim leaving?"

In response to this question, Alan sees himself in Jim's office, being offered the chance to take over as marketing manager.

"What's to think?" he says as he struggles to quash the flashback. "Unless the new guy's some kind of Simon

Legree it probably won't make a difference one way or the other."

Rick makes a face. "I still don't understand why they didn't post the job. Other companies post their job openings and at least give their employees a crack at moving up the ladder.

"But I'm telling you, Alan. I'm going to figure out a way to get promoted to marketing manager if it kills me."

Alan, who's heard this song before, can't imagine how Rick—a mediocre copywriter at best—could ever find a way to get the promotion he's after.

For a while they remain silent. Then Rick says, "So your father proposed on Christmas Eve?"

"It was an event. He said he was going to do it in private, but then he made a big show of it in front of everyone. And Dolly—God, I can't believe someone could go through life with a name like Dolly . . . Dolly made a big show of it too. Tried to pretend it was a total shock, when the fact is she's been trying to snag my father ever since my mother died."

Rick pours more beer into his glass and takes a sip. "Sounds like you don't like the woman," he says at the tail end of his sip.

"I don't really have a problem with her. . . . Okay, I hate her guts, but only because she hates mine more."

"Why? What did you do, spray shaving cream on her car when you were twelve?"

"Haven't I told you that story?" Alan says.

"What story?"

"About her daughter? Vera?"

"Vera . . . The name rings a bell but I don't remember any story. Tell me again."

"There's nothing much to tell. When I was fifteen and she was fourteen she invited me to her birthday party, which I grudgingly went to, but then she started hanging around trying to get me to ask her out and eventually I had to make it clear to her that I wasn't interested."

"Oh, right," Rick says. "I remember. You broke her heart. I always knew you were a cad."

"Worse than that—I was an insensitive clod. I don't recall my exact words, but I made it clear that I thought she was ugly as sin."

"Right, and then she goes crying to her mother, and her mother has had it in for you ever since."

"That's about it," Alan says. "It's a variation of the boy-meets-girl story: boy meets girl and insults her."

Rick is shaking his head, smiling. "And now it's come back to haunt you—she's going to be your stepsister. Poetic justice, if you ask me."

"Thanks for your compassion."

"Don't mention it."

Alan stifles a yawn and tries not to look at his watch. Eagle-eyed Rick picks up on it.

"You look beat, Alan. Have you been getting enough sleep?"

Here's his opportunity. Rick is his best friend—the closest thing he has to a best friend, at any rate—yet he hasn't mentioned a thing to him about Brooke. Why not? He knows it would probably help to get the male perspective, and maybe Rick's feedback would lead him to a decision about the whole mess. For some reason, though, he just doesn't want to get into with Rick. Is this a failing of Alan's, maybe his basic mistrust in people? Or is it a comment on the nature of his friendship with Rick?

"Have I been getting enough sleep?" Alan says. "No, not really. I think it's the holidays. I always get stressed out on the holidays."

He sits up, and for a moment he could swear he's looking across at Rhonda.

"I'm going to ask you a serious question," Rick says. "Do you miss Claire?"

"God no! That's about the only thing that's going right in my life."

"Because I could understand it if you did. Even though you and Claire had your differences, you were together for a long time."

"Far, far too long," Alan says.

Rick leans back again on the couch. "Just wondering," he says. He seems to be saying something in addition— maybe *Then what's been eating you?* (It's clear he doesn't buy the holiday-stress story.) And maybe he's also saying *Don't you trust me enough to confide in me?* For a moment Alan feels guilty, but Rick's next comment seems to indicate that he wasn't thinking these things at all.

"I never told you this, Alan, but I never could warm up to Claire."

"Join the club. I was married to her for however many years, and *I* couldn't warm up to her."

"That's sad," Rick says, and he glances toward the hallway, where he last saw his wife and his child. "It's sad," he repeats, but this time he can't suppress a slight smile, no doubt at the thought of his own good fortune.

"Uncle Alllaaan!"

Sally's musical voice preceded her down the hall, and now Sally herself comes into view. "Emily's ready for her story," she says smiling at Alan, and he tries to quash his visceral reaction to her undeniable radiance.

He gets up and walks toward the hall. Sally has joined Rick on the couch, and Alan realizes they won't be joining him in Emily's bedroom.

"Don't worry," Rick says, "we won't eavesdrop."

Alan doesn't know what to make of their trust in him— not that he's given them reason to think he's the kind of person who would molest a child. Still, they're relatively new parents and he's a male non-family member. . . . He just has no idea of the protocol that goes along with being a parent of a young child. He's out of his depth—that much is clear to *him*, at any rate—but he's touched by their trust in him and their sensitivity to his need to remain unobserved as he reads to their daughter.

He walks down the hall into Emily's room. She's sitting up in bed—all scrubbed and brushed and eager for the next moment in the series of unfolding moments that make up her life.

"Uncle Alan!" she says, and she reaches down and grabs a book and practically shoves it in his face. "You read this."

Alan looks at the book. "*Leandor the Farm Puppy*," he

reads under his breath. "Are you sure you don't want me to read the Warren report?"

"Puppy," she says.

"Okay, I'll read this, but on one condition."

Emily looks at him suspiciously. "What's 'condition'?"

He's tempted to play around with the word at her expense, but to do so, he tells himself, would be a form of child abuse. Like Mike telling him they were going to get to the Catskills by climbing up a rope. "What I mean is," he says, "I'll read to you, but only if you lie down."

Emily seems to think this is a fair deal, for immediately she curls up—one hand grasping her stuffed elephant, the thumb of the other hand in her mouth.

Alan opens the book. "My name is Leandor," he reads. "I'm a puppy. I live on a farm." That was the first page. He turns the page and continues. "Every morning I wake to the rooster's 'cock-a-doodle-doo.'" (Alan has made sure to moderate his cock-a-doodle-doo so as not to arouse Emily.) Again he turns the page. "I run to the barn to watch Bud milk the cows." He looks up from the book to see if Emily might be nodding off, and he can tell she's trying hard not to. "Maybe you should close your eyes," he says to her.

She looks at him wide-eyed but he knows it's her last hurrah.

"Why don't we make another deal," he says. "I'll keep reading if you close your eyes." He's aware that this is an abuse of power, but his main job isn't really to read to Emily—it's to send her off into another realm.

She closes her eyes and Alan returns to the book. "After

breakfast I chase the hens around the henhouse. Sometimes I watch the pigs in their pen." So much for that page. "After lunch I take a nap in my favorite corner of the barn."

He becomes aware, now, of quiet, steady breathing; she's asleep. He could turn off the lamp and leave the room, but he wants to see how the story turns out.

"Later," he reads, lowering his voice a little, "I run to greet the school bus. Bud and Cindy play fetch with me all the way back to the house. After supper I watch them do their homework." Now he's on the next-to-last page. "After Bud and Cindy fall asleep I go outside and look up at the stars." He stays with this page for a minute, looking down in the dim light at the picture of Leandor the puppy looking joyously up at the sky as if to embrace every star and everything else life has to offer. He turns to the last page. "Then I curl up in my doghouse and dream of all the fun I'm going to have tomorrow." Alan closes the book and sets it down, then turns off the lamp. For a moment he stands looking down at Emily in the darkness.

When he steps out of her room he's surprised to see Rick and Sally standing a few paces down the hall.

"Bravo!" Rick says in a hushed voice.

"You said you weren't going to eavesdrop," Alan whispers back.

"I lied."

Back in the living room he takes his place in the armchair across from Rick and Sally, but everything seems different to him in a way. Rick seems to have picked up on this for he says, "What did I tell you? Kids are great."

Alan says nothing and Rick and Sally say nothing, and for a while they just sit. Finally Rick says, "So Alan, how was your Christmas, aside from your father proposing?"

"Boring. How was yours?"

Rick glances over at Sally. "We went to Sally's parents' in Connecticut," he says. Then he leans toward Alan as if confidentially. "It was boring too."

"Rick!" Sally says, and she gives him a little punch on the shoulder. Alan interprets the punch—and Rick's reaction to it, which is to turn to his wife and hold up his hands in mock self-defense—as the first sign of foreplay. It's time for him to leave.

"I really should be going," he says, stretching his arms to emphasize his point.

"You can't go yet," Rick says.

"Why not?"

"Because you haven't told us whether you're going to help us ring in 1975."

"I don't know," Alan says. "Your party sounds like fun, but the idea of going home on the subway at three o'clock in the morning doesn't really appeal to me."

"Subway? What about your car?"

"Didn't I tell you? My transmission went. The car will be in the shop till a week or so after New Year's."

"Bummer," Rick says. "But as far as your transportation goes, you don't have to go home on the subway, you can stay here. The couch opens up into a bed." He turns to Sally for confirmation.

"Sure," she says to Alan after the slightest hesitation. "It makes a pretty comfortable bed."

"I'll have to think about it," he says.

"Alan, my man," Rick says. "It's bad enough you left the Christmas party before the dancing started. Now you're turning down a New Year's Eve party?"

Alan says nothing, hoping Rick will drop the subject. He honestly doesn't know which way he's leaning, now that Rick has come up with a solution to his transportation problem. He doesn't have any other offers, and the idea of spending New Year's Eve alone in his apartment is depressing—in principle, if for no other reason. Then again he can just see himself lying on the foldout bed in Rick and Sally's living room while they're down the hall fucking their brains out.

"Let me think it over," he says again. "I'll let you know Monday, Rick."

"As you wish," Rick says. "But remember—if you come to the party you might meet someone who'll help you get back into the swing of things."

Alan mumbles something about "the swing of things" not being a problem, then stands and stretches his arms again.

Almost immediately Rick and Sally stand as well. It takes another ten minutes, but eventually Alan finds his way out into the hall and into the elevator and out onto the streets of Brooklyn Heights and onto the subway and finally back to Manhattan.

A little while later he's in his apartment, sitting across

from the TV. After some channel hopping he settles on a 1940s detective movie that promises to be interesting. It isn't. Or, at least, it can't compete with the thoughts that keep racing through his head: thoughts of little Emily, and Vera and her vindictive mother, and Claire's father, for some reason. And, of course, the thought—the image, really—that he's been unable to shake for weeks now: the image of the new Brooke—groomed, polished, attractive, self-confident—getting on that crosstown bus. It's becoming clear to him that his obsession with Brooke concerns more than the question of paternity. It concerns, as well, the possibility that even after all these years, and despite what went down between them, his relationship with her might in some way be salvageable.

Part II

7

1969

Sitting in a language lab is not exactly exciting. Especially on a Friday afternoon. And especially on a beautiful spring day. But when you have nothing to do, you find something to do.

He tried to refocus on the tape he'd been listening to. No luck. Maybe he should give himself a break, he thought. Go downtown and stare at the paintings in the Bevington Art Museum, for instance. Or maybe take in a movie, though he knew there was nothing playing that he wanted to see.

He made another attempt to focus, but then he became aware that someone had sat down in his row, a few carrels down from his. He glanced over and his eyes meet those of a somewhat homely, badly dressed young woman. Instinctively he looked away but then, for some reason, looked back. The woman had her eyes fixed on his, and she seemed to be leaning in his direction—a question mark knitting her brows, as he was sure a question mark was knitting his.

"Aren't you Thomas's roommate?" the woman said.

Now he recognized her. She'd been at his apartment on at least one occasion when he and Thomas were actually there at the same time. He'd been introduced to her, he recalled, but he wasn't good with names.

"That's right," he said in a stage whisper, which, considering that the two or three others in the lab were wearing headphones, was entirely unnecessary. "You're . . ."

He tried to make it look like her name was on the tip of his tongue, but the woman gave him a sly little smile which he interpreted to mean that she'd seen through his pretense.

"You're Alan," she said. "And I'm Brooke."

"Right," he said. "I met you a couple of weeks ago."

To his surprise Brooke stood up and moved two carrels closer to him, only one carrel remaining between them. That's when he smelled her. It wasn't an overpowering case of body odor she had, but it was unmistakable—that musty, slightly rank but somehow sensual scent of female perspiration.

"So," she said. "I see you're like me. Nothing to do on a Friday afternoon."

Alan was struck by the offhand manner in which Brooke had delivered this comment. She was smiling as if having nothing to do on a Friday afternoon was nothing in the world to be embarrassed about.

"I have some French I have to listen to," he said, but

then realized that his response had been an attempt to justify a companionless state that, according to Brooke, needed no justification.

They chatted for a couple of minutes and then, quite suddenly, Alan realized he was looking into a set of rather large, dark blue eyes. He'd never seen eyes of such a deep shade of blue, and immediately he thought of those high, cloudless, bluer-than-blue skies that come along every so often.

"... And so it would be illogical to conclude that Fellini has a mother fixation," he heard Brooke say.

"I'm sorry," he said. "I missed that. What were you saying?"

"I was just refuting what you said about Fellini having a mother fixation. Freud's theories are only valid if you accept his premises, and as far as I know there's no law that says you have to accept his premises."

Brooke's remark took Alan by surprise, and all at once it struck him that they were on the same wavelength. Here was a woman, he could see now, who wasn't content to go through life on the surface of things. Like him, she was fascinated by ideas, and since she looked at things obliquely her ideas made sense to him. He couldn't remember the last time he'd met someone he could really talk to.

Why, then, had he begun to think about her body? The answer was simple: she was a woman who'd taken some interest in him. Alan, despite what he'd been told were his good looks, had never had much luck with the opposite sex. Certainly, being a little shorter than average narrowed the field, but the main problem was that women seemed to think he was just too different. What he needed was a woman who saw his "differentness" as a plus—a woman who embraced it, who was attracted to it. And now, only a single carrel removed from him, was just such a woman. Or, at least, that seemed to be the case. Considering that he was not just lonely but horny as well, it was logical that he would cross over into the realm of the physical. But on the other hand it was ludicrous. The woman not only had b.o. but she was poorly dressed, poorly groomed (it occurred to Alan that it might have been a month since she'd washed her hair), and sported what appeared to be the remains of a severe case of adolescent acne. What was he doing sizing up a woman who looked like this? Was he that desperate? No, the idea of a physical relationship with this woman was out of the question. Besides, he would be leaving for New York in a few weeks.

At Brooke's suggestion they decided to quit the listening lab and drive down to Taylor Park. They each took their own car but arrived almost simultaneously at their designated meeting place (the parking area at the east entrance to the park).

They climbed to the top of a little hill that overlooked the main part of the park—a large open field perfect for kite flying or touch football games—and targeted one of the many large trees that, in Alan's opinion, made the park so idyllic. Brooke had brought a blanket from the trunk of her car, and now they settled beneath the tree, not close together physically but close together in an intellectual

kind of way colored by a remarkable affinity of temperament. Based on Brooke's appearance and on what she'd
volunteered about having nothing to do on a Friday afternoon, Alan assumed that she, like him, was no stranger to
the Saturday night bath. This only added to the sense of
kinship he felt with her.

They spent the next couple of hours locked into each
other's world and largely insensible to the world around
them. When the time came to say goodbye, though, things
turned a bit confusing—at least for Alan. They were standing in the parking area, leaning on their respective cars,
and he felt both drawn to Brooke and repelled by her. On
the one hand he really liked her, and not just her intellect
and temperament. He liked her eyes, of course, and he
also liked the fact that he and she seemed to be exactly
the same height, which he took as a sort of cosmic proof
that they belonged together in some way. Plus, in the time
they'd spent together that afternoon, he'd come to accept
her peculiar body odor—deciding, finally, that it was more
sensual than rank. And he'd begun to see her acne as a sym-
bol of her accepting nature. (His reasoning, here, was that
someone flawed in this way would surely tolerate the flaws
in others.) Above all, though, as Alan had noticed when
Brooke stood up back in the language lab, her body was not
unshapely, even though she was trying to obscure it in an
ankle-length pioneer-woman skirt and a ratty sweater that
was clearly a size too big for her. No, there was no denying
it: he was attracted to Brooke in just about every way a man
could be attracted to a woman. So why did he feel as though

he were impaled on some kind of torture device that was stretching his arms to opposite sides of the earth? So what if her physical appearance was sub-par! Surely he'd grown to the point where he could put his real needs ahead of his concerns about what people might think of him if he were to become involved with a woman who looked like this. But as he stood there in the parking area, his eyes focused on Brooke's, in part to keep from taking in the entirety of the physical self she'd chosen to present to the world, his growth didn't seem such a sure bet.

Although Brooke was leaning against her car as if casually, it seemed to Alan that her body was reaching out toward his body. He was confident he wasn't imaging the sexual energy coming from her, any more than he was imagining a certain wistfulness about her. He told himself that Brooke, like him, was reluctant to initiate anything physical between them, but for a reason very different from his. For whatever reason, she'd fashioned herself into a physically unattractive woman. Her choice of clothes and her choice to make only a glancing gesture at basic hygiene—such choices spoke to an apparently deep-seated fear of physical intimacy, or more precisely to a fear of the painful emotions that can result from such intimacy. Like the stereotypical pretty-but-fat woman who pads herself in flesh to keep men at bay, Brooke padded herself in homeliness. Alan's guess was that her wistfulness was a reflection of her "inner woman" crying out in an effort to break through her self-imposed paralysis, even as she clung to it as to a lifeboat. At any rate, this explanation let him off the hook;

she has her own reasons, he told himself, for keeping this platonic.

They ended up standing in that little parking area for at least half an hour, each of them making little stabs at ending the conversation, only to be caught up in its thread again. Finally, beginning to feel overwhelmed by the intensity of the situation, Alan said, "I really should be going. I've got some studying to do."

"Me too," Brooke was quick to reply, but he wondered if she would study when she got back to her apartment or just sit there and think about their unexpected afternoon together. He envisioned them on a split movie screen— each sitting in their respective apartments thinking about the other.

He opened his car door but turned back to her. "Can I ask Thomas for your number?"

"That would be nice," she said before she got into her car and drove off.

On Sunday night Alan called Brooke and they talked for nearly two hours. The next day they met on campus and from that point began to spend considerable time together. They often ate lunch together in the cafeteria—long, lingering affairs in which the food and the coffee were entirely incidental. Sometimes they found themselves walking about the campus so deeply engrossed in conversation that they were barely walking at all, the enormity of their shared ideas having slowed them to a crawl and sometimes to a dead stop. Such moments, Alan supposed, were the equivalent of a long, spontaneous kiss executed in a vacuum as the rest of the world went about its business. Up to that point in his life he would have preferred the kiss, but he and Brooke shared so special a communion that he didn't feel deprived of anything. He'd found an intellectual companionship he'd never dreamed of finding, and it relegated his sexual impulses to second-tier status. Or so he told himself.

Brooke was an oboist. A few weeks after their afternoon in the park, Alan attended her senior recital. She played beautifully, but more than anything else Alan was impressed by her demeanor onstage. She held herself completely erect, in contrast to her usual slight slouch, and seemed to be swept away by the music even as she was master of it. Decked out in a long black evening gown that showed off her figure to good advantage, she looked reasonably attractive. Plus she'd obviously washed her hair for the occasion. It was this latter observation that led Alan, for the first time, to take a long, hard look at Brooke's face. And what he saw was not entirely surprising. He'd already acknowledged to himself that she had a cutish face (and something beyond cute if you narrowed your focus to her eyes). But framed now by her newly lustrous honey-brown hair, her face actually seemed pretty. He began to imagine what it would look like stripped of its acne. He began to imagine all sorts of things, like Brooke in her black evening gown and her long, clean hair, gliding into the front seat of his car and beginning with him the journey that would take them to their new life together in New York. He imagined their wedding day on a beautiful spring afternoon, in an outdoor setting somewhere in Central Park, and all their friends celebrating with them, and Mike and Aunt Marie and his grandparents throwing rice at them and demanding to know how many children they were planning to have. He imagined himself happy. Imagine that!

Alan wasn't surprised, however, when he ambled up to the stage after the concert and found himself peering at the same less-than-stellar-looking woman he'd come to know in the last few weeks, except in an evening gown and with clean hair. Still, his imaginings had planted a bug in him, and this bug helps to explain, if not to excuse, what happened about two weeks later.

Two weeks later took them to the end of May, a few days before finals were to begin. Although Alan and Brooke had been spending a good deal of time together, they'd never been to each other's apartment (with the exception, that is, of Brooke's previous visits to Thomas). In fact, Brooke seemed to be going out of her way to avoid being alone with Alan except in locations where they were at least partly visible to others. This played into his theory that her physical unattractiveness was by design.

One day they were on campus seated in one of their favorite nesting places, the bottom steps of a landing in the student union.

"Do you like Stan Getz?" Brooke said after one of their infrequent but entirely comfortable silences.

"I *love* Stan Getz, but I thought classical musicians hate jazz."

Brooke kind of screwed up her face. "You think we're all a bunch of snobs, don't you."

"No, I just thought—"

"That's okay," she said. "Lots of classical musicians are snobs, but I think it's more like sour grapes. They know they can't improvise, so they pretend jazz is beneath them."

"I'm not that much into jazz, really, but I love the way Stan Getz plays. I have the original *Jazz Samba* album— the one he did with Charlie Byrd. And I have the one he did with Joao Gilberto."

"I've never heard that one," Brooke said. "Is it good?"

"It's great!"

She was quiet for a while. Finally she said, "Do you have it with you at school, or is it at home?"

This confused Alan for a moment but then he understood that she was talking about the album with Joao Gilberto. "I have it here," he said. "Back at the apartment."

A few minutes later, and much to Alan's surprise, they were in his car headed to his apartment. Soon they were climbing the stairs and he felt his head shift gears from neutral to suspicious. Had Brooke's question about Stan Getz been a ruse to get him to ask her to his apartment? Had she learned from Thomas that Alan had some Stan Getz albums, and had she introduced Getz into the conversation as a circuitous way to get into his pants? And if so, why now, after a month of avoiding being alone with him? More to the point, was Brooke the kind of woman who would make up a story just to get what she wanted? Unless he'd completely misjudged her character, the answer was no.

They entered the apartment and Brooke began to walk

down the hall to Thomas's room, which also functioned as kitchen and living room.

"The record player's in my room," Alan said.

Brooke hesitated a moment, and Alan added, "I can bring it into Thomas's room if you want."

"No, that's okay," she said.

She followed him down the hall to his room, which was perhaps ten feet by ten feet and almost entirely taken up by a double bed. There was, however, a couch against one of the walls, and this was where she sat, making sure, it seemed to Alan, to plant herself on the end of the couch that put her a little farther away from the bed than otherwise.

He found the Getz/Gilberto album, turned on the record player, and carefully placed the needle into the first groove. Then, after deciding that sitting on his bed might send a message Brooke apparently didn't want to receive, he sat down at the other end of the couch. This left about two feet separating them—a significant distance in couch terms, perhaps, but a meager distance in fact.

"This is terrific," Brooke said after listening to maybe twenty seconds of the first cut. "But where's Stan Getz?"

Alan held up a finger to indicate that she should wait, and then suddenly the golden sound of Stan Getz's tenor sax came soaring into the room. Brooke gave a little start— almost a gasp—at the initial sound of the sax, and then Alan watched as she closed her eyes, clearly transported by what she was hearing. He envied her ability to throw herself into the music, but in truth the music was weaving its spell on him as well. At the end of the first cut she looked over at him and said, "I love it!" In the meantime, the space between them had somehow contracted. He looked at her and she looked at him and something gave way. Suddenly they were upon each other. She was clutching at him, it seemed, with every part of her—her lips, her fingernails, the entire weight of her sexuality—and he was beside himself with sexual excitement, his erection bearing down hard against the inside of his jeans, threatening, it seemed, to burst through them into the open air. In the next moment they were on the bed, thrashing about, with Stan Getz wailing around them and through them—the scintillating bossa nova rhythm of guitar, bass, and drums having transformed Alan's lumpy mattress into what he would have sworn was a magic carpet. And then, as if someone had tapped him on the shoulder to remind him that practical matters must be tended to, even at times like this, he remembered the roll of condoms sitting in his night table drawer. By now he and Brooke were only partly clothed, and he could feel his erection begging to enter her, and he could feel her body begging to pull him in. . . . And then it occurred to him that there might not be time for him to reach into his night table drawer and prepare himself. He was at a crossroads. He made his choice.

Again he heard Brooke gasp, but this time it was because he'd entered her. It was all over in a matter of seconds. Alan rolled over onto his back, his body spent but his mind reveling in what he'd just accomplished. Almost at once the refrain *I've done it, I've lost my virginity!* became fused with the crystalline tones of Stan Getz's tenor sax, and he felt himself drifting off into that sweet post-coital slumberland all men know and love.

"Alan!!"—this was Brooke shrieking. "Alan, what the fuck did you do!?"

The sound of her voice—a maddeningly plaintive, incredulous sound—pulled him back from the edge of oblivion. He opened his eyes to see her standing at the foot of the bed, staring down at him in disbelief.

"I guess I got carried away," he said, feeling he was half in a dream.

"Carried away? Alan, you . . . Why didn't you use a rubber, for God's sake!? You just . . . Wait a minute. Did you think I'm on the pill? I'm Catholic, you *know* that. I'd *never* go on the pill!"

Brooke was clearly waiting for an explanation, but what could he say? He opened his mouth as if one or two exculpatory words might spill out, but then he saw something almost mask-like descend upon Brooke's face—something so powerful it transformed her features to the point where he felt he was looking up at a total stranger.

"Alan," she said, "are you telling me . . . Are you a *virgin!?*"

"Not anymore," he said, aware at once that he could have given a better answer.

"My God!" she said. She stepped around the bed to the small space between it and the couch, and now she was looming over him, half-clothed, looking far more like a harridan than the beautiful woman he'd perceived her to be during his orgasmic bliss of a few moments earlier.

Alan lay there, dumbly looking up at her. Brooke had pulled up her panties probably the moment he withdrew from her, and now she stood before him, her jeans bunched around her ankles. Then she seemed to remember that she was half naked. Quickly she pulled up her jeans and grabbed her blouse and put it on, then smoothed back her greasy hair.

"My God, Alan," she said, "I'm in mid-month. I could get pregnant."

Stupidly, he adopted the tone of an expert. "Oh, that won't happen. What are the chances?"

"What the hell do *you* know?" she shot back. "All the women in my family are fertile. *Very* fertile. My mother, my three sisters, my aunts—everybody. We're all fertile."

In the meantime, Alan's mind was clearing and he could see that his act had been both irresponsible and opportunistic. A wave of guilt passed over him and he promptly sat up and began to reach for his own clothes. Then he noticed that Brooke had picked up her handbag and was on her way out of the bedroom. He thought of pleading his case, trying to reassure her that she wouldn't get pregnant from this one time, but something occurred to him that might have occurred to him at the moment of entry had he not been preoccupied. The thought—the sudden realization, really—was that he'd slid into her like Willie Mays into third base. Brooke, he saw now, wasn't herself a virgin. For all he knew she was quite experienced, maybe even promiscuous. This last thought—a surprising one considering her physical appearance and in contradistinction to the sexually frustrated wallflower Alan had painted her to be—was enough to distract him from trying to stop her from leaving the apartment. A moment later he heard her shout, "Asshole!"—this followed by the sound of the apartment door slamming. Then he became aware again of Stan Getz's lyrical tenor sax, weaving its way in and out of that infectious bossa nova rhythm, oblivious to the travesty that had just taken place in his bedroom.

During finals Alan stayed as far away as he could from the music building and even the student union, feeling that he and Brooke would each be better off if they could avoid running into each other. Besides, what would be the point in rehashing the bedroom debacle? He would be heading down to Columbia soon and she would be heading over to Boston and they would never see each other again anyway. As it turned out, Alan managed to get through those few days of finals without seeing Brooke, and by the time he'd reached the city—having skipped commencement, which he'd been planning to do anyway—he'd put the whole thing behind him. Or so he told himself.

8

It's February 15, 1975, and upwards of eighty people cram into Sacred Heart Church in downtown Morehead, New Jersey, to witness the marriage of Dolores La Forgia to Michael Agnalini.

After the ceremony everyone gets into their car and drives the quarter mile to the local Moose hall. Dolly has insisted on a Valentine's Day wedding, probably so that she can have a "theme" reception and thereby indulge her passion for supervising things—in this case, the decoration of the hall. It was Dolly La Forgia, after all, who supervised the preparations for any number of the junior high and high school dances Alan might have gone to if he'd been the kind of kid who went to dances. Dolly, in fact, was known as the mother superior of the neighborhood. The one who organized the block parties and the bake sales and the Easter egg hunts, year in and year out. Now, as he walks into the Moose hall, Alan can see that Dolly has outdone herself. From the red tablecloths to the giant red crepe paper hearts that line the walls to the red streamers hanging from the ceiling to the pink, heart-shaped napkins that sit primly at each table setting—the entire hall reeks of Valentine's Day. And Dolly is glowing, less so because she was just married, it seems to Alan, than because she achieved her goal of creating the perfect ambiance for a wedding reception.

"Oh, Dolly," one of her sisters is saying, "you did such a beautyful job the way you decorated the hall. Just beautyful."

"And it's so romantic," another sister chimes in. "It makes me feel like getting married all over again." The woman gives a sidelong glance at a bald, pot-bellied *gibbone* whose paper plate is overflowing with hors d'oeuvres, and the other women roll their eyes and cackle.

Mike has told Alan that Dolly's three sisters and two brothers are mostly from Sheepshead Bay and Canarsie. How, then, did Dolly end up in New Jersey? And on Alan's block!

He has no reason to feel sorry for himself, though. He isn't the one who just married the woman and now has the honor of sleeping in the same bed with her, and hearing her gargle every morning, and then watching as she struggles into her girdle. As a mere stepson Alan is far removed from any of this. It's Mike, a man whose only redeeming quality is his undying love for Alan's mother, who will suffer these particular slings and arrows. *It ain't the same the second time around*, he said to his son a few weeks ago. And he didn't have to add that he's getting old and needs some companionship. Alan understands. And he's determined to be a dutiful son, to do whatever propriety demands he do in the situation. Once the cocktail hour has run its course they'll all sit down to dinner and he'll stand up and raise his champagne glass and make a toast to the newlyweds, and he'll finish by looking Dolly in the eyes and saying *Welcome to the Agnalini family*. May you choke on your prime rib, he'll be thinking, but no one will know this. No, he'll do things by the book. He's determined to be there if Mike needs him at some point down the road—if he calls up some day to intimate that being in a loveless marriage has begun to take its toll on him. If he wants to reminisce about what it was like when he and Alan's mother were young, and then complain about the present state of things—*Dolly did this*, or *Dolly said that*—Alan will be there for him. He owes it to the man. Or if not to him, then to his mother.

During the cocktail hour Alan makes it a point to stay on the move and to keep a glass (in this case, of seltzer) in his hand at all times. He discovered this trick during the cocktail hour at his cousin Evelyn's wedding reception, and now, several years later, he finds it equally effective. By the time the hour is up he's covered the equivalent of who-knows-how-many city blocks but has managed to avoid a plethora of small talk.

Slowly everyone makes their way to their tables. Soon Alan will be making the toast, but that won't be a problem. The first dance, on the other hand, promises to be a thornier issue. He looks up at the stage and there's Lenny, his fifteen-year-old, saxophone-playing second cousin, flanked by a pubescent accordion player and a barely pubescent drummer, playing "This Could Be the Start of Something Big." Lenny has one eye on Uncle Vini, who is to give him the high sign to segue into "The Sheik of Araby"—Dolly's choice for the first dance. Alan realizes he's holding his breath and tells himself to calm down. After all, he reasons, there are worse things than having to dance with a cow. And then he thinks of one: having to dance with the cow's daughter. It hadn't occurred to him until this moment that after he dances with Dolly he'll be expected to dance with Vera. Instinctively he looks around the room for the nearest exit, and then he hears an abrupt break in the music followed by a poorly executed drum roll. He watches as Uncle Vini waddles up onto the stage and blows into the mic a few times, then waves an arm to quiet the crowd.

"Can I have your attention," he says over the squealing mic. "It gives me great pleasure to introduce to you, for the first time: Mr. and Mrs. Michael Agnalini!"

Lenny and the boys launch into the first number, and Mike and Dolly stride out onto the floor and begin fox-trotting around to the polite applause of their relatives and newly acquired in-laws. As for Alan, he's all too aware that in a few seconds he'll be the one dancing with the cow. Suddenly he seems to hear his old high school friend Burt saying *Cheer up, Agnalini, it'll all be over soon,* and to his surprise Burt's words give him the little jolt of courage he needs. He smiles and waits for his cue to cut in on Mike and Dolly, and when the time comes he pulls the whole thing off with aplomb. He and Dolly dance around at arm's length, each of them smiling and making small talk, and the same thing happens with Vera. Before he knows it, Alan is sitting at the head table next to Mike, feeling not just relieved but rather proud of himself for having acted like a mensch for once in his life. Riding this wave of self-confidence he makes an excellent toast, and when he looks at Dolly and welcomes her to the Agnalini family he almost means it.

After dinner he's sitting alone at one of the tables. He knows he should get up and mingle a little, at least make a show at being in a festive mood, but what's the point? Everyone knows he isn't a mingler, and he certainly isn't a dancer. And besides, who within a ten-mile radius of where he sits would have anything to say that he wanted to hear? And who would be interested in anything *he* had to say? *You need practice,* he can hear Rhonda saying. *It doesn't matter if you're bored silly or if you're boring the other person silly. The point is, you're getting practice in conversing, and therefore you're getting better at it.* But Alan is in no mood to practice anything. He just wants to get back to Manhattan, back to a world that makes sense to him. He looks around the room at the relatives he grew up with and at the new relatives he hopes he won't have to see for another ten years. Everyone seems to be having a good time. They're in their element, while Alan, having been thrust into their element, is out of his own.

"What's the problem, bro? You look like you just lost your best friend."

Vera, of all people, has sat down at the table. Ever since

Mike and Dolly began "keeping company"—their term—
Vera has been acting not only civil to Alan but nauseatingly
familiar. And now she actually called him "bro." What is he
supposed to say to her? That he looks forward to getting to
know his new stepsister better? That he doesn't wish she'd
get a job in some remote outpost of the North Pole? He has
nothing to say to her.

"Oh, hi Vera," he says. "No, I was just daydreaming."

She gives him her best mother-hen look. "Now that
we're brother and sister, Alan, I want you to know you can
confide in me if there's something you got on your mind."

Confide in her? In *her*?

"That's very nice of you," he says. "But no, I was just ... I
was thinking about work, if you can believe it."

"Thinking about work? At a wedding? You gotta lighten
up."

He takes a sip of beer, hoping Vera won't ask him to
dance by way of lightening him up.

"Vera—Alan. You two making plans for another wedding?"

Alan looks up and sees his cousin Ralph—all two hundred seventy-five pounds of him—standing across the table.

"Don't go starting nothing, Ralph," he hears Vera say.
"You're always instigating something. You been that way
since I can remember."

"I was just making a joke," Ralph says, and the two childhood neighbors share a couple of yuks.

Relieved of the burden of being in a one-on-one with
Vera, Alan leans back in his chair to take in the sideshow.

"So Ralph," Vera says, "I was just now saying to my mother how beautyful Glenda looks tonight. How much weight did she lose?"

"If you ask me, Vera, she's too thin. She lost, I think, forty pounds on that peanut butter diet. But if you ask me she's too thin."

"I never had that problem," Vera says. "I always been thin."

As if anyone who grew up on Carter Street needs to be reminded about Vera La Forgia's bony ass!

"I lost some weight too," Ralph says. "Nine, ten pounds."

"Good for you, Ralph." Then after a moment: "So Ralph, how're things going in the real estate business? I heard you opened up a new branch in Philly."

"Actually it's Cherry Hill—right outside a Philly. I think it'll be a big addition to the business, to corner that part a the Jersey market."

"How many branches you got now?"

Ralph pauses for a moment and seems to be counting in his head. "That's our ninth branch," he says, "but I see the business getting much bigger. I been putting out some feelers in upstate New York and New England. But the goal is to go national. That's where the *real* money is."

Alan has always wondered if Ralph had been able to wrest control of what was once McNabb Realty the same way he rose from senior-class vice-president to president in high school: by starting false rumors about his rival while maintaining for himself an appearance of flawless integrity—and then, when the time was right, going in for the kill. (This was just one of many such exploits Ralph boasted about to Alan when they were growing up.)

Alan notices, now, that Ralph seems to be waiting for Vera to comment on his business plans, but she seems distracted. A trace of surprise crosses Ralph's face, and he turns to Alan.

"Remember when we were kids, Alan? I used to be a pretty good athlete. I was a little thinner back then, of course."

"I remember when you two boys used to play stickball in the street, it used to drive my mother crazy. 'Those two kids are gonna break somebody's window and it better not be mine.' I can still hear her now."

After a moment of silence Ralph turns back to Alan. "But we used to have some pretty good stickball games, right Alan? And you were pretty good for a little kid."

"I could hit your fastball when I was eight years old," Alan says. "And you were practically full grown by then."

"When you were eight? That would make me what— fourteen? I wasn't full grown by then?"

"You could've fooled me."

"Alan was always good at sports," Vera says. Then she turns to him. "How come you didn't try out for the baseball team in high school, Alan? Or did you?"

"He didn't," Ralph volunteers. "Cause I didn't let him. His grades were slipping—what was it, eleventh grade?— and my uncle Mike calls me at work and says, 'Ralph, you gotta give Alan a call and straighten him out. He wants to try out for baseball, but his grades ain't up to snuff.' And I called and straightened you out, remember Alan?"

"You was always such a good brother," Vera says to Ralph. Then to Alan she adds, "You were lucky to have a big brother like Ralph, Alan."

"I did what I could," Ralph says. "Growing up next door like that—we *were* almost like brothers sometimes, right Alan?"

"Sure," Alan says, no longer able to drum up contempt for the charade he's had to pay lip service to his whole life.

"Daddy, Mommy has a headache and she says she wants to go home!"

Alan looks up to see Ralph's three sons—Moe, Larry, and Curly—running toward the table.

"Angelo, didn't I tell you not to interrupt grownups when they're talking?"

Angelo, the oldest boy, begins to pout, but Louis, the middle boy, tugs at his father's sleeve. "But Mommy says she's gonna throw up!" he says.

"My wife gets migraines," Ralph explains to Vera. Then he turns back to Angelo. "Tell your sister to get our coats, they're in the hall closet when you come in."

A minute later Ralph and his male heirs have gone, and Alan is left alone again with Vera. He begins to stand up—though he hasn't decided what he'll say to her by way of making an escape—when, to his surprise, Vera herself stands up and without a word begins to walk across to the

Sheepshead Bay-Canarsie side of the hall. Alan sits back down, feeling slightly miffed.

After a few minutes his guilt gets the better of him. He can't exactly go into Rhonda's office on Tuesday having spent the bulk of his father's wedding sitting off by himself. He pulls himself to his feet and begins to walk in the general direction of a group of his cousins who are standing near the dessert table.

"Alan," his cousin Loretta says, "you look snazzy in your tuxedo."

Snazzy? This curious word, inherited from an era Loretta never came close to seeing, is all it takes to remind Alan of the insurmountable gap that separates his world from that of his cousins. In spite of this, he's determined to meet them half way. "Thanks," he says. It's a start.

Then his cousin Evelyn says something and he says something back, but he can feel his mind wandering far from the Morehead Moose Hall. For some reason he begins to think about his plans for tomorrow, which include going to the Ninety-second Street Y to do some running. That—the running—was one of his New Year's resolutions, and he seems to be getting some results from it; he feels better physically, he's less stressed generally, and he's even sleeping a little better.

"So Alan, you got a girlfriend?"

His cousin Loretta's question has pulled him back to the present, and he launches into his standard I'm-not-even-divorced-and-you've-already-got-me-married defense. Unfortunately the word "girlfriend" has reminded him about another of his New Year's resolutions, which was to make a real effort to find Brooke, and immediately he begins to feel guilty over his failure to follow through in this regard. *Why don't you just go to the musician's union?* This was Rhonda's suggestion when he announced to her that he'd made a few fruitless calls to B. Hadleys. And her point is well taken; if he really wanted to find Brooke, he could do so with relative ease. But here it is the middle of February and he's done next to nothing to locate her. Is it simple procrastination he's guilty of, or is his inaction the result of something more diabolical—self-sabotage, perhaps, or some childish propensity for doing the opposite of whatever an authority figure might want him to do?

Just then his cousin Dominic, the garbage man, approaches the group, and Alan remembers Vera's admonition that he needs to lighten up.

"So Dom," he says, "how's the garbage business? Probably stinks, huh?"

Neither Dominic nor any of Alan's other cousins get his joke (or think it's funny), and he takes their non-reaction as his cue to politely excuse himself and wander back to the table.

He settles into his chair and looks up at the stage. Once again there's Saxophone Lenny, just fifteen years old and the most arrogant son-of-a-bitch you'd ever want to meet—exempt, by virtue of his talent, from the social pressures that befall mere mortals like Alan. Ah, to be a talented fifteen-year-old *putz* like Lenny!

Alan scans the room and notices his aunt Gertie sitting alone at a table near the emergency exit. Because he kind of likes Aunt Gertie, and because he always feels more comfortable sitting near emergency exits, he walks over to her table and sits down.

"Alan," she says. "You look so handsome in your tux. How you been doing?"

"I'm good," he says with as much conviction as he can mount.

"Good," she says. "I'm glad. Do you believe your father after all these years getting married? But it's for the best, he needs somebody, nobody should be alone at his age."

Alan can see that his aunt has downed an extra sip or two of wine, so he discreetly moves her glass out of her reach. She doesn't seem to notice.

"So how's life as a bachelor?" she goes on. "You getting enough to eat? You look a little thin, you should find a nice girl she'll cook for you."

"I'm fine," he protests mildly, knowing that comments about food and nice girls are the price you pay when you approach the Aunt Gerties of this world.

"That's good," she says, "cause you gotta keep up your strength."

His strength? Apparently he's looking not only thin but exceedingly frail.

"I'm fine," he says again.

His aunt gives him a skeptical look. "So you like your job, Alan?"

He shrugs.

She reaches in the direction of where her wine glass was sitting and says, "It's just a job, right? That's okay, you're young, you got time to find what'll make you happy. I thought you were gonna be a professor, weren't you gonna be a professor all those years?"

"That didn't seem right," he begins. "It's not the real world. . . ." But then he notices that she's not paying attention.

"Did you see Grandpa crying before?"

"No," Alan says. "When?"

"Before."

"No, I didn't see that."

"Yeah, he was crying to see Mike getting married, it reminded him of your mother may she rest in peace. You don't know what it's like, Alan, to lose a child."

Alan is about to say something like *No, and I wouldn't want to find out* when his aunt says, "Your mother was Grandpa's favorite. She was everybody's favorite, it's like that when you're the baby of the family. But you didn't know your mother when she was young. She was a spitfire, and so pretty! I was surprised when she ended up with Mike. Don't get me wrong, your father's a good man, but my sister she—"

Alan's aunt begins to fiddle with one of her earrings—an obvious attempt to distract him from whatever she was about to say.

"My mother what?" he says.

Aunt Gertie looks back at him. Of his mother's four sisters, Aunt Gertie has always been the one who most resembled her. For a moment it seems to Alan as though he's looking across at his mother—the way she might have looked had she survived into her sixties.

"I shouldn't say," Aunt Gertie begins in answer to his question. "It's not my place. Besides, Aunt Marie was the only one who knew for sure, and she never told. We all knew Rudy was the one your mother had eyes for, but he was always on the road—he was a traveling salesman—and even when he was in town you'd see him with this one or that one. 'He ain't husband material,' we used to tell Agnes but she wouldn't hear it she was so ga-ga over this guy. And then when she comes in one day outa the blue and says, 'I'm marrying Mike Agnalini'—well, you had to wonder."

Again Aunt Gertie pauses. She seems to be questioning whether she might have said more than she intended to.

"In case you're wondering," Alan says, "I know about the miscarriage."

His aunt seems a little surprised. He thinks of moving her wine glass back within her reach (one more sip might be enough to get her to say what she's only implied to this point) but he doesn't do this. Besides, the implication told the whole story. So his mother was pregnant by some guy named Rudy when she married Mike! Somehow this doesn't surprise him, and what's more he would bet money not only that Mike knew about Rudy and the baby but that he volunteered to give the baby a name and raise it as his own. After all, this was the same man who voluntarily stepped in to become Ralph's de facto father a couple of years later when Ralph's father died. What is it with Mike Agnalini and other men's children?

"How we doing over here, Gert?"

Alan looks up and there's the devil himself. Or is he a saint? Or just someone who likes to play the hero?

"Mike, this was a lovely affair," Aunt Gertie says. "Dolly did such a good job with them decorations."

"Sure did," Mike says.

Mike's attempt to sound proud of his new wife is transparent—at least to Alan. He looks at Mike standing there in his rented tux, trying to pass himself off as the lucky groom, and he actually feels sorry for him. For one of the few times in Alan's life, he feels compassion for the man whose obvious preference for Ralph tormented him throughout his childhood and well beyond it. But now, at twenty-eight, Alan is past all that, and it isn't just a matter of not having the energy for the old anger. Maybe he isn't an adult yet—Rhonda, for one, says he has some work to do in that department—but he's mature enough to know that, for better or worse, the man he's looking up at is his father, and that he did his best raising his son, and that he's hurting.

9

"Well, that's all she wrote," Alan hears Rick say.

He looks up from his typewriter and sees that Rick is on his feet, tossing a folder to a corner of his desk.

"I'll meet you over there," Alan says. "I just have to finish up this jacket copy."

"Alan, it's Friday afternoon. The copy can wait till Monday."

"I just want to finish it up. I don't like to leave stuff hanging."

Rick is at the door now. "There's a word for people like you."

"What word is that?" Alan says.

"You tell me. You're the one seeing the shrink."

Alan catches the back of Rick's head as he slips out of the office. "I'll be over there in twenty minutes," he calls after him.

He turns back to his typewriter and writes a few lines,

then reads what he's written. "No, this isn't right," he mumbles, tempted to abandon the copy and begin his weekend. A few minutes later he does just that.

Alan enters The Kopper Kettle and spots Rick over in a corner.

"You're early," Rick says as Alan approaches the little table he's commandeered for them. "Finally saw the wisdom in the Friday afternoon jailbreak?"

"I suppose," Alan says.

He's sitting now, and he catches the eye of a waitress and orders a beer. Then he says, "So how's Sally? And Emily?"

"They're great, Alan, but we're not here to talk about them. You said you needed my advice about something, so shoot. I'm all ears."

Alan looks out into the room as if something has caught his attention, but he's merely buying time. Then he says, "There's this situation. Rhonda and I have been going back and forth about it for months, and finally she suggested I talk to you about it."

"To me? She should give me a kickback. But what situation?"

Alan takes a sip of beer and then another. "There was this woman in college," he begins. "Brooke."

After Alan has finished his story Rick sits uncharacteristically silent. As for Alan, he feels quite relieved—almost giddy—now that he's finally revealed to someone other than Rhonda that he was a twenty-two-year-old virgin. But he's surprised Rick has shown no visible reaction to his disclosure. Maybe he assumed all along that Alan was slow to lose his virginity.

"And you want my opinion," Rick says at length.

"Well . . . yeah. I'm stuck, here."

Rick leans over the table and lowers his voice. "Forget it ever happened, Alan. You don't need something like this complicating your life."

Alan sits back in genuine surprise. "This from you?" he says. "Mr. pro-marriage, pro-family?"

"Mr. pro-*legitimate* family. This was an indiscretion, Alan—and a damned funny one, if you ask me—but it's not the kind of thing you should rearrange your life over. Let it go."

Alan looks across at Rick, not knowing what to make of his advice.

"Don't get me wrong," Rick says. "It's not just for your own good that I'm telling you to steer clear of this. This woman, Brooke, and this child—if there *is* a child: they have a life, a history. It's way too late for some stranger to come waltzing into the child's life without expecting repercussions. Confusion, alone, is hard enough for a young child to deal with. You can't expect a little kid to say, 'I'm sorry you missed the first four years of my life, Daddy, but you're here now so let's go fishing.' It doesn't work that way."

Just what Alan needs: something *else* to consider. Rhonda has been telling him to find Brooke for his *own* good. But the issue of whether it might be detrimental to the child's welfare if he were to insinuate himself into its life? That was an issue they never discussed. Does this mean that Rhonda is ethically or morally bankrupt in some way? Or is she simply looking out for her patient—namely, Alan—rather than for some hypothetical child? What a mess! If only he'd been looking east instead of west when Brooke got on that crosstown bus.

Later he's walking up Second Avenue, taking his usual Friday-night slow trek home. Rick has pointed out to him what should have been obvious, and now he can see that he's not only damned if he does and damned if he doesn't—he's doubly damned if he does. Come to think of it, though, doesn't that make his choice a simple one? If the child's welfare is indeed the paramount issue, then his course of action is clear: he'll stay away from the situation and thereby spare the child. Unless Rick's argument was specious in some way. But how is he to know? Does he have the life experience to make such a judgment?

Alan stops off at a Baskin-Robbins. About twenty minutes later—satiated but no less confused—he comes to a grocery store and glances in the window. What he sees there stops him in his tracks; the name "Brooke Hadley" is staring out at him in big black letters. He stares back at it, then takes in the entire poster:

IN CONCERT
Brooke Hadley, oboe
David Ketts, piano
Saturday, February 22, 1975, 8:00 PM
Church of the Good Shepherd
142 E. 38th St., Manhattan
donations accepted

10

Alan is sitting in a cab on his way to the church. Was it chance last night, or some kind of divine intervention, that led him to the poster advertising Brooke's concert? Not that it matters. What matters is that he's finally about to confront Brooke, he's about to get his answer.

His plan is to arrive after intermission, find a seat in the back of the church somewhere, and then, when the concert is over, approach her.

I'm sure you're surprised to see me, he'll say, *but I've been having this crazy idea that you had a child from that time we were together, back in our senior year.*

A child? she'll say. *From that one time? Don't be silly, Alan. If anything, I should apologize to you for overreacting the way I did.*

And that will be the end of it. They might go out for a cup of coffee for old times' sake, or he might disappear from the church without another word. In either case it will be over. What has he been worrying about all this time? Rhonda's right: he's not happy unless he's making himself miserable.

As the cab inches its way downtown, though, Alan can feel his optimism waning. In fact, by the time they've reached Fifty-ninth Street he's certain Brooke's reception of him will be icy at best. And by the time the cab pulls up in front of the church he's tempted to tell the driver to turn around and take him back uptown.

Instead he pays the driver and gets out. The weather has warmed a bit recently and now it looks like it might rain. As Alan steps into the church, people are still milling around. He hangs back near the door, and eventually everyone begins to take their seats. The church seems to be about half full (or half empty, depending on your perspective). He slips into a back row and sidles over until he reaches a seat that's partly obscured by a pillar. Confident that he'll be invisible to the performers but still having a good view of the front of the church, he settles back to await Brooke's arrival onstage.

After a minute the house lights dim and the musicians come back onstage. He doesn't recognize Brooke at first. She seems taller and a little slimmer than she seemed to Alan when he caught a glimpse of her, back in November. Her hair, which is tied in a single braid, seems longer as well, reaching to at least the middle of her back. And not just her hair but all of her seems to be glowing. He attri- butes this to the spotlight that shines on her and the pianist, although the pianist doesn't seem to share quite the same glow.

The pianist plays a note and Brooke tunes to it. Then there's a pause—he can't help thinking of it as a pregnant pause—and they begin.

Alan sees from his program that they're playing something by Mangiapoli. Who the hell is Mangiapoli? Whoever he is, his idea of music is far removed from Alan's. Even so, he sits back and tries to lose himself in whatever it is he's hearing. This works for maybe a minute and a half. Part of the problem, of course, is the music, but a bigger problem is Brooke herself. She sits onstage as if on a pedestal—elegant in her black evening gown, her body moving subtly to the music, her lips enveloping the oboe reed with studied determination and an obvious symbolism it would be useless to try to ignore. That's when it hits him: he came to the concert not merely so that Brooke could clear something up for him. He came here to behold the new, grownup version of the homely girl he remembers from their college days. The fact is, he's fascinated by the transformation she's undergone, and, as he'd realized some months ago, his obsession with her isn't simply about paternity. Nor, however, is it simply about salvaging their relationship in some way. What he wants from Brooke, he can see now, is for her to excuse his past indiscretion so that they can start over as two adults, child or no child. And if things move beyond friendship? Well, so much the better.

The two musicians finish the Mangiapoli and go into

something by Mozart. Alan glances at his program and sees that there are two pieces after the Mozart. He thinks about leaving the church and wandering around the neighborhood for a while (seeing Brooke in performance is proving to be far more agitating than he assumed it would be), but he nixes that idea. Instead he sits back and for the next forty minutes or so does what he can to keep his mind off fantasies of Brooke making love to him, or Brooke and him in bed playing with their little girl (so he envisions the phantom child as a girl!), or Brooke and him standing hand in hand on a deserted beach looking out at the ocean, with their little girl running up to them shouting *Mommy, Daddy, look what I made!* And then they turn and there's a huge sandcastle staring up at them. *Can we live in that castle?* their little girl says, and Brooke says *We already do.*

Eventually the final piece comes to a close, and after the musicians take their bows the house lights come up. Alan watches as Brooke places her oboe on her chair and she and her accompanist begin to mingle with some of the audience. The concert is over, but for Alan it's showtime. And, as it turns out, it's a different showtime from the one he rehearsed. No longer is it a simple matter of confirming the existence or non-existence of a child. Now it's also a matter of trying to reestablish a relationship with someone he, in a sense, violated. Is such a thing possible? Could Brooke really forgive him his irresponsible arrogance? Will she even say two words to him, or will she turn her back on him and pretend he doesn't exist? Or worse, will she sneer at him and say *Yes, I have a child and yes she's yours, but you*

will never be part of her life. You're dead to me, Alan Agnalini.
Still, he can't run away from the situation. He's so close to
a resolution—and a new beginning?—that the idea of running away is tantamount to jumping into the East River.

Feeling like an exposed nerve ending, Alan stands and
begins to make his way toward the center aisle. Suddenly
he hears a small voice shout "Mommy!" He looks up to see
a little girl, perhaps four or five years old, running up the
center aisle from the vestibule in the back of the church.
He can see the girl only in profile, but her dark brown hair
seems identical in shade to his. He watches as she runs into
Brooke's arms. *You're getting so big,* Brooke seems to say to
her, and he feels a rush of something—maybe some spe-
cies of joy or wonder he's never had an inkling of. In the
next moment he sees Brooke's eyes travel to the back of the
church. A tall, dark-haired man—good-looking, maybe a
few years older than Alan—is striding up the aisle like a
movie star at a chamber of commerce meeting, his eyes
trained on Brooke, who, with her daughter trailing behind
her, has begun to approach him from the front of the
church. When they meet somewhere midway down the
aisle, they kiss. Not passionately like new lovers, but com-
fortably as if they've been married for some years and have
no regrets about what they got themselves into. It's a happy
family they make, the three of them—standing there in the
aisle, partly obscured by the thinning audience. And it isn't
Alan's family.

He quickly makes his way down the row and out the
church, willing himself not to look back at them. When he

hits the street he feels suddenly deflated. You'll feel better in the morning, he tells himself. This whole thing about having a life with Brooke was just a pipe dream anyway. And you finally have your answer: the child is not yours.

Part III

11

The first two weeks of May were chilly, almost winter-like, but now the weather has turned. Alan spots the restaurant from down the block and sees that there are tables set up on the sidewalk in front of it. Seconds later he sits down at one. He's never been to a restaurant in the East Forties before. The neighborhood seems kind of quiet, as if everyone is home preparing for the start of another work week. For a moment he feels envious of all the people in the world who have nothing to worry about other than what they're going to wear to work the next day. Life can be moving along smoothly, but then you get a phone call and suddenly you don't know what's coming next.

It's about ten of seven. He's ten minutes early, and that's if she's right on time. More likely she'll be fashionably late and he'll be sitting here like a moron for twenty minutes. He takes out the book he's been reading but only to appear occupied. A few sentences later a waitress appears at his table.

"Are we dining alone tonight?" she asks.

The waitress's use of the royal "we" has been enough to prejudice him against her. That, plus she looks somewhat like his lovely stepsister, Vera.

"Someone's joining me," he says, not matching her toothpaste smile with one of his own.

"I'll keep an eye out," the waitress says before she scoots off to more fertile ground.

Alan goes back to his book but he can't concentrate. In a few minutes Brooke will be sitting across from him, and then what? Why did she call him out of the blue, and why couldn't she just tell him what she had to tell him over the phone? What's the big mystery that requires a sit-down dinner?

He glances at his watch and sees that it's twenty after seven. He's been sitting here half an hour, and he's beginning to think that maybe he's in the process of getting stood up. He turns back to his book but then all at once Brooke is upon him.

"Sorry I'm late," she says, sitting down across from him. "I was at a rehearsal and it went over. Have you been here long?"

"A while," he says, "but it's okay. I'm enjoying being outside."

She picks up a menu and begins to pore over it.

Their eyes still haven't met, not for more than a second—proving that even the new, *improved* Brooke can feel ill at ease under the right conditions. It isn't until they've each ordered that she looks across the table at Alan.

"I was shocked, Alan, when I saw you as you were leaving that concert. It's been so long. How have you been?"

"I've been okay. But you. You look great."

"Thanks," she says, "but how is it you ended up at the concert?"

"I, uh . . ." he begins. "I happened to see a poster advertising the concert and was kind of flabbergasted to see your name. And I guess I was curious to see you after all these years. Not to see you and talk to you—we didn't exactly part on good terms—but just to see you. That's why I sat in the back. So you wouldn't be able to see me."

Brooke seems to accept this explanation, though Alan had noticed her face tighten when he alluded to their sexual encounter.

"But what have you been up to?" she says now. "I know you were married, right?"

She does? How does she know that?

He supposes his confusion is transparent, for she says, "Thomas told me he'd gotten a wedding invitation from you. You must have met someone as soon as you got to Columbia."

"Pretty much," he says.

A moment later the waitress comes by with a basket of bread. Alan takes out a roll and breaks off a piece and begins to butter it, but he can feel Brooke's eyes upon him. Then he hears her say, "There's no point trying to pretend it didn't happen, Alan. That's why I wanted to see you. Indirectly, at least."

He looks up. For the first time since Brooke sat down some minutes ago, he allows himself to really look at her. It's Brooke Hadley, all right. Except that her acne is gone and her hair isn't greasy and her eyes seem even bluer than he remembers them being.

"I can't believe it," he says. "It's really you. Do I look like a stranger too?"

"No, you look the same. But older, I guess."

"I'm sorry," he says, "I wasn't trying to change the subject. But before we get to whatever it is you want to say to me, I need to apologize for that whole thing. I was a real jerk."

Brooke says nothing, and Alan takes her silence as confirmation of his need to apologize.

He takes a nervous sip of water. "Anyway," he continues, "don't think I haven't berated myself over the years."

More silence, until finally he realizes she isn't going to let him off the hook. In fact, unless it's his imagination he thinks he sees the shadow of a scowl cross Brooke's face.

Alan waits for her to say what's on her mind but she remains silent. Finally he says, "So why exactly did you want to see me? You mentioned it has something to do with our . . . with that afternoon in my apartment."

Just then the waitress descends upon their table. "Swordfish," she says with a flourish as she places Alan's dinner in front of him. "And the chef's salad," she continues, setting Brooke's salad in place. "I'll be back in a minute with the wine."

Brooke turns to her entrée and Alan does the same with his, although his question hangs in the air. Why did Brooke want to see him? A minute later the waitress appears with their wine and he finds himself wondering whether he should make a toast or repeat the question. His debate ends when Brooke takes a sip of wine and says, "Anyway, Alan, the main reason I wanted to see you was to tell you about Stephanie."

"Who's Stephanie?"

"Stephanie's my daughter."

"Oh, right," he says. "I saw her at the concert. She looks like a sweet little girl. I'll bet your husband can't get enough of her."

Brooke gives him a quizzical look. "My what?"

"Your husband," Alan says. "You know . . . that guy I saw at the concert. He was your husband, right?"

She gives a mirthless chuckle. "No," she says. "He wasn't my husband."

Alan steals a glance at Brooke's left hand and sees five ringless fingers. Now he's confused. If this guy isn't her husband, but is the obvious father . . . Then it occurs to him that, in the spirit of the late Sixties, they never married. Well, husband or common-law husband or live-in boyfriend—what's the difference?

"That was Kyle," Brooke offers. "He and I split up. Not too long after that concert, in fact."

Alan tries to piece this together. "So . . . But Kyle is Stephanie's father, right?"

"Kyle and I only met about six months ago. He's definitely not Stephanie's father."

Alan feels himself plummet into a kind of limbo. *Kyle's not the father.* Something tells him there's a significance to these words, something . . . And then he asks himself why Brooke would have contacted him unless there was something important . . . That's when his mouth falls open, he's sure, for Brooke reaches across the table and puts a hand on his forearm.

"That's why I wanted to see you," he hears her say. "Stephanie is yours, Alan. She's your daughter."

Alan looks across the table in wonder, as if he can't quite comprehend what he just heard. At the same time, he tells himself that this was the outcome his gut was telling him to expect all along.

"I know this is a shock," Brooke says, "but it's been going on too long. I should've told you the moment I knew for sure that I was pregnant."

I can't believe it, Alan keeps repeating to himself. That little girl . . . mine? He tries to formulate some question, some configuration of words, that might help him make sense of what he's just been hit with.

"It was just that I was so angry," Brooke says. "I was really pissed, Alan, when I found out I was pregnant. And by the time I calmed down a little you'd already been in New York for weeks. I thought of writing you—I could've found your address easily enough—but then some friends convinced me I should raise the baby on my own. Finally when my due date was approaching I changed my mind and decided to contact you, but when I called Thomas and asked him if he had your address he told me you were getting married. It didn't seem right to give you information that might cause a problem in your marriage, so I let it go. I knew that eventually my child would start asking about its father, but figured that no father at all might be better than a father who was never around. Anyway, I made my decision and stuck to it. Until now, that is."

Her explanation seems plausible enough—except for her alleged concern over his marriage. Because if she knew he was married then, how does she know he isn't *still* married? And if he's still married, then why would she be any less concerned now than she was then that his marriage might suffer if he learned the truth? Unless she knows he's getting a divorce. But how could she know that?

"How do you know I'm not still married?" he says.

"You're not, are you?"

"No. Well, technically I am; the divorce won't be coming through for a while. But no, I'm about as unmarried as you can get. But how did you know?"

"I put two and two together. I saw you alone at that concert on a Saturday night, and then I looked up your name in the phone book and saw that you live in the four-hundred block of East Eighty-third. I have a friend who used to live on that block and I know the apartments are small. Plus, the listing said Alan Agnalini, not Alan and *blank* Agnalini."

"It was one of the world's worst marriages," he volunteers. "But as far as your reasons for not telling me about the baby—you don't owe me an explanation."

But *doesn't* she owe him an explanation? Certainly it was his blunder that precipitated the whole mess, but does that mean he doesn't have a right to know about his own child?

"I don't know what I owe you," Brooke says now, "but I need to explain it. When I realized I was pregnant I convinced myself that you wouldn't have had any interest in the child. But that was just my anger talking. I knew better." Here she pauses, and for a moment she looks vulnerable, like the old Brooke. "But I was young and confused," she continues. "And scared. I didn't know how I was going to support myself, let alone myself and a child. Next to preparing for the baby, supporting myself became my first priority. So it was easy to put you out of my mind. Then, as I said, I did decide to contact you, but when I found out you were getting married . . . Well, you know the rest of the story."

But I could've helped with the money, Alan wants to say. Really? Could he have done that? *Would* he have done that? Maybe Brooke's initial supposition was accurate. Maybe learning that he had a child would have meant nothing to him.

"Anyway, I was already in Boston when I found out for sure I was pregnant, and one way or another I made ends meet. I was able to get a few concerts and some studio work, plus I had a handful of students. But it wasn't really enough to get by on. For a while I was waiting table, but then I got too big. Finally I had to move back home to have the baby. That's a story in itself. My parents were pissed—*beyond* pissed. But they helped me out when I needed the help. And they didn't insist on knowing who the father was."

"They probably would've shot me," Alan says, but his remark is funny neither to Brooke nor to himself.

Brooke pauses again and shoves around some of the salad in front of her. Alan takes a bite of baked potato, but only to restore a sense of normality to the moment. He's far too confused and far too unworldly to know what he should say in response to her revelation. Does she want him to respond at all? Why, come to think of it, is she telling him any of this? Why, after all these years, has she suddenly decided that he needs to know?

He glances around at the other patrons and then out into the street. "It's getting a little chilly," he says. "Should we move inside?"

A couple of minutes later they're settled in a booth in a corner of the dimly lit restaurant. They've each returned to their dinners, but there's something nagging at Alan— something he can't quite put into words. He takes a stab anyway. "So Stephanie's my daughter!"

Brooke looks at him with some surprise. "There's no question you're the father," she says. "You were the only man I'd been with in a while, and I didn't sleep with anyone else until after I learned I was pregnant."

In response to this information, Alan sees himself lying on his bed celebrating the loss of his virginity as an outraged Brooke stands over him, shouting something or other. But that's ancient history, he reminds himself. What matters now is that he's a father and he needs to decide what to do about it. This thought triggers another—namely, What does *Brooke* want him to do about it? He opens his mouth to ask this question but realizes he's in too much a state of shock to know what would be wise or what would be foolish for him to say.

He returns to his dinner but then becomes aware that Brooke is fumbling around in her wallet for something.

"Where did I? . . ." She looks up from her wallet. "I always keep Stephanie's picture in here, but I can't . . ." She begins to dig around in her purse but then stops abruptly. "*I* know what I did with it. This quartet I'm in had a rehearsal at my apartment the other day and I remember taking it out to show the new clarinetist. I must have left it on the coffee table.

"Anyway, Alan, I thought you should know. I don't know what I expect from you, or if I expect anything at all." Here Brooke takes a sip of wine, not out of thirst, it seems to him, but to deflect whatever she might be feeling. Then she says, "That's not entirely true. Stephanie's been asking about her father ever since she was old enough to talk. 'Where's my daddy? Why doesn't my daddy live with us? Will I ever see my daddy?' And whenever a man would come into my life she would say, 'Is *he* my daddy?'"

Brooke spears a piece of lettuce but doesn't put it in her mouth. Alan waits, and finally she says, "You would love her, Alan. She's such a delightful child."

"I'm sure she is," he says, but then the import of Brooke's

statement hits him. She's implying that he might want to be part of her—that is, *their*—daughter's life. That's when his habitual skepticism kicks in. His mind darts back to earlier in the conversation when Brooke mentioned that she split from her boyfriend. When, precisely, did that relationship end? She said *not long after the concert.* She didn't say *immediately after the concert.* For some period of time—a week or two, maybe a month—she was still with this guy. Which raises the question, Why did she wait until after she broke up with him to contact Alan? Was it because the thought of contacting him didn't occur to her until after the breakup? This seems plausible. After yet another boyfriend/father figure abandoned her and her daughter, she decided to take advantage of Alan's sudden appearance on the scene. *Why not tell Alan he's the father?* she might have asked herself. *He's a nice guy, the kind who wouldn't walk out on a little girl he thought was his daughter. And Stephanie would get the father she's been longing for. A neat solution all around.*

"Does Stephanie have any half-brothers or half-sisters?" he hears Brooke say.

"Half-brothers . . . Oh, do you mean did my wife and I have any children? No, no children."

"Don't mind me," Brooke says. "I was just wishing out loud. Stephanie has cousins but they're all in Poughkeepsie. She doesn't see them nearly as much as I'd like."

"That's a shame," Alan says, but in the next moment he sees Brooke's question about the half-siblings in a more sinister light; she's applying a subtle pressure—one he's far from ready to deal with.

He looks around the restaurant and catches the waitress's eye.

"Dessert?" she says as she approaches them.

"I could go for coffee," Brooke says.

"And you?" the waitress says, looking at Alan.

"You know," he says to Brooke, "I really should be going. I just remembered I have to be in early for a meeting tomorrow morning."

It's a lame excuse and he can see that Brooke doesn't buy it for minute.

Soon the waitress is back with Brooke's coffee and the check.

"I've got it," Alan says, reaching for the check and handing the waitress a twenty.

He's on his feet now. "I know we have to talk," he says to Brooke, "and I'm sorry I have to run. Call me, you have my number."

Out on the street it occurs to him that Brooke spent the last couple of minutes with a look of total confusion on her face. But what does she expect from him? He needs some time to sort this out. Maybe she's lying and maybe she isn't. But how is he supposed to know? The Brooke he knew from the past would never have lied about such a thing. But this new Brooke? Who could say?

He thinks about this for a minute and has to acknowledge the unlikelihood of Brooke's character having done a complete about-face. Still, her daughter's desperate need for a father, combined with the sudden appearance of opportunity, might have been enough to push her over the line from honesty to mendacity. In any case, he's certain that if he'd stayed at the restaurant they would have gotten around to the question of his skepticism. *It's only natural for you to wonder, Alan,* she might have said. *But I swear I'm telling you the truth. If you want, we could arrange for a blood test.* And here she would have paused, knowing he wouldn't take her up on her offer. *That won't be necessary,* he would have said. And he might have added *I just need some time for this to sink in,* knowing he would need more than time to decide what his next step should be. And *then* he might have come up with the excuse about the early meeting. Either way he's in a pickle. All of a sudden he's being asked to turn his world upside down. And all based on the word of someone who—former best friend or not—is for all practical purposes an unknown quantity to him. Is he to take a leap of faith, or a giant leap in the opposite direction? Is he to trust her or to trust his well-honed instinct to *mis-trust*? What in the name of a problem-free existence is he to do now?

At this point Alan is on Second Avenue, somewhere in the Fifties, headed home. He's always been able to do his best thinking when he's meandering through the streets with no immediate destination. Now he finds himself speculating about Brooke's former boyfriend Kyle. What kind of father substitute was he to Stephanie? Did he try in any way to fill that role or did he resist it, perhaps leading to the eventual breakup with Brooke?

Suddenly Alan sees that breakup in a new light: Brooke is a free agent, not the married lady he presumed her to be.

Maybe she's already seeing someone new, but maybe not. True, the old rapport between them was missing at dinner, but that was to be expected given the way things had ended for them. And then the bombshell about Stephanie—that would have trumped anything that might have been brewing between them. But in claiming that Alan is the father, hasn't Brooke opened the door to the possibility that the two of them might get together? Well, perhaps not intentionally, but the possibility is inherent in the situation. He can see them—the three of them—on a playground somewhere, sliding down the slide or climbing the monkey bars, a happy family. . . . But he's getting ahead of himself. After all, in a very real sense he and Brooke are strangers. For all he knows, there's only the slimmest chance they could ever revive their friendship, let alone fall in love with each other. And he isn't about to be a father to Stephanie just to find out one way or the other about Brooke and him. No, if he's going to be a father to Stephanie then he'll do so for a million selfless reasons and the most selfish reason of all: because she's *his child*.

12

In the past forty-eight hours Alan has done little more than replay his dinner-long conversation with Brooke. Replay it, turn it inside out, analyze it to death, and replay it again. Something tells him it would be a bad idea to bring up his dilemma to Rick, but Rhonda is a different story. He can't *wait* to get her feedback.

"Something happened this week," he says as he enters her office.

"This must be important, Alan. Why don't you sit down and tell me about it."

He watches Rhonda settle into her chair, then settles into his own.

"It concerns Brooke," he says.

"Brooke," she observes, leaning forward the way she tends to do whenever something has especially piqued her interest. "I haven't heard that name in a while."

Alan recounts the scene with Brooke, and when he finishes, Rhonda writes something in her notebook. Then she says, "Tell me, Alan. Do you really think this is all a big lie?"

He considers the question. "Probably not," he says.

"*Probably* not? The idea that this is a lie is preposterous! It's straight out of a soap opera: 'Honest woman turns con artist to give daughter the father she's always wanted.'"

The shrink has a point, but what about the timing? Why did Brooke wait so long after the concert to tell him?

He puts this question to Rhonda and she gives him what amounts to a look of near disgust.

"Did it ever occur to you, Alan, that you're not the only person in the world who might have trouble making a decision?"

Okay, she has him there, but he isn't ready to concede that a hoax is out of the realm of possibility. "I guess I'm the kind of person who needs proof," he says.

"Then start with a blood test. If the blood test rules you out, then you can forget the whole thing."

Right, a blood test. But a blood test is out of the question. If there's ever to be a chance that he might have a relationship with Brooke, he can't start by implying a lack of trust in her. Besides, if a blood test doesn't rule him out it still doesn't prove he's the father.

Again he watches Rhonda write something down, perhaps a note on his non-response to her suggestion.

"Tell me, Alan," she says now. "What is it that so frightens you about the idea of fatherhood?"

Is *that* what he is? Frightened?

"I don't know that I'm frightened," he says. "Cautious, maybe."

She gives him a half smile, informed by equal parts forbearance and exasperation. "There's reasonable caution, and then there's caution that serves another purpose. But humor me. Let's *assume* you're frightened about the prospect of fatherhood. What is it, specifically, that *most* frightens you?"

Alan closes his eyes. Suddenly he sees Mike's face. Then it's Mike playing catch with Ralph as he looks on, too young to play. But *that* couldn't be it. Surely he isn't afraid that he would be the kind of father Mike had been. If anything, he would be the opposite. He would be *too*—He stops short, as if an iron wall has slammed down in front of his thoughts.

After a moment he can hear Rhonda asking him something, but the words don't register. He looks across at her. She's sitting there, waiting.

The room is silent. He can hear the faint hum of the ceiling fan and the ticking of a clock mounted on the wall behind him. Outside are the sounds of the city—the endless din of traffic, someone shouting, a siren in the distance.

"Alan, what were you thinking just now?"

He realizes that this was the question Rhonda asked him just moments ago. What was he thinking before his mind went blank?

Then it comes to him. "That I might be too . . . I don't know, loving. That I might love her more than . . ."

Once again he finds himself unable to complete a thought. It might be a minute before he says, "That I might love her more than I could stand."

He looks up and sees Rhonda smiling at him. In fact, she's beaming. Is this what therapists get off on? Other people's suffering?

"You've had a breakthrough, Alan."

Breakthrough. She said the word with such reverence, as if she herself were its primary beneficiary. But he knows this isn't the case. He has someone on his side—someone who's not a friend and not a relative and whom he has to pay. But she's on his side.

He would like to say something to lighten what he's feeling, but he knows his voice would fail him.

"Here," Rhonda says, handing him a tissue.

Alan dabs at his eyes, grateful that he hasn't broken down and bawled like a baby. The moment has passed, he's in control again—though he knows that a lack of control is precisely what she wants from him.

For a while neither of them speaks.

"It's scary," Rhonda says at length. "But it doesn't have to be overwhelming. You're a victim of your own sensitivity, Alan. In many ways. But this is one of the ways where your sensitivity would work to your advantage."

She pauses, perhaps waiting for a response. Then she says, "Did you ever hear a mother say of her child: 'I love her so much it hurts'?"

He nods.

"Fathers say that too, Alan. Not all fathers. Not your father. But the lucky ones."

Right now he feels anything but lucky. Aside from being emotionally drained, he feels himself at the mercy of a thought which is hanging just out of reach. . . . Suddenly he sees a faceless Stephanie sandwiched between Brooke and some faceless man, walking down the street toward him. And past him. What if he became invisible to his own child? Sure, he would have his visitation days, but joint custody would never happen. But the other *could* happen. A new man could come into Brooke's life, someone who would be there for Stephanie round the clock. Someone with good fatherly instincts of his own—who would listen to her and play with her and actually *be* her father. Alan would become an afterthought, nothing more than a biological encumbrance with certain legal rights. No, he can't risk it. Not if he breaks down at the mere thought of being a father.

"What's wrong, Alan?"

He looks up, and there, poised to be of service, is Rhonda—a statuesque, middle-aged black woman who happens to have a knack for getting him to feel things he didn't know he felt.

He tries to collect his thoughts, not wanting to misrepresent himself. "It's what you just said," he begins. "About fathers. For some reason it occurred to me that I could easily be preempted. Brooke wants me in Stephanie's life. For now, anyway. But what happens if some other guy comes along? What happens if they get married? What happens if they move to California?"

"What happens when families split up?" Rhonda says. "It's not pleasant and it's certainly not convenient. But people survive. Even the children, sad as it is for them, survive. The point is, Alan—and this is what you're not ready to acknowledge—you're already emotionally involved in this child's life. What-if questions are no longer relevant. Sorry to say, but you've passed the point where you can extricate yourself from this without batting an eye."

Tethered, in spite of himself, to a child he never met? Is it true?

"Besides, why do you assume the worst? Brooke's a musician. What better place for a musician to be than New York? And as for another man in her life, that doesn't automatically mean you'll be out of the picture. This whole thing is your fantasy, remember. Things might turn out great. On the other hand, how would you feel if twenty years from now your daughter comes to me as a patient complaining that her father never loved her, that he was never even part of her life?"

Once again Rhonda has made her point. Alan is out of excuses. And if, as she said, he's past the point of no return emotionally, then it's all academic anyway. It's no longer a matter of if, but when.

He sits there awhile longer and then excuses himself, although there's still some time left in the session. On his way downstairs to the lobby he recalls the words Rhonda said to him some months ago: *I now see exactly what it is that keeps you from taking action where Brooke is concerned.* Was it his breakthrough, the one he supposedly just had, that she was alluding to back then? Had she been able to intuit, despite his resistance and his denial and the rest of his bag of tricks, that he was scared to death of being swallowed up by love? And if this is indeed a breakthrough— *the* breakthrough—then in what *way* is it a breakthrough? After all, Alan has known from the outset that he's afraid of being consumed by love for the child. Then again, as he's learned only too well in his months of therapy, knowing something isn't the same thing as feeling it.

When he reaches the street he notices a phone booth. It's been there all along, of course, but now he sees it as if for the first time, as if it's been transplanted there for the sole purpose of daring him to make the call. *When can I see her?* is all he would have to say. Instant fatherhood for a dime.

He walks past the phone booth and on toward the bus stop. No, it's not really a question of *when* he might go about establishing himself in Stephanie's life. It's a question of courage, and whether or not he has enough of it to take the plunge.

13

"Okay, Alan. Takes *one* to hit it—only takes one."

The first pitch bounces three feet in front of home plate.

"Good eye," someone shouts, as if it takes a good eye to lay off a pitch that bounces three feet in front of the plate.

"Just meet the ball, Alan. Don't try to do too much with it." This is Rick, their self-proclaimed captain.

The next pitch is low and outside. Will Alan ever get anything to hit?

He looks out at the mound and glides his bat across the strike zone a couple of times as the pitcher goes into his windup. Then comes the pitch—high and outside but not as far off the plate as the last pitch. He leans into it and drives it over the first baseman's head for a double, easily scoring Michelle Sennert from accounting and Julio from the mail room.

"Way to go, Alan," he can hear coming from the third-base bleachers.

A few pitches later, Grace Maiser—the same Grace Maiser who asked Alan to write her copy test for free—singles through the left side. Alan races around third as if he's at Yankee Stadium instead of the ball field in back of Holy Name School on West Thirty-second Street. His slide into home is unnecessary but it feels good.

"Way to hustle," Rick says as they exchange high-fives on the sidelines.

Alan acknowledges the shouts of congratulation coming from his other teammates. Then, as Barbara Hencken from graphics strides to the plate, he looks out at the field and beyond it at the sun, which is just beginning to sink behind the trees in right field. The TV weather reports have been forecasting a chance of showers for tonight, but from the look of the sky—and to the delight of Spaniel Publishing and their opponents, Knowles Press—it appears the reports were wrong.

"Sally said she'd be here by six," Ricks says, looking at his watch.

Alan looks at his own watch. "Relax," he says, for a change playing big brother to Rick. "It's only twenty after."

One of the secretaries from the eighth floor bounces one past the pitcher and through the second baseman's legs, setting off a series of miscues that results in the secretary's landing on third base. Alan's side of the field erupts into cheers, but he can feel himself drifting back into the malaise he's been stuck in for the past couple of weeks. Despite Rhonda's claim that he's already emotionally involved with Stephanie, he can't shake a sense of doubt that seems to be flitting around him like a gnat. Was it like this for Hamlet? Or Lyndon Johnson? One thing is certain: you simply can't act until something tells you it's time to act. Still, the fact that he hasn't mentioned any of this to Rick, who, he knows, would advise him against accepting paternity—this would suggest that accepting paternity is precisely what he wants to do. For some reason, though, he can't take that first step.

"Here they are," he hears Rick say.

Sally and little Emily are walking toward the bleachers from the parking lot, and Alan watches as Rick jogs over to meet them. As the three of them near the bleachers, Alan can see that Emily has grown since he last saw her. Then he sees Rick point in his direction and watches as Emily comes running toward him. He crouches down to give her a hug.

"Uncle Alan!"

She smells of talcum powder and some flowery scent.

"I wanna play," she says, breaking free from his arms and taking a step toward the batting cage.

Rick whisks her up in his arms and sits her on the second-to-bottom row of the bleachers. "You sit here," he admonishes. "There are people swinging bats around here."

"Right," Sally says. "You don't want to get plunked in the noggin."

Emily breaks into peals of laughter, tickled either by the word "plunked" or by the word "noggin," or perhaps by the idea of getting hit in the head with a baseball bat.

The little girl's laughter is contagious; everyone within

earshot has been infected by it. Everyone but Alan, that is, whose mind darts back to the brief sighting he caught of Stephanie back at that concert. Will he ever see her again? *Should* he see her again?

He becomes aware that Bruce, one of the copy assistants, has popped up to end the inning. For the next inning-and-a-half both teams score prolifically, but as they enter the bottom of the sixth the game is tied again, this time at fifteen. Since both teams have agreed it's getting too dark to consider extra innings, this will be Spaniel's last chance to win the game.

Julio from the mail room leads off with a line-drive single past the shortstop but advances to second when the left fielder misplays the ball. Alan moves from the on-deck circle into the batter's box.

"Okay, Alan," he can hear Rick shout, "here's your chance to shine. All we need is another base hit."

The first pitch is above Alan's shoulders but is called a strike. As he steps out of the batter's box he can hear shouts of "Kill the ump!" coming from the third-base bleachers. He steps back into the box and digs his heels into the rust-colored earth around home plate, then cocks his bat into position as the pitcher goes into his windup. The pitch comes spinning toward him on the inside corner and he turns on it, ripping it down the third-base line. Julio coasts home and the celebration has begun.

Later he's walking up Second Avenue, his baseball glove dangling from one arm then the other. Everyone has gone to a bar across from Madison Square Garden, but Alan has opted out of the festivities. Far from raising his spirits, his heroics have made him feel like the biggest loser west of the East River. Sure he had a few hits including the game-winning hit, and sure he made a couple of stellar plays in the outfield, but this was a company softball game, not the World Series. And it was typical of him: a star on the small stage, a washout on the big one. He's twenty-eight years old and what has he accomplished? His dreams of a life in academia fizzled. The idea that he might want to get a better job in publishing has never motivated him to actually look for such a job. Other people his age, maybe with less ability than his, are writing books, publishing stories in magazines, ghostwriting for whomever. What's *he* writing? Junk mail, which can be reduced to the single word "trash." Maybe he needs to get his professional life in order before he can deal with his personal life. No, that would be a cop-out. Your life is your life, he tells himself. Personal, professional, sexual—it's all one life.

Alan looks up and sees that he's approaching Forty-sixth Street. Sometime later, after thousands upon thousands of additional thoughts and not a single conclusion as to what he could possibly do to make his life a little less demoralizing, he turns onto his block. Maybe the legion of his critics has been right all along. Maybe he does think too much.

He enters his building and stops in the vestibule for the mail. Four flights later he turns on the kitchen light and drops his baseball glove and the stack of mail onto the kitchen counter. After a tall glass of orange juice he begins to sort through the mail. Bill. Bill. Junk. Bill . . .

The bottom letter in the stack is addressed to him in ballpoint pen. Then he notices the name on the return address: Hadley. He opens the envelope and reaches inside. There's no note, just a snapshot of some kind. He turns it over and there, looking at him with eyes he could swear are his own, is a little girl with an impish grin on her face and a yellow bow crowning her long brown hair. Stephanie!

Alan moves to the front room and sits down on the couch, then reaches up to turn on the lamp. For some time he sits motionless, clutching the photograph, looking down at it, looking away, looking back again. Eventually he grows drowsy. Returning to the kitchen he sets the photograph on the counter, where he'll be able to look at it tomorrow at breakfast.

14

It's around eight-thirty on Saturday morning, two days after a snapshot in an envelope changed Alan's life. He steps out of the shower and a few minutes later he's sitting at the kitchen counter, about to make the call to Brooke.

He picks up the phone but then it occurs to him that he might want to delay the call a few minutes in case she's sleeping in. On the other hand, if he waits too long she might already be out for the day. Why didn't he leave a message with the babysitter yesterday afternoon when he had the chance? *Please have Brooke call me tomorrow morning before she leaves the apartment*, he might have said. *She'll know what it's about.*

Deciding to err on the side of not disrupting anyone's sleep, Alan places the phone back on the receiver and wanders into the front room, only to have the phone ring.

"Alan, I'm glad I got you in."

It's Mike, and Alan can tell something is up.

"What's wrong, Dad? You sound upset."

Mike pauses, perhaps for dramatic effect. Then he says, "It's Dolly. She left me."

The news is shocking but not entirely surprising. And knowing Mike, Alan is certain it has something to do with money.

"Gee, I'm sorry to hear that," he says, stumped for anything else to say.

Mike continues as if he hasn't heard Alan's remark. "Yesterday, it was. I come home from work five-thirty like always, and I walk in the house and right away I know something ain't right. Then it dawns on me—the house is half empty. Alan, you're not gonna believe this. She cleaned out all the closets—the hall closet, the bedroom closet, the closet upstairs by the attic stairs—all a them. She took everything that wasn't nailed down that belonged to her. She musta been planning this for weeks, but you know what they say. The husband is always the last to know."

Alan begins to say something but Mike cuts him off.

"And then I walk into the kitchen and there's a note on the table. Can you believe she didn't even have the decency to tell me to my face, she had to leave a note? Here, I have it right here."

There's silence for a few seconds and then Mike comes back on the line.

"Here, you're not gonna believe this, Alan. 'Dear Mike, I moved back across the street but don't come over I don't have nothing to say to you. Sincerely, Dolly.' Can you believe it, she don't even have the decency to call me up on the phone even. It was never this way with your mother. Your mother and me we had our fights—what married couple don't?—but we always worked it out right when it happened. We had a rule—"

"Never go to bed mad," Alan says.

"Right," Mike says, "never go to bed mad. And in twenty-seven years a marriage not one time did we do that, go to bed mad. Cause you know why? Cause when something would come up—she'd get mad about something or I'd get mad about something—we'd sit down right then and there and work it out. Like grownups. We didn't have no secrets, your mother and me."

Mike falls silent and Alan can hear him sighing from way across the Hudson River.

"But Dolly's only across the street, Dad. I'm sure you can work it out, just give her some time."

Again Mike goes on as if he hasn't heard his son, which is a possibility considering his hearing loss. "There, I can see her right now through the front window. . . . Here, lemme pull the phone in here. . . . There, she's across the street watering her tomatas. Do you think she's giving me another thought? What does she need me for, she's got her daughter, she's got her house, she's got her tomatas—what does she need with me? And that's the problem right there. The daughter's been in between us, me and Dolly, from back even when we was keeping company. It's always Vera. 'What would *Vera* say?' or 'What would *Vera* think?' That's the problem. They been cooped up in that house the two a them for too many years—the husband walked out when the daughter was a baby. And I tried to tell the mother, I can't *tell* you how many times I tried. 'You gotta let her grow up,' I says. 'She shouldn't be always in the house. A girl her age needs to have a social life. Friends, she needs.' But you think the mother listens? No way. 'She'll start getting out when the time's right,' she tells me. 'My daughter Vera she ain't like you and me, she needs to do things in her own time.' Her own time, my eye! She'll be an old maid before you know it—sitting home on Saturday night like she does, watching television. . . ."

Alan glances at the kitchen clock and sees that it's approaching nine. If he's going to reach Brooke before she starts her day he should call soon. Then he remembers a vow he made to himself back in February at Mike's wedding—that he would be there for Mike if the marriage started to go downhill.

"But you must have some idea what's bothering her, Dad."

There's no response, and Alan wonders if Mike might have spotted Dolly walking across the street that very moment, perhaps about to make the first move toward a reconciliation.

"I know what's bothering her, all right," Mike says as if on a three-second delay. "She wants to keep the house."

Keep the house . . . *Which* house?

"Oh," Alan says, "you mean she wants to keep *her* house?"

"Yeah, she *thinks* it's her house, but it ain't. It's *our* house now cause when you get married that's the way it works. She can't get it through her head that she can't go operating like she was still single. That's one thing your mother understood from day one. When you're married, you're married. There ain't no separate checking accounts and separate this and separate that. What's mine is yours and what's yours is mine, we used to say. That's the way it should be, and Dolly's gotta understand this. Besides, she ain't being practical. We could turn a pretty penny on that house. And we're gonna need it, we'll be on Social Security before you know it. But no—she's gotta keep the house for Vera, she says. For when she gets married and starts a family. Lemme ask you. How's that girl gonna meet anyone what'll marry her when she spends her whole life in that house? You think she's gonna meet somebody at the supermarket? Who goes in that supermarket? Old ladies, that's who. But does Dolly listen? No, she don't listen. She's so wrapped up in her daughter she can't see the situation . . ."

Mike pauses here, evidently searching for the right word.

"Objectively?" Alan says.

"Right, objectively. She don't see it like that cause she's too close. She needs to let her daughter have a life a her own. 'Let her get an apartment in Paterson,' I says to her the other day. 'Or Hackensack. Someplace where there's people. How's she gonna meet Mr. Right in this little town, going back and forth from the house to the supermarket?' But Dolly won't hear it. 'Vera's gotta do things her own way,' she says. But I know the real reason, Alan. The real reason Dolly don't wanna sell the house is she's waiting for me to drop dead."

"That can't be true. She just married you, she's—"

"I know these things, Alan. She married me for my money."

His money? What money?

"I know how these women think. She figures, He's sixty-three years old, he's had health problems, in a year or two, maybe, he'll have a stroke or a heart attack. And then she'll have *both* houses and she can sell one a them. But she don't know about the codicil to my will. If anything happens to me, Alan, you get the house. That's if things stay the way they are right now. But if we sell *her* house, then when we're both dead you and Vera split *our* house."

Alan isn't sure how to respond to this. Finally he says, "That won't be for a long time, Dad."

"Cause if I don't do that—give you the house—then who ends up with it? Vera, that's who." Mike sighs again and somehow Alan can tell he's about to change direction.

"I tell you, Alan, it wasn't supposed to be like this. Your mother and me had plans for our old age."

Mike continues on in this vein for several more minutes, but finally Alan can tell he's talked himself out.

"Look Dad, if there's anything I can do . . . If you want, I can take a drive out there and talk to Dolly."

"Thanks, Alan, but we'll work it out—one way or the other. But why don't you come out to the house tomorra like you say. I'll make you spaghetti. Or would you rather have ravioli?"

When Alan finally hangs up the phone it's nearing nine-thirty. He calls Brooke but there's no answer. Could his timing be worse? In any event, he can't sit around all day calling an empty apartment.

He moves into the front room to get his wallet and keys and notices the gift-wrapped box that's sitting on the coffee table. On his way home from work yesterday he stopped off at a toy store and bought Stephanie a stuffed puppy. Now he begins to question whether a puppy had been the right choice. Perhaps he should have gone with the giant panda bear, although that might have been too bold a statement. The alligator was cute, maybe he should have bought the alligator. If only he'd been able to reach Brooke yesterday, he could have asked her what Stephanie would like. Maybe she doesn't like stuffed toys. Maybe she's allergic to them. Maybe he should stop off at a book store and pick her up a couple of books, just in case.

Alan is about to leave the apartment when the phone rings again. A minute later he's racing down the stairs, the words *This can't be happening* like an incessant drumbeat that's taken up residence in his brain. When he hits the street he sprints up to Second Avenue and looks for a cab. With nothing in sight he turns and begins to run south on Second Avenue, weaving in and out of pedestrians and vehicles alike and every so often looking over his shoulder to see if he can spot a vacant cab. He reaches Seventy-ninth Street just as the crosstown bus is about to pull away from the curb. The brief ride across town seems to take forever, but finally he reaches Central Park West. This time he finds a cab almost immediately. "Twelfth Street and Seventh Avenue," he says, almost forgetting to close the door behind him.

At Twenty-third Street the traffic starts to back up. "I'll get out here," Alan says a block later.

He pays the driver and races down Seventh Avenue, thankful he's been jogging on a regular basis. After he crosses Thirteenth Street he begins to look for the hospital on the left. Then he sees it just beyond Twelfth Street and puts on a final burst of speed.

"I'm here to see Brooke Hadley," he's able to get out between breaths. "She was an emergency patient but she's just been admitted."

The woman behind the desk consults a chart and directs him to Room 1608.

On the sixteenth floor he finds the right hall, then suddenly slows his pace. What is he going to say? What could he possibly say to her?

The door to the room is open and Alan steps in and tries to adjust his eyes to the relative darkness. He can see there are two beds in the room. In the one nearer the door an older woman is sitting up doing needlepoint. She gives him a maternal smile as he passes her and approaches the other bed.

For a moment he's not sure he's in the right room but then he recognizes Brooke. She's lying on her back, her head bandaged and both eyes blackened.

"Alan," she says in an unsteady voice that's barely louder than a whisper.

He pulls a chair toward her bed and sits down, his back facing the window. He has no idea what to say, but Brooke seems content just to have him there. Finally he says, "I'm sorry."

"No reason," she seems to say.

"She's a little groggy from the painkillers."

A nurse has entered the room—an older woman, like the woman doing needlepoint. She explains to Alan that Brooke has suffered a mild concussion as well as some deep bruising and a few minor lacerations. "But no internal injuries," she adds.

Alan looks over at Brooke and sees that she's nodded off, then indicates to the nurse that he'd like to speak with her out in the hall.

Outside he says, "And what about the little girl? The woman on the phone said she was in critical condition."

The nurse seems to scrutinize him. "You're Mr. Agnalini, correct?"

"That's right."

She lowers her voice, although at the moment no one else is in the hall. "I can't lie to you, Mr. Agnalini. Your daughter has suffered extensive internal injuries. She might pull through this—I've seen worse cases pull through—but it's just too soon to know. She'll be in surgery for another forty-five minutes or so, and then we'll have to keep our fingers crossed."

Back inside the room Brooke is still sleeping. Alan sits down and thinks about what the nurse said. She was direct with him, which he appreciates, but she didn't give Stephanie a death sentence. For instance, she used the word "extensive." *Extensive* internal injuries, not *massive* internal injuries. That had to be a good sign. Worse cases have pulled through, she also said. Surely Stephanie will be one of those cases. If she has anything like Brooke's spirit, her inner strength, she'll pull through.

Alan opens his wallet and takes out the photograph of Stephanie. She has the Agnalini eyes, he thinks to himself, and suddenly he remembers Mike. For the first time, it occurs to him that Mike too has a stake in Stephanie's life. Mike Agnalini, the man Alan has defiled in his mind for the greater part of his life, has a granddaughter who's lying on an operating table fighting for her life, in part so that one day Alan will be able to drive her out to Morehead, New Jersey, to meet her new grandfather. And isn't that something Alan would want—for Stephanie to meet, and to know, and to be loved by her grandfather? Because he can't imagine that Mike, now that he's approaching old age, would be anything less than enamored of a little child who's presented to him as his flesh and blood.

The sound of Brooke stirring wakes him from his daydream. He looks over at her but she's gone back to sleep. There's nothing for him to do but wait. Except for the muffled sounds coming from the street below, the room is perfectly still. He can hear the wall clock ticking off hours instead of seconds, and every sound from out in the hall makes him jump to attention. Is there news?

Now he stands and looks down onto Sixth Avenue. The traffic is going about its business, oblivious to its potential to maim and to kill, concerned only about covering a certain distance in a certain period of time. *They were in a taxi. Something involving a pedestrian. I don't know all the details.* The woman on the phone sounded compassionate. *Try not to worry,* she said.

Alan hears a sound and turns from the window. Brooke is awake. She starts as if to smile at him, but then he can see her eyes reflect the memory of where she is and why she's there.

"How do you feel?" he says, sitting back down and moving his chair closer to the bed.

"Stephanie." She's saying *How's Stephanie? Is she going to be okay?*

Alan looks at his watch and sees that only fifteen minutes have passed since he spoke with the nurse. "She's still in surgery," he says to Brooke. "Can I get you anything? A glass of water?"

Brooke indicates that, yes, she'd like some water, but when Alan returns from the hall with a cupful, she's once again asleep. For close to another hour—alternately sitting and pacing and attending to Brooke whenever she happens to emerge from sleep—Alan tries to will Stephanie to pull through the operation. Finally he hears a sound and he looks up as a bearded, turbaned man in a white coat enters the room.

"Miss Hadley?" the man says as he approaches them. "I'm Dr. Omprakash, the attending physician."

Part IV

15

Alan steps into the elevator and presses L, then watches the numbers light up one after the other. When he reaches the lobby he isn't surprised to see that it's deserted; who in their right mind would be working late on a Friday?

Outside he hails a cab but takes it only as far south as Twenty-third Street, having decided to walk the rest of the way to the Village. The air is brisk but not cold, and there's a gusty breeze that sends the leaves scattering.

He walks over to Twenty-second Street, then turns down toward Eighth Avenue. After a block or so of commercial buildings he comes to a residential area. Most of the brownstones are already sporting their Halloween decorations—the witches and goblins and skeletons that so delight little children. Halloween, according to Brooke, was Stephanie's favorite holiday. *This year she wanted to go as a kangaroo so she could hop from apartment to apartment and put the candy in her pouch. She made me start sewing a costume for her all the way back in April, but then* . . . But then she fell off the edge of the world into the void. And there was no way she could climb back up. And there was no one who could answer the question, Why?

I'm sorry, we did everything we could. Over four months have passed since Stephanie's death, but Alan can still hear the doctor's words as if he's hearing them for the first time. Each syllable came like a blow to his stomach, but for Brooke it was far worse. In the next moment he was kneeling beside her, cradling her in his arms as her body convulsed with the physical trappings of whatever unspeakable emotion had overtaken her. Later he was lying on a cot at the foot of her bed, the curtain pulled around her half of the room. It was sometime in the middle of the night and he was still awake. Brooke had been given a sedative and he could hear her breathing gently. And from down in the street he could hear the traffic that in New York City stops for nothing, not even for the death of a child.

The next thing he knew he opened his eyes and sunlight was flooding the room. Brooke sat on the edge of her bed taking in the sunlight, which, in this case, had no power to heal or to uplift. She turned toward him.

"Hi," she said, her voice insubstantial, as if her larynx—not just her heart—had been severed.

Alan sat up on the cot and flung his legs over the side. It was painful for him to witness Brooke's attempt at a smile and nearly as painful to try to smile himself. Not that he had a chance of pulling this off. And faced with the task of

finding the right thing to say—of finding anything to say—
he failed again.

Brooke stood up and took a step to the only chair in
the makeshift room. She was sitting diagonally across from
him now.

"I'm sorry, Alan."

She was sorry?

"What do you mean?" he said. "You have nothing to
apologize for."

"No, not apologize. But when I sent you that picture
of Stephanie I knew you would want to be in her life. And
yesterday when the doctor"—here her voice broke, but she
rallied herself. "When the doctor said what he said, I could
tell you weren't just consoling me. You were grieving too.
She was your daughter too, Alan, and I know you wanted
to get to know her."

Brooke's words had pierced the most vulnerable part of
him and he had to summon all his will to keep from breaking down in front of her, although he wanted to fall to his
knees and clutch at her as if *he* were the one who'd lost the
child he'd carried in his womb, as if *he* were the one who'd
loved and nurtured her for five years. . . . His loss was insignificant compared to Brooke's, but *she* was comforting *him*.

Suddenly, like a subliminal message that flashes across
a movie screen, Alan saw the old Brooke—the girl with the
acne and the ill-matched clothes and the greasy hair. And
then just as suddenly the new Brooke was back. Except she
was no longer the stranger he'd fashioned her to be, no lon-

ger someone whom time had transformed into a different being. She was Brooke—the same sweet, compassionate young woman he'd grown so close to for that one brief month back in 1969. She was his friend, and why in the name of God did this have to happen to her?

Brooke was released from the hospital the following day, and at her request Alan contacted her older brother to break the news to the family. On the drive up to Poughkeepsie she told him that she'd called her brother as well, sometime after Alan's call, to explain that he was not just a friend but Stephanie's father, and that he would be coming up for the wake and the funeral. Alan imagined himself entering the family home for the first time. *There's the bastard that knocked up my little girl! Off with his head!* But when the time came, Brooke's family was gracious to him—though in truth they were far too grief-stricken to give him much thought one way or the other.

It was in that house, sitting amid the large Scottish-Welsh family, waiting until it was time to leave for the funeral home, that Alan began to feel like an impostor. Who was he, after all? He hadn't even known the child and couldn't begin to feel what they were feeling. Stephanie, to him, was a mere idea—the idea that he was linked to her biologically and in some genealogical, blood-ties kind of way. True, he felt some kind of visceral connection to her that seemed to defy logic, considering that he'd never known her, but the connection stopped there. Who was he to insinuate himself into the lives of people who loved her not just for biological and genealogical reasons, but because she'd been an actual part of their lives—a child they'd known intimately, whom they'd watched grow, whom they'd loved beyond reason? And yet, Brooke wanted him there. He could see her across the room, the object of all the love and emotional support her family could give, yet he could feel her reaching out to him. *Stay with me, Alan.*

And he stayed, and he endured his private, indefinable grief—which intensified and became even more indefinable once they were all settled in the funeral home. The sight of the tiny casket was more than he could bear, it seemed, but he stayed with it, trying to imagine Stephanie's spirit rising up through the lid and through the ceiling and through the roof and into the unknown. At one point he remembered the stuffed puppy he'd bought her. Why hadn't he thought to bring the puppy? It was too late to give Stephanie any part of him, but he could have given her that much. Had Brooke thought to have an object—a keepsake—placed in the casket? Probably. Probably a necklace or a photograph or maybe Stephanie's favorite stuffed toy. What had been her favorite stuffed toy? What had she been like? What made her laugh, what frightened her? Was the sound of her voice like music?

Stephanie Amy Hovell (a musical colleague of Brooke's, Ben Hovell, had volunteered to put his name on the birth certificate to keep the hospital administrators from hassling her) was buried in a cemetery in a blue-collar section of Poughkeepsie, just down the block from the family home. Brooke's grandparents and great-grandparents on her mother's side were buried there, along with assorted great-aunts and great-uncles. And now her daughter was with them.

"It's better this way," she said to Alan on the drive back to the city. "If she was in New York somewhere I would either be visiting the cemetery or feeling guilty when I wasn't. I have to let her go."

Then she burst into tears, but it was Alan's first indication that Brooke had begun the process of accepting the unthinkable. It wouldn't be a cakewalk and he wanted to be there if she needed him. To do what he could to help her through it. But would she want him there? Wouldn't he just be a reminder of her loss?

He was surprised, then, when he got a call a few days later.

"Alan, can we meet?"

They met at a restaurant on the Upper West Side, not far from Rhonda's office and, therefore, not far from the bus stop where Alan had spotted Brooke about six months earlier. At first they were hesitant, each of them ill at ease, but gradually they began to talk—about things in general, about life, about Stephanie. There were long silences, moments when Brooke appeared about to break down, but eventually they were able to pick up the conversation. They parted that night with the unspoken understanding that they would be seeing each other again soon.

In fact they became friends. It wasn't, and couldn't have been, the same as it was when they were in college. They were different people now, and life had turned out to be more formidable than either of them could have imagined.

But they still connected on a fundamental level. And they needed each other, for reasons they didn't begin to explore.

Meanwhile Alan was having a hard time accepting the idea that a foolish twist of fate had kept him from having his daughter in his life.

"It's a shame," Rhonda told him one day. "Maybe even an injustice, you could make that case. But here's the important thing. Stephanie may not have actually been part of your life, but she'll always be part of *you*. The sense of loss you're feeling right now will never completely go away. You need to understand this and accept it. The good news, if there's any good news, is that you're a young man, Alan. You have to believe that one day there'll be another child, or other children. You can't let yourself become jaded because of this. Life is too precious."

On his good days Alan was able to remain optimistic, as Rhonda had encouraged him to do. On other days, along with a sadness that seemed to overwhelm him at times, he would fall into a mix of anger and self-pity at having been shortchanged by life—although he knew that if anyone was justified in feeling such emotions it was Brooke, not he.

Aside from this one issue, though, his life was gradually returning to normal. It was a *new* normal, to be sure, but with the passage of time and the help of his therapist and some surprisingly compassionate help from Rick, each day became a little easier to get through than the last.

Then in late September he attended a concert of Brooke's at a church on the Upper East Side. Afterwards they had a late supper at a restaurant that had just opened in his neighborhood. Brooke was in especially good spirits considering what she was going through. For one night, at least, she seemed to have set aside the memories that had been shadowing her at every turn.

Later they stepped outside and Alan offered to hail her a cab.

"Why don't we walk awhile," she said.

They began to walk slowly down the block and, as if by mutual agreement, toward Alan's apartment building. It was a gorgeous night, the first real autumn night of the year. The aroma of a wood-burning fireplace, mingled with the glass or two of wine they'd each had, must have set something off, for suddenly they were in each other's arms, his lips smothering hers, their bodies trembling with all the force of the six years that had passed since their one encounter and all the pent-up emotion and accumulated sexual tension of the past four months.

Alan turns onto Bleecker Street and spots Luigi's. He isn't in the mood for Italian, but tonight isn't about food. Will he and Brooke pick up where they left off after their night in bed? Her response to him that night would indicate that, yes, she'd like to see where this goes, but maybe her behavior the next morning indicates the opposite. Why did she disappear from the apartment while Alan was still asleep? Was it a fact, as her note said, that she had to get back to her apartment to pack for her flight? Or was her abrupt departure a way of saying that their lovemaking had been a mistake?

These thoughts spin around in Alan's mind as he approaches the restaurant. Then he hears his name and there she is, walking toward him.

"Brooke," he says. "It's good to see you. How was Seattle?"

And that's the way the conversation goes throughout dinner: impersonal, noncommittal. Brooke seems nervous, rambling on about things that ordinarily would bore her, deflecting Alan's attempts at more meaningful conversation with one non sequitur after another.

Finally, over coffee, he says, "I don't know about you, but I rather enjoyed that night a couple of weeks ago."

She smiles at him—wistfully, it seems. "It was wonderful, Alan, it really was. But it's not going to happen again."

He's prepared himself for this, but now he's too stunned to think, let alone to say anything.

"I've been a coward," Brooke says. "I've been sitting here talking about everything and nothing, when the fact is I have something important to tell you. I didn't really have any work out in Seattle. I went there to make sure I was going to be doing the right thing."

"The right thing?"

"I did some work out there a few years ago, and I really liked it. Seattle, I mean. The Pacific Northwest has a whole different feel to it. Anyway, for the last couple of months I've been thinking about moving there, and I went out now to make sure it would be the right decision."

Alan feels his heart give way inside his chest even

before the words have fully sunk in. Then he hears, "I signed a lease on an apartment the other day. I'll be moving next week."

Brooke pauses as if expecting a response from him, but what can he say? Finally she says, "I'm sorry if it seems like I was leading you on. I never should've let it happen, knowing I might be moving away. It's just that—"

"No explanation is necessary. And *I'm* not sorry it happened."

Again Brooke smiles sadly. "I'm not really sorry either," she says. "But I'm sorry if I hurt you."

"I'll live."

The words are out of Alan's mouth before it occurs to him that you don't say *I'll live* to someone who's just lost a child. And there, in a nutshell, is the problem: she lost her child. Brooke needs a change in her life, and is it his place to stand in her way? Maybe not, but is he just going to roll over? To give up?

Then he says something he's tried not to think about. "But what if I'm in love with you, Brooke?"

She gives a little chuckle. "You're in love with me?"

"Well . . . I could see myself falling in love with you, given half a chance. . . . The thing is, you've never been just a friend to me, it's always been something more than that. Even when things were going well in my marriage I could never completely get you out of my head."

Do it, Alan, he can hear Rick saying. *If you want the girl, fight for her.*

"Call me selfish," he says, "but I don't want you to move

to Seattle. I know you've been through hell and I know you need to make a fresh start, but I have feelings too."

Brooke says nothing and for a long time they sit—both of them silent, each of them grappling with their separate needs, their separate confusion.

Finally she says, "I have to do this. Please try to understand."

Outside Alan steps off the curb and hails a cab. But when it stops and he opens the door for Brooke, she stands in front of the interior as if blocking his entrance.

"I don't want to prolong this, Alan. Try to be happy. You deserve it."

She touches her lips to her hand, then touches his face for an extended moment. *In another life we might have been something to each other*, she's saying. Or maybe she's just saying goodbye.

Alan watches the cab speed down the block and out of sight. For some time he stands there, huddled against the wind. Then, since he isn't ready to hop into a cab himself and go home to bed, he begins to walk slowly up Bleecker Street.

Who knows, Brooke said before they left the restaurant, *maybe it won't work out. I might be back in New York someday—maybe sooner than you think.*

But even if that were to happen would she call him? Would he *want* her to call him? If they ran into each other on the street would they stop and talk or would they each pretend they hadn't seen or recognized the other?

He cuts across Washington Square Park, ignoring the

drug dealers and the winos, and soon finds himself on a residential block. He doesn't need the pumpkins and witches to remind him of Stephanie. Stephanie, the daughter he never met, is gone. And now Brooke, the woman who might have become the love of his life—gone as well. He's alone again. So what else is new?

Part V

16

Alan emerges from the Holland Tunnel and after a couple of false turns finds his way through the streets of Jersey City to his cousin Loretta's house. After maneuvering into a parking space a few houses beyond hers, he gets out of his car and looks around. The street is just as he remembered it, though it must be at least three years since he's been here. Not that he recognizes anything specifically—there's little to distinguish one small, unpretentious bungalow from the next—but the block holds for him a sense of familiarity, one that probably lies closer to nostalgia. Except for being a good deal bigger, Jersey City isn't much different from Morehead (his childhood prison yard, as he likes to think of it). Back then the little houses that made up his neighborhood seemed huge to him. Now the world has shrunk, along with his sense of the time that's passed since he was a child.

He begins to walk down the block toward Loretta's

house—the one with the blue-and-white-striped awning, she reminded him over the phone. What possible reason could she have had for inviting him to this party? He doesn't have children of his own, is totally out of the mainstream as far as his extended family is concerned, so what made her think he'd want to attend a child's birthday party? But more to the point, why did he say yes?

As he approaches the front door, armed with the toy dump truck he bought for little Anthony, Alan can hear the muffled sounds of voices and children's music coming from inside the house. He rings the bell but after a few seconds tries the door, which proves to be unlocked. As he steps into the house, he sees a few women standing in a cluster talking, and one of them calls out to him.

"Come on in," she says, a little too cheerfully for his taste. "You're Loretta's cousin Alan, right?"

Alan nods and the woman adds, "Loretta's been waiting for you."

"Loretta!" one of the other women bellows. "Your cousin's here, the one from New York."

The first woman, the cheerful one, takes Alan's coat, and he watches her disappear with it into a room off the living room. Feeling conspicuous, he glances around at the other women and exchanges faux smiles with them.

"Alan, hey, how you doing?"

Loretta's husband, Joey, has entered the room. At five-six, Joey has always made Alan feel tall, though there's not much else about his cousin-in-law that Alan responds positively to.

"It's good to see you, man," Joey says, extending his hand. "What you been up to?"

"Not much," Alan says, knowing it was the kind of answer Joey was hoping for.

"Alan, you finally got here. I thought maybe you weren't coming."

He turns to see that his cousin Loretta has emerged from downstairs, and he offers up his cheek to be kissed.

"You're just in time," Loretta adds. "Anthony just started opening his presents. Oh, and before I forget. My mother's having Thanksgiving at her house, and she wanted for me to invite you."

"To invite *me*? Well, uh . . . I'll have to check. . ."

Loretta has begun to move toward the stairs, and Alan follows.

"Don't worry, Alan," she says. "Just call and let me know if you can make it."

As Alan descends the stairs behind his cousin he's greeted with the full force of a five-year-old's birthday party. The sense of motion, even of the children who sit in one place and attend to the ceremony of opening presents, strikes him even more so than the laughter and screams and giggles and the seemingly irrelevant but age-appropriate comments that seem to fly around the room and bounce off the walls like some of the children themselves.

After a moment he notices a little girl with long brown hair, and immediately he thinks of Stephanie. Nearly a year-and-a-half has passed since her death, but Alan always feels a pang of renewed grief whenever he's reminded of her. He wonders if this is a normal response, especially considering that he never even met Stephanie, but he supposes there's no timetable when it comes to a person's feelings. In any case, he's prepared himself for this—the experience of being in the presence of a group of children this age—so now he's able to chase away the flurry of emotions he feels by refocusing on his surroundings.

"Anthony, look," he hears Loretta say to her little son. "Your cousin Alan came from New York just to see you, he brought you a present."

The little boy glances in Alan's direction, then goes back to ripping the paper off an oversize box.

"He doesn't recognize me," Alan says to Loretta, but she's already turned away from him.

He glances absently around the room and again asks himself why he agreed to come to the party.

"Have something to drink," he hears now. "There's beer in the fridge in the other room."

A woman has approached him and is pointing toward what he remembers to be a small room off the main basement room. He takes a closer look at the woman and recognizes his cousin Edwina, who, he's heard, just moved back to Jersey from Idaho.

"Alan, is that you?" Edwina says. "Loretta said you might be coming. I ain't seen you in years." The two cousins exchange kisses and the kind of platitudes you exchange with someone you haven't seen in years and never had much to say to in the first place, then fall into an awkward silence. Edwina takes up the slack when she waves her arm with an indefinite gesture and says, "Kids! They're something, ain't they?"

Alan has to agree but has nothing to add, and once again they fall silent. Then Edwina excuses herself, citing some crisis that's taking place on the other side of the room, evidently involving a little girl's barrette and another little girl's ankle bracelet.

Alan redirects his attention to little Anthony, who's now opening *his* present. That is, the one he brought for the boy.

"Look at that, son! It's a dump truck!" This was Joey, who just emerged, beer in hand, from the room Alan was directed to.

"And it's yellow," Loretta chimes in, for a reason that's probably known only to the nuclear family.

After a few more minutes of this, Alan decides to take advantage of his escape clause. He slips out of the main room and around a corner into the little one. And then his jaw drops. Across the little room, standing in conversation with another woman, is the most breathtakingly beautiful woman he's ever seen. Ever. The two women notice him at once, and the good-looking one gives him a tentative smile, revealing a set of perfect—and brilliantly white—teeth. Then the other one, perhaps sensing that an animal connection has been made within feet of her, excuses herself and disappears from the room. Alan is left alone with the most beautiful woman in the world.

The woman—her chestnut hair long and shimmering, her huge brown eyes dancing out at him with bemused interest—hesitates a moment and then seems to make a move in his direction. Alan responds to the attenuated movement of her legs by rousing himself from the stupor he was thrown into at the sight of her. He too puts one leg in front of the other and, since the room is not at all large, he finds himself, a moment later, standing face to face with her.

"Hi," she says. "I bet you're Alan, right?"

And then Alan's jaw drops again, but for an entirely different reason than it did the first time. The sound of the woman's voice has reminded him that he's in Jersey City, not at a midtown Manhattan art gallery. Of *course* she would have a New Jersey accent. What else is she going to have?

"I'm Marissa, by the way," the woman says. "Marissa Liotti."

She extends a slender hand to Alan and he shakes it, although—and in spite of her voice—his impulse was to kiss it.

"Alan," he says, remembering she just introduced herself. "Alan Agnalini."

"Well, Alan Agnalini," Marissa says, "it's nice to make your acquaintance. Loretta mentioned you. She didn't think you'd come to the party, but here you are."

And so he is. What he didn't count on, though, was being both here and in the presence of a woman whose beauty simply overwhelms him but whose whining, grating voice and overall demeanor (Hudson County chic, he likes to think of it) disconcerts him, to say the least.

Marissa tilts her head slightly, evidently in response

to the near-catatonic state he's fallen back into. *What's up with you?* she seems to be asking, and it behooves him to come up with an answer, and quick. He decides to ignore her aspect and concentrate, instead, on the male-female dynamic that's taking place between them.

"How do you know Loretta?" he says now, a reasonable if banal question.

"She works at my shop," Marissa says. "Or I work at *her* shop. You know, in Hoboken. I only just started there, I used to be at a shop up in Guttenberg."

Alan feels his insides plummet like an Otis elevator. A New Jersey accent isn't bad enough, she has to be a beautician on top of it!?

"I was wondering where you two were?"

Alan turns his head, and once again there's Loretta.

"I see you two are getting to know each other," she says, and suddenly it all becomes clear to him: Loretta fixed him up.

Marissa seems to blush at Loretta's remark, which makes Alan wonder if she knew about the fix-up. He'd like to think not—for one thing because he doesn't like being manipulated, but more so because he's fishing for reasons, other than Marissa's beauty, to be favorably disposed toward her.

"But don't let me get in the way," Loretta says grabbing a few cans of soda out of the mini-refrigerator. She's gone a moment later.

In her wake Marissa says, "She means well. I had a feeling she was trying to fix you and me up."

"Loretta's been after me since the moment my wife and I separated. She apparently doesn't believe that single people can be happy."

Alan notices a hint of what seems to be sadness cross Marissa's face. "Are you happy being single?" she says.

"Happy? I wouldn't go that far, but being single isn't so bad. It beats being married to the wrong person."

Marissa's face remains sad, or maybe pensive would better describe what he's seeing. Was it something he said? Did she think of him as damaged goods because he's been married? Or maybe she had a bad marriage herself.

"How about you?" he says. "Have you been married?"

This time a look of genuine consternation crosses Marissa's face, and she turns her head away for a moment. "Me?" she says, turning back to him. "No, I never been married. Maybe someday. I'd like to have a baby, that's for sure."

"Babies are good. That is, if the parents are ready for the job."

"Did you and your wife have a baby? You're a father, Alan?"

The second question hits him like a torpedo. Yes, he *was* a father—or maybe you're *always* a father even if your child has died—but this isn't something he can get into with Marissa.

"No," he says in answer to the first question. "My wife and I both knew we weren't ready to be parents. That's a pretty big responsibility."

"Responsibility?" Marissa says. "I see it as a blessing, having a baby. Alls I ever wanted to be was a mother. From the time I was a little girl. I guess someone like yourself, though—you know, someone from New York and all—they have bigger ambitions in life."

Alan can tell that Marissa's last remark was in no way sarcastic. If anything, she seemed to be putting herself down for being . . . well, a Jersey girl.

"Nonsense," he says. "Parenthood, especially motherhood, is the most important job in the world."

Marissa makes no response to this, and Alan wonders if it was arrogant of him to tell her something she instinctively understands.

"So," he hears her say after a moment, "Loretta said you're a writer."

"A writer? That's too kind. What I write doesn't qualify me for the title, at least in my estimation."

"What do you write?" Marissa says.

"Junk."

"Junk? Whata you mean junk? I don't get your meaning."

"You know—junk mail. The kind of stuff you get in the mail and throw away without reading."

"But you write it, right?"

"Right," he says.

"Then you're a writer."

Alan is not about to argue with Marissa's logic, considering that it was based on a total misunderstanding of what he was actually saying.

Silence descends on them like a sudden fog. He scrambles for something to say but comes up empty. Then he sees Marissa glance at her watch.

"Geez," she says, "I didn't realize how late it's getting to be. I gotta be going."

She doesn't, however, turn on her heel and vanish from the room, which Alan takes to mean that she does in fact have to be going. In lingering, she seems to be giving him a chance to rise to the occasion, as it were. To meet her on her own terms, if such a thing is possible. And then he realizes she's waiting for him to ask for her phone number. But does he want her phone number? She's drop-dead gorgeous, no question, and he can think of worse things to do on a Saturday night than to spend it with her, but would he survive? He couldn't go five minutes without running out of things to say to her, how could he get through an entire date? And besides, he could always get her number from Loretta later on, if he decides to pursue it. But wouldn't it be insulting not to ask for her number?

"Can I call you?" he hears himself say.

His ambivalence has clearly not been lost on Marissa, for she doesn't respond at once. Then she reaches into her handbag and fumbles around for a couple of seconds.

"Here," she says, handing him a business card.

"'Mr. Kenneth's Hair Emporium,'" Alan reads. "'We do hair with flair.' Catchy."

Marissa is on her way out of the room now. "Just ask for me," she says, then adds with a wink, "but don't worry. I won't shrivel up and die if I never hear from you."

17

"Well Alan, alls I need is six pins. If I can keep the ball in the pocket, there shouldn't be a problem."

Alan, sitting at the scoring table, can only look up in wonder at Marissa's radiant smile and dancing eyes. The woman is proving to be far more than just a pretty face.

He watches as she steps to the ball-return and retrieves her ball, then takes up her stance as the ten little Indians at the far end of the alley await their just deserts.

Now she goes into her approach—in a slight crouch, moving slowly at first. As Marissa swings her right arm back, Alan can't help focusing on the most enchanting part of her dorsal side. Then he hears the ball meet the floorboards with a perfect "pflunck," and the sound awakens him to the ball's path. He watches it glide seamlessly down the alley as if on a conveyor belt and he knows what the outcome will be. As the ball moves to within a couple of feet of the pins, it takes a sharp detour to the left and, a moment later, makes contact with the head-pin and the three-pin simultaneously. The result is the explosion he predicted: random but with its own seemingly ordered beauty. The final holdout, the seven-pin, teeters on the brink of life and death and then topples into the gutter, but this is a moot point; all she needed was six pins.

He watches Marissa raise her arms to the sky and then do a quick pirouette so that she's now facing him in triumph, even as cheers and applause break out courtesy of more than a handful of alley rats.

"I did it!" she exclaims. "You lose again!"

Alan can only smile in defeat.

"So," Marissa says as she approaches the scoring table, "you gonna congratulate me or what?"

"You won fair and square," he says. "And twice. I'll happily buy you dessert and coffee, which I was going to do anyway."

"No you weren't. If you'da won, then I would be the one doing the buying. That was our bet."

"And a bet's a bet," Alan says, not sure to what degree he's humoring her or to what degree he's genuinely enjoying the world as she sees it.

This world of hers is something he thought he might not be seeing again, since for nearly a full week after he met Marissa he remained conflicted about calling her. Finally, no longer able to justify passing up an opportunity to have a date with a woman of such stunning good looks, he called her but was met with a surprising response. *You almost passed my sev-*

en-day limit, Marissa told him. *But I won't hold it against you. I got doubts a my own.*

Now they're out in the parking lot, and Alan opens the car door for his date.

"See, what did I tell you?" she says. "Bowling was a great idea. I always like going bowling on the first date. It breaks the ice."

"As long as it didn't break any part of my body," Alan says.

He walks around to the driver's side and gets in. "So," he says, turning on the ignition, "how do I get to the diner?"

Marissa directs him and a few minutes later they arrive at a gaudy rectangle in a predominantly residential part of Weehawken.

"Here we are," Marissa says. "Dinah's Diner."

To Alan's ears the words sounded like "Dinah's Dinah," but he's getting used to the strange juxtaposition of Marissa's physical beauty and her less-than-beautiful way of speaking. The juxtaposition, he supposes, is quirky. Marissa herself, he's seeing, is quirky.

They enter the diner and Alan looks around, trying to spot an out-of-the-way booth. "How about that booth over there," he says to Marissa, but when he turns toward her she's nowhere. A second later he sees her running toward the counter.

"Moira?" he hears her shout. "Is that you?"

The waitress behind the counter turns, and Alan sees a look of surprise light up her face. "Marissa!" she exclaims. "Marissa Liotti, I can't believe it, I ain't seen you in years."

Alan watches as the waitress comes out from behind the counter and the two young women embrace. This Moira person isn't bad-looking. In fact, he realizes, she looks something like Brooke. The thought of Brooke predictably triggers a thought of Stephanie, but he wills himself to direct his mind back to Marissa.

"I thought you were dead," he can hear her saying, and he's unsure whether to take a step toward the counter or just stand there in the middle of the room and wait for his cue to join the conversation, assuming there would be one.

"Dead? Who told you that?"

"I don't know," Marissa says. "I heard it somewheres. But . . . But lemme look at you." Marissa moves back a step and looks her old friend up and down. "Are you pregnant?"

"Not even three months and I'm starting to show already, I can't believe it."

"Oh my God, Moira, I'm so jealous. I can't *wait* to have a baby a my own."

"I can't wait either, I'm so excited. I met this guy in Buffalo. That's where we ended up after my dad lost his job in Pittsburgh. Anyways, I met this guy and one thing led to another. We just moved back down here from Buffalo. We'll be getting married next month, you gotta come to the wedding."

"Sure, I'd love to."

"But don't hate me, Marissa. I been meaning to call you, but what with all the unpacking and everything I kept putting it off. But I'll send you an invitation. I'll come by your table later and get your address, I forget what it was."

Alan tunes out the conversation at this point and focuses, instead, on how ridiculous he feels. He feels, perhaps, like a two-year-old in a shopping cart waiting for his mother to choose the three best melons out of the dozen vying for her attention. Or maybe a three-year-old in the same predicament.

Deciding to take action he steps toward the counter only to have Marissa turn toward him.

"There you are," she says. "I didn't know where you went to."

She turns back to her friend. "Moira, this is Alan Agnalini. And Alan," she adds, "did you know that Moira and me were best friends since eighth grade? And then a couple years after we finished high school she goes and disappears on me."

Alan, who knew none of this, is suddenly famished. He wants to sit down in a nice booth and eat something. He'd even accept prolonged silences between Marissa and him, so long as food is part of the equation.

"It's good to meet you," he hears Moira say, and he accepts the heavily ringed hand she extended to him.

"Alan's from New York," Marissa says. "He's in publishing."

"Hey, miss, can I get some service over here?"

Alan looks down the counter to see a burly trucker-type with his fat neck craned in Moira's direction.

"I gotta get this," she says to Marissa. "I'll stop by your table later and give you my new number and all."

Finally Alan finds himself sitting across from Marissa in his coveted booth.

"She's such a sweetheart," Marissa says. "It's so good to see her after all these years, her family moved—what was it? I think 1972. . . . But I'm sorry, Alan, I was being rude keeping you waiting like that."

"Not at all," he says. "It's always nice running into an old friend. Especially when you thought they were dead."

"What are you two having over here?"

Alan looks up at the sound of a man's voice but does a double take when he sees that the speaker is a woman.

"You still got that coconut custard pie?" Marissa says to the woman (who, over the phone, could fool a lot of people as to her gender).

The waitress says yes to the pie and then asks Marissa if she wants coffee with that.

"Natch," Marissa says.

Natch!? It's been years since Alan heard anyone say, "natch"—short for "naturally." He has a sudden yearning to be back in Manhattan. He can almost see himself swimming across the Hudson in desperation.

"And that's one lump with the cream on the side," he hears Marissa say.

He looks up and the waitress turns to him.

"And what about you?" she says.

"Apple pie would be fine. French apple, if you have it."

"We got that," the waitress says, writing all this down.

"And just black coffee for me," Alan adds.

The waitress disappears, and Alan and his date sit in silence for a minute. Then Marissa says, "So," but seems unable to expand on this.

"I like your friend," Alan says, jumping on the first thing that comes to mind. "She's Irish?"

"Irish, right," Marissa says. "Flynn. Her name's Moira Flynn."

"Sounds Irish."

Marissa resettles herself on her side of the booth, and Alan takes this as a sign that things aren't going well between them. He thinks of asking her what high school she went to, but he has no interest in knowing. He settles on asking her if she has any brothers or sisters.

"Nope," she says. "I'm an only child. Actually, I'm adopted. I bet you didn't know that."

How could he know that? Unless Loretta told him, which she didn't.

"You're adopted?" he says. "From infancy or later on?"

"From when I was eight months, I think. My parents— my real parents, I mean the ones who raised me—they told me my other parents drowned on the Staten Island Ferry, but maybe they just said that."

Alan thinks of a clever remark but this is no night for clever remarks. "Do your parents live in Hoboken too?"

"They're dead."

"No, I mean your parents who raised you."

"That's what I meant. They're dead."

"Oh," he says. "I'm sorry to hear that."

"It happens," Marissa says, looking away.

After an extended lull, the waitress appears with their order. Alan makes no attempt to reestablish the conversation, nor does Marissa. They tackle their pie and coffee with deliberation, and Alan looks around surreptitiously to see if he can spot a clock anywhere. (He doesn't dare look at his watch).

"Loretta says your cousin's rich," he hears now. "You know, the one who's like your big brother."

Just what he needs: Ralph to insinuate himself into the conversation.

"My cousin Ralph?" Alan says, resigned to the series of questions he knows will follow. "Yeah, you could say he's rich."

"He's in real estate, Loretta says?"

"Right. Commercial real estate."

Marissa screws up her eyes in a way that makes her seem even prettier to Alan than she already is.

"How old was he when your parents adopted him?"

This is another misconception that casual students of Alan's extended family are often prey to.

"He was never adopted," Alan says as if by rote. "When he was a baby—I think two—his father died, and my father became a kind of surrogate father to him. But my aunt Fiona, his mother, was very much alive. And living right next door to us, in fact."

"Yeah, I remember that. Loretta said you grew up in a duplex."

"Loretta knows her family lore," Alan says with sarcasm that sails over Marissa's head like a flock of migrating geese.

They fall into a strained silence, and finally Alan decides it would be better to reintroduce the topic they were discussing, distasteful as it is for him, than to deal with the awkwardness of a stagnant conversation. "Our parents," he says, "—I mean my father and my aunt Fiona, not so much my mother—insisted that Ralph and I think of ourselves as brothers, not cousins."

"But were you like brothers?"

"No," Alan says, "we were cousins."

"I know, but were you close like brothers or close like cousins?"

"We weren't close period. Except in terms of physical—"

He was about to say "proximity" but he'd promised himself to try not to talk over Marissa's head. "The only way we were close," he says, "is that we lived next door to each other. You could say we were geographically close, but that was about the extent of it."

"Why? Didn't you like each other?"

Alan stifles a sigh. This line of questioning, he reminds himself, is part of the price he has to pay to keep the conversation going. "I can't speak for my cousin," he says, "but I didn't have a problem with him. In fact, when I was a little kid I idolized him."

Marissa takes a sip of coffee. "How much older is he?"

"Six . . . Something like six and a half years, I think."

"That's too far apart to be friends when you're growing up," she says.

Alan takes a bite of pie, hoping Marissa will remember that she just saw her friend who turned out to be alive after all, and that this would lead her to start reminiscing about good old Moira, and so on. But evidently Marissa's curiosity hasn't been slaked, for now she says, "But he's rich though, right?"

Her question reminds Alan of his cousin Dominic, who has a tendency to ask a question over and over, as if he's so delighted with the answer that an isolated instance of it simply isn't enough to satisfy him.

"He's definitely rich," Alan says.

"And you're not."

"Neither are most people," he says, feeling an internal cringe despite the veracity of his statement.

"But he's your brother—I mean your cousin, but he's like your brother. So how does that make you feel, that he's rich and you're not?"

Beautiful though she is, Alan observes, Marissa is no paragon of tact. But to her credit, she's direct. The kind of person who cuts to the heart of a matter.

"It makes me sad," he says, answering her question in spite of its bluntness and in spite of himself. "But not because he has money and I don't. It makes me sad because of the way people—my family, mostly—see me in relation to him."

Alan is silent—having said all he has to say on the matter, and willing, on second thought, to endure excruciating silence if that's the only alternative—but Marissa's mind seems to be in overdrive.

"I think I know what you mean," she says. "They see you as less than him. Cause he *has* more, then he *is* more. That's the way they think, right?"

Alan is surprised by this observation. "You hit the nail

on the head. I've always felt like the weak one, but only because I'm *seen* as weak, not because I *am* weak."

Marissa has no response to this, and he wonders if he said too much. This was supposed to be a date, and here he is getting all heavy on her. Of course, she was the one who asked the question.

"It's like me," she says now. "People think that just cause you're a beautyful woman that your life is perfect. So they see me as perfect, and that puts pressure on me cause I'm not, I'm just Marissa. But people expect me to be happy all the time, or smarter than I am, or more ambitious than I am. And all cause I happen to be beautyful."

Alan is impressed. Marissa? A thoughtful—as in "thinking"—person? Who would have guessed?

They fall silent again for a moment. Then she says, "Loretta says your father always favored Ralph. That musta been hard on you growing up."

"I dealt with it," Alan says as if casually, but he feels an urge to unburden himself, to let Marissa know how hard it was to grow up in the shadow of a looming presence like Ralph Passacantando.

"How're you two kids doing over here?"

It's the androgynous waitress, back to ply her trade.

"I'd like another cup a coffee," Marissa says.

"And you?" the waitress says turning to Alan.

"No, I'm good."

A minute later the waitress returns with Marissa's coffee. Encouraged by Marissa's desire to plumb somewhat beneath the surface of things, Alan looks forward to the next leg of their sputtering conversation but with a new topic, he hopes. What he gets from her is a question which, though peripherally related to what they were talking about, is far less emotionally charged for him.

"Loretta says your father had a stroke?"

"I'm afraid so," Alan says. "It wasn't a major stroke, but he'll never be what he was. His speech isn't too bad, and he can get around with a walker. . . . At least he has Dolly to take care of him."

"Who's Dolly?"

"Dolly's his wife."

"Your father remarried? They're divorced, your parents?"

"My father's a widower," he says. "My mother died a while back. When I was twenty-one. Didn't Loretta mention that?" he can't help adding.

"No, she never said nothing. And I'm sorry about your mom."

"It happens," Alan says, realizing he used the exact words Marissa had used about her own parents' death. "But eventually he married the lady across the street. It was a marriage of convenience and at first they had some problems, but I guess it's paying dividends now."

Alan steals a glance at his watch but Marissa doesn't appear to notice. Unless he's mistaken, she decided to shift gears but seems at a loss as to what precisely to say next. Finally he hears: "So Alan, you like living in New York?"

"I love it," he says.

"Wheres exactly to do live in New York?"

"Yorkville. It's the non-swanky part of the Upper East Side, over by the East River."

Marissa seems to have no interest in any of this, and he wonders why she asked the question. He tries to come up with a non sequitur that might lead them onto a topic more to her liking, but he finally gives up and asks her if she gets to the city much.

She quickly glances away as if rattled by the question, but then turns her gaze back to him. "I used to go to New York all the time," she says. "But it's been a while since I been there."

On its surface, Marissa's answer was straightforward enough, but something in her delivery, coupled with the expression on her face, tells Alan he's not getting the whole story. In any case, and unlike Marissa, he isn't about to explore territory he considers too personal for a first date.

After a few moments Marissa's mood seems to lift, but she remains silent. As for Alan, he can't think of another thing to say. Their mutual awkwardness quickly intensifies. For the next twenty minutes, interrupted only by a brief visit from Marissa's old friend Moira, they make false starts and go off on tangents and misunderstand each other and endure increasingly longer silences. By the time Alan pays the check and they leave the diner he's totally demoralized. And ready to pack it in and drop her off in Hoboken and chalk the whole thing up to experience.

Outside they walk silently to his car at the far end of the parking lot. The night is crisp, a little on the chilly side even for November—the sky blue-black and flooded with stars. Alan sees himself as if he were in a movie, walking with a gorgeous woman beneath a starry sky on the kind of night that makes a young couple want to huddle together, for warmth and in appreciation of life's beauty. But Marissa remains distant from him and he from her. Physically distant and metaphysically distant, as if they're in different dimensions.

Inside the car Alan turns the key in the ignition and turns up the heater. He glances over at Marissa and sees that she's clinging to the passenger-side door.

"It can't take too long to get to your house from here," he observes as he pulls out of the parking lot.

"Ten minutes tops," she says.

Ten more minutes of this, Alan thinks to himself. He envisions, now, the moment of truth that awaits him ten minutes down the road. *The two of them ascend Marissa's front stoop. He wonders if he should try to kiss her goodnight, though he's certain if he does she'll just turn her head and offer him a cheek. But he goes ahead and does it anyway, and, as predicted, gets the dreaded cheek. "I had a nice time, Alan," he hears her say, and then he watches as she slips through the front door, thus putting an end to their ill-fated experiment. . . .*

He hears a car horn blaring and realizes that he's stalled out at a red light. After a few tries he manages to get the engine turned over, and they proceed down the winding hill from Weehawken into Hoboken.

"Take this street here," Marissa says a few minutes later.

Alan turns onto a quiet street that's lined with rather dreary-looking row houses. Hoboken isn't Beverly Hills but it has an unassuming charm about it—a kind of old-world timelessness. He understands how someone like Marissa might be perfectly content living here.

"You should try to find a parking space now," she says.

Alan slows down and they both scout for a space. Finally Alan locates something a couple of cars ahead. He has to resort to parallel parking, not his most polished skill, but he gets the job done.

He kills the engine and gets out of the car, then goes around to the passenger side. The little town of Hoboken is tucked away in bed. There will be no witnesses to whatever is about to take place on her front stoop, and for that much he's grateful.

"It's just at the other end a the block," Marissa says as she gets out of the car.

He tries to read her mood but can't. Has she, too, given up on them, or is she waiting for him to pull a rabbit out of a hat?

They begin to walk down the street. Alan, who feels like he's on his way to the gallows, slows his pace to match Marissa's. She's in no apparent hurry to get home, which could be a good sign; she might be delaying the moment when they'll have to say goodnight. On the other hand, she might be dreading what she assumes will be an attempt on his part to kiss her.

But then she does something completely unexpected: she sidles over a little closer to Alan and slips her arm through the crook of his arm.

"It's lovely out tonight," she says. "Don't you think?"

Marissa's action has caught Alan off guard, and he scrambles to regain his composure.

"Yes, lovely," he says, trying to make it sound matter of fact.

"I love this time a year," Marissa says. "I don't like it *too* too cold, but weather like this is perfect."

Now they come to her house—the next to last in a long block of row houses. She begins to mount the few steps to her front door and Alan follows at a respectful distance. He's been given an opening and he's determined not to blow it.

The front door of Marissa's house seems menacing to Alan as he stands with her now on the top landing. Not that he has any hope of seeing the other side of it on this particular night. Marissa, he figured out early on, isn't the type to sleep with a man on the first date. And he respects that. And, if truth be told, prefers it.

He looks diagonally across the street at a corner of what he guesses might be a large park.

"Do you spend much time in the park?" he asks.

"Not really. But I like to look out the window at it. It makes me feel, I don't know, peaceful."

Alan turns his face back toward her. "God, you are so incredibly beautiful," he says, and he can tell she's blushing, although she's probably heard those words a million times before.

"I had a good time tonight, Alan, and I'm not just saying that. Even when we ran outa things to say, it still felt right being with you."

Marissa raises her head slightly and Alan responds to the classic invitation. He inclines his head toward hers and in the next moment their lips meet, tentatively at first but then with a rush of mutual passion. And then he loses all sense of time and place. All he knows is that Marissa is in his arms and he's kissing her and that she's responding to him with a heat he never could have predicted. And then, finally, after what seems to him like a full minute, the kiss comes to a close. Except it starts back up only moments later, and then Alan finds himself kissing her neck repeatedly and then burying his face in her hair. . . .

He feels Marissa pull back from him—not abruptly but with conviction.

"Whoa," she says, wagging a finger at him. "You're getting a little carried away there, mister. I'm afraid you're gonna have to wait for that."

Alan, put in his place and still reeling from the kiss, watches her turn and disappear through the front door.

18

"That was a good dinner, Alan, don't you think? See, not all the good restaurants are in New York."

Alan and Marissa have just finished their meal at the Clam Broth House, Hoboken's world-famous seafood restaurant, and now they turn the corner onto Washington Street.

"This is pretty neat as far as main streets go," Alan says. "It has an old-time quality to it, kind of like something from the early part of the century."

"You think?" Marissa says. "To me it's just Hoboken, but I guess that's cause I live here."

They walk in silence for a time. Then Marissa points up at the sky and says, "Look Alan, it's snowing. I love it when it snows like this."

Alan feels a sense of well-being come over him. In the next moment, almost as if he's been rewarded for appreciating life's ability to simply astound us at times, he feels

Marissa's arm slip through his and he stops and turns to her and they kiss. It's a lovely, snowy kiss—lacking some of the surprising intensity of their first kiss, but containing a promise of things to come that would have been premature a week ago.

Now they continue down Washington Street, huddled together as if slow-dancing through time toward a timeless destination. When they come to Fifth Street they cross Washington and turn down the hill. Minutes later they enter Marissa's bedroom and make love for the first time. For Alan it's like coming home after a long journey. It's like discovering a part of himself he's always sensed but whose existence he's been uncertain of.

About mid-morning, after yet another round of pyrotechnics, Alan and Marissa finally pull themselves out of bed. Alan, clothed only in a pair of jeans, is standing now at one of Marissa's front windows—the middle one, which gives the best view of the park.

"I see what you mean, Marissa," he calls out to her in the kitchen. "The park definitely gives you a sense of peacefulness. And all this snow doesn't hurt matters."

Marissa, wearing only an oversize football jersey and driving Alan crazy as a result, appears in the doorway off the living room, and once again he's floored by her beauty.

"I'm glad you're enjoying yourself," she says, "but it's time you got dressed. The neighbors are gonna get the wrong idea seeing you standing there bare-chested in front a that window."

"Actually, I think they'd get the right idea," Alan says. "*I* sure think it's the right idea."

Rolling her eyes, Marissa turns and disappears back into the kitchen, but not so fast that he's unable to catch a glimpse of his favorite part of her. Absent her face, that is.

A few minutes later, Alan, fully dressed now, is sitting at the kitchen table as Marissa puts the finishing touches on breakfast. He's surprised that the breakfast she's prepared for them is relatively simple—a cheese omelet, juice, toast, coffee. But he supposes that a woman of Marissa's physical attributes needn't bother to aim at a man's heart through his stomach.

Later, when the breakfast dishes have been cleared and washed and put away, they sit over coffee and talk (and hold hands across the table and play footsies, and so on). But now Alan notices that Marissa's mood seems to be downshifting on him. Finally he says, "Are you okay, Marissa? Do you have a headache or anything?"

"No, I'm okay. But there's something I need to tell you. I don't tell just anybody, so you should take that as a compliment."

Alan wonders what this could be about. Could she be sick? Maybe he was making love all night to a dying woman. Or maybe she's losing her eyesight as a result of some rare congenital disease. . . .

"So," Marissa begins. "Remember when I told you my parents died? Not my birth parents, but my real parents?"

Alan nods.

"Anyways, I didn't say that night how they died. It was in all the papers, maybe you read about it. 1968, it was."

"Maybe," Alan says, although the possibility is remote considering that he was in Vermont at the time.

"What happened is, my parents were up on Washington Street doing some shopping. My father was just retired from the railroad, just a few days before, and he was helping my mother with her shopping. So anyways, there was this little grocery store on Washington Street in the middle a the block between Tenth Street and Eleventh Street, but close to Eleventh. Genovese's Market, it was called. And next to it on the corner there was this apartment house with a dry cleaners under it, and it was being torn down to make way for a new parking lot they were gonna be putting up. So my parents, like I said, they were shopping that day, and they went into the grocery store—"

Marissa is silent for a long moment. "You'd think it would get easier after all this time," she says finally, "but it don't."

She wipes a tear from beneath one of her eyes and continues. "So like I was saying, they had just went into the grocery store—I know this cause there were a couple witnesses who saw the whole thing—and there was this wrecking ball that they were using to tear down the building next door, but somehow the wrecking ball swung into the grocery store, which it wasn't supposed to do. . . . And everybody in the store was crushed to death."

Alan can feel his body stiffen. He scrambles for the right thing to say, settling on, "I'm sorry."

Marissa pauses a moment, silently acknowledging Alan's condolences, then goes on with her story. "This was in 1968, like I said. I was in twelfth grade by then and just like that I didn't have my parents no more. I didn't have nobody, really, cause my parents didn't have a lot a relatives, either one a them. But my father told me a couple times about his will, and he made sure I understood it in case something happened to them, which it did. So I knew to call my father's lawyer and to call my uncle Harry in Delaware, who I didn't know too good, I only met him a couple times when I was little. And the lawyer arranged for a real estate company to rent out the house while I was in Delaware, cause I had to go down there, that was part a my parents' will in case I wasn't eighteen yet when they died.

"Anyways, I went down to Delaware—Wilmington, it was—and at first it was okay. Different, that's for sure. My uncle and his wife, Aunt Edie, they tried to make me feel at home, but my cousins, at least the two girls—they were both in tenth grade, they were twins—they treated me like I was Cinderella and they were the mean stepsisters. The only one who was really nice to me was my cousin Ned, who was outa high school already and had a job in a hardware store. Ned was a sweet boy—I still think a him that way, even after what happened—but he was a little slow. You know, kinda retarded-like.

"So what happened is, they sent me to this private school. My uncle Harry was rich but not so rich like your brother, I mean your cousin is, from what it sounds like.

But Uncle Harry was doing pretty good and they had a big house on a farm just ten minutes from downtown, with horses mostly but some other animals too. But I didn't like the private school they sent me to cause all the kids in it were snobs, it seemed like to me. All they cared about was the 'things' they had—you know, their cars and their trust funds and their country clubs and like that. And they all thought I talked funny, but I thought *they* talked funny. And then the girls didn't like me cause a my looks and the boys were always trying to get to first base with me, but I've had that my whole life.

"Anyways, the time passed and since I wasn't gonna be turning eighteen till May I couldn't've went back home before the school year was out because a what my parents' will said. So I stayed there, but at least I had Ned to talk to—we'd talk about things sometimes and he was nice to me. But what really helped me get through it was Robbie, who was my boyfriend back home. It was hard being away from him, but at the same time he'd send me letters and sometimes he'd call me on the phone and he kept reminding me that time passes. So it made it easier being there.

"So before you know it, it was June and I was graduating. And my uncle decided he was gonna throw me a big graduation party even though I only had a couple friends. So that's what he did. They had this big graduation party for me, and while all the other kids were going to everybody else's parties I went to mine, even though I didn't know half the people there and only had a couple friends a my own there. But I think my uncle did it cause he knew I wouldn't be invited to any a the parties, so he wanted to keep my feelings from being hurt.

"And I was having a pretty good time at the party, cause even though I didn't know most a the people—they were mostly people my aunt and uncle socialized with, or people he did business with—a lot a them would come up to me and talk for a minute and ask me questions about my plans and all.

"But when the party was starting to break up I noticed that my cousin Ned—you know, the retarded one—that he looked a little drunk to me. He was drinking beer and he musta had one too many, but no one seemed bothered about it cause Ned never got in trouble so I guess they figured being a little drunk wouldn't hurt him none. But after the party I was up in my room getting undressed and I hear this sound from out in the hall. And the next thing I know Ned walks into my room without even knocking and he starts lunging at me and saying what he wanted to do to me—you know what I'm talking about—and then he pinned me on the bed ..."

Marissa is silent. Alan feels a wave of nausea pass over him and he wants to reach out to her physically, to wrap her in his arms and somehow take away the memory of what obviously happened to her. Since no amount of comforting could do this, though, he remains motionless.

Time passes, whether a minute or five minutes Alan has no idea. Finally Marissa speaks.

"He raped me, Alan. I just wasn't strong enough to

fight him off, but I was screaming and calling for help and I guess he didn't have the sense to gag me some way. Cause a minute later my uncle comes running into the room and he pulls him off a me, but by then it was too late."

Marissa appears now to have sunk into herself, as if in reliving the nightmare of her rape she took reflexive shelter in her body. From out in the street Alan can hear children shouting, probably as part of a snowball fight, and he finds himself wishing that somehow their joy at being alive—and presumably ignorant of things like rape—will be enough to bring Marissa out of herself and back to the present.

He reaches across the table and puts his hand on Marissa's. "I'm sorry this happened to you," he says.

But Marissa surprises him with her response. "I'm just getting started. I wish that was the end a my story, but it's not."

She takes a sip of coffee now and it seems to fortify her. "So after my uncle pulled Ned off a me and they got him settled down, my aunt spent the next couple hours in my room—you know, trying to calm me down and all. And she said in the morning they would take me to the hospital but that I needed to rest now, and that I didn't have to worry about Ned, my uncle would take care a that end of it. But after they left my room I waited till I was sure they were asleep and called a cab—I had my own phone in my room. And I called a cab and left a note on the bed, and I had the driver take me to the train station downtown—me and my two suitcases. And I had to wait in the train station all night, but in the morning the train came and I took it to Newark and then I took a cab to Hoboken."

Marissa pauses to take another sip of coffee, and Alan asks her where she stayed when she got to Hoboken.

"I stayed here."

"Here, in this house? But I thought you said they rented out the house while you were away. Wasn't there someone living here?"

"No, they only rented it out for a few months. Then my father's lawyer hired a contractor and they changed it around to make it into two apartments. It was simple. Alls they had to do was put a kitchen in the upstairs and a bathroom in the downstairs and change around the entranceway a little. And when they were done they mailed me all the keys, so when I got back to Hoboken from Delaware I moved right into my own house—only just on the second floor now. And then I rented out the first floor."

They sit in silence for a minute, holding hands across the table but in a nonsexual way. Then Marissa resumes her story.

"As soon as I got settled back in Hoboken . . . By the way, I didn't get pregnant from the rape in case you're wondering. That was *one* good thing anyways.

"But like I was saying, when I got back to Hoboken I got a job at a greeting card store up in Union City and then I started thinking about going to beauty school. And me and Robbie started up again like we were never apart and before long he popped the question and I said yes. So things were going good for me for the first time in a long time, but then—right around Valentine's Day it was—Robbie came down with the flu except it wasn't the flu after all, and they had to rush him to the hospital and that's when they found out he had meningitis. And by the next day he was dead."

Alan becomes aware that for several moments he's been holding his breath. He lets out the air now, a massive expiration which seems to him to be in keeping with the tragedy upon tragedy upon tragedy Marissa just laid out for him. "My God!" he says now. "How did you have the strength to get through it all?"

Marissa's response—again a surprising one—is to shake her head and smile to herself. "That's not the whole story," she says. "There's two more things."

"Two more!?" Alan says. He's overwhelmed by her story, and he almost wishes there was a way to avoid learning what came next, not to mention what came after that. At the same time, he feels a sense of stewardship toward her now, and he knows she needs to tell the story in its entirety.

"So," she says, "I pulled myself back together little by little and a couple years later I met this guy Tom. We hit it off pretty good and by that time I was going on twenty-one and I started to think that this might be the guy for me. So to make a long story short we got engaged and had a big engagement party on the night a the day I turned twenty-one, since it happened to be on a Saturday. You could probably guess what happened next—or at least the *kind* a thing that happened next—so I'll just say it without any more introductions. Tom fell off a six-story building in Jersey City—he was a construction worker and they did a whole investigation but he wasn't pushed or nothing. And the doctors said he was lucky he died cause otherwise he woulda been paralyzed from the neck down."

"My God!" Alan says for the second time. "I . . ." But he has no words—nothing that might express his sense of disbelief, nothing that might convey what he feels is deep compassion toward her, and certainly nothing that could magically erase her tragic past. And to look at her, he says to himself now, you couldn't begin to guess . . . But this too is a shallow thought; sometimes the abuse life can heap upon us is resistant not just to words but to thought itself.

"So that's my story, Alan. I wanted to tell you cause I have a feeling you're not just in this for a couple rolls in the hay. You're not that kind of a man."

Alan is confused. "I thought you said there were *two* more things."

"Did I say *two* things? I meant one." Marissa looks away for a moment but turns back to him. "You're right, Alan," she says. "I meant two, but I think it's better to leave it off there." Again she looks away, and Alan can tell she has no intention of telling him the final part of her story.

Given the magnitude of the tragedies she told him about, he can only imagine the magnitude of the one she chose to withhold from him. For a moment he feels almost insulted by her decision to leave her story unfinished, as if he somehow has the right to know her innermost secrets. But this idea is ludicrous; he barely knows the woman. What makes him think she would want to open up to him about *anything* of importance to her? Why, in fact, did she tell him any of this in the first place? He thinks about this for a moment and then the answer comes to him: she told him about her past to give him an out.

"Anyways, I could understand it if you just walked out that door and never came back," she says, proving him right.

"Why would I want to do that?" he says.

"Why? Cause I'm a jinx, that's why."

In spite of himself Alan can't suppress the beginnings of a laugh. "You're a jinx? No you're not. You're a lot of things, Marissa, but a jinx isn't one of them."

"That's sweet a you to say, Alan, but facts don't lie. Look at all the tragedy around me. And not one but two fiancés go and die on me. If I'm not a jinx then who is?"

"That's the whole point. *Nobody's* a jinx. There's no such thing."

Marissa gives him a look which he can't quite read. Half skeptical, he supposes, and maybe a tad resentful.

"Is that what they tell you in those books a yours?" she says.

"Among other things. But think about it. In what way are you responsible for what happened? Any of it. Did you swing the wrecking ball that killed your parents? Did you push your fiancé off that building? Did you . . ." He'd been about to say *Did you rape yourself?* but caught it in time. "None of this is your fault. Surely you can understand that, if you really think about it."

Marissa puts her head in her hands, and Alan has a sudden vision of what she must have looked like as a child.

"I know what you're saying, Alan. I'm not a *complete* imbecile. I know what it means to think straight and to think not straight. But that don't change how I feel about it. I feel like I'm a jinx, so I'm a jinx."

It occurs to Alan that Marissa could use some psychotherapy. He thinks about asking her if she's ever seen a shrink but decides to let it go.

"It's all coincidence," he hears himself say.

Marissa looks across at him as if she's heard this explanation before but is willing to listen to it again if it makes him happy.

"I mean, life is full of coincidences," he goes on. "Back in the Forties, for instance, there was this guy walking along Flatbush Avenue outside Ebbets Field and he was hit in the head with a foul ball and he died on the way to the hospital. All because a baseball and his head happened to converge at the exact same point in space at the exact same moment—even though the chances of this happening were probably one in a million. Plus it hit him in the precise spot it did. If it had hit him in a different spot, maybe a fraction of an inch up or down or to the side, he might have ended up with only a concussion or something else non-life threatening. He might never have died. That's coincidence. There's no getting around it, life is full of coincidences. Your parents, for example. What if they'd met a neighbor on their way to the grocery store and stopped to talk for a minute? Then by the time they'd got to the store it might already have been demolished. They would never have been killed."

Suddenly he thinks of Stephanie. He would like to be able to tell Marissa about Stephanie and, in this context, about how things might have turned out differently if only he hadn't hesitated when Brooke implied that she'd like him to be part of Stephanie's life. If only he'd put aside his fears. Will she hate me? Ignore me? Run away from me? If he'd been man enough to face these possibilities from day one, then it might have been he, not Brooke, who took Stephanie to her ballet class that morning, and almost certainly with benign results. Or if not that, then if Brooke had been just a little bit behind or a little bit ahead of schedule they wouldn't have ended up in the cab they ended up in—again with almost definitely benign results. Either way it was a perfect example of coincidence doing its best to mess with people's lives, but he can't use it; no one in his family knows about Stephanie, and if Marissa were to let it slip to his cousin Loretta, then before long everyone would know, including Mike, who certainly could do without the information that he used to have a granddaughter but she died when she was barely five years old.

"I think all a this has been too much for you, Alan." Marissa stands now and comes around to his side of the table. "You're such a sweet man," she says, stroking his face. "But think about what I said today. You didn't know what you were getting yourself into when you met me, but now you know."

What Alan knows about Marissa has increased dramatically in the last hour, but what he knew about the advisability of getting involved with her in the first place is still a mystery. It was the reason he took nearly a week before he decided to go ahead and ask her out—and her story, tragic though it is, hasn't changed any of this. He knows that once he starts to think with his head rather than with the contents of his briefs, he'll have to reexamine his involvement with her—although what started out as a simple matter of sexual attraction seems to be evolving into something more complex.

19

Even under normal conditions, parking spaces are hard to come by in the part of Hoboken where Marissa lives. So when Alan spots an empty space just past Ninth Street he maneuvers his car into it—no easy task considering the surprise snowstorm that sprang up earlier in the day.

He gets out of the car and begins to make his way through the snow toward Marissa's house. The row houses on Park Avenue are festooned with Christmas lights of red and green and yellow mostly, but one house, a house which has been strung exclusively with blue lights, stands out to him. The aura created by the blue lights—a less festive, almost wistful aura—seems fitting to him. Because even now, years after he's outgrown his childlike fascination with everything surrounding this holiday, Christmas still holds a sense of mystery for him. It isn't the religious component (he long-ago jettisoned the tenuous hold Catholicism had on him), but there's something about Christmas in its purest, most non-commercial form that still gets to him. And it doesn't hurt that he has somewhere to go on this particular night that he's dying to get to. Someone he can't wait to be with.

He crosses Eighth Street and breathes in deeply. All around him is silence—the fat snowflakes careening downward in the soft glare of the streetlamps and mingling with their predecessors to form an astonishing blanket of whiteness, the bite of the cold air, the aroma of a wood-burning fireplace off in the distance . . . It all speaks of silence and timelessness and the incomparable hum of life. He feels alive, *is* alive—young and healthy and very much alive. Earlier this evening he was reminded of this fact all too clearly. Mike, out of the hospital finally but compromised significantly, reminded him of it simply by being in the state he's been reduced to. Alan's uncle Vini, recovering from a quadruple bypass and lacking the energy, it seemed, to so much as pick up a cup of coffee, reminded him of it. His aunt Yolanda, who, like Aunt Marie a few years ago, has been stricken with breast cancer, reminded him. And Alan's grandparents, his mother's parents, who, though ostensibly healthy, probably won't survive more than another couple of years simply because time will finally have caught up with them—they reminded him too. *You're a young man,* Aunt Yolanda said to him as she ladled out a serving of his grandmother's lasagna onto his plate. *Enjoy your life while you can.*

Now, as Alan crosses Sixth Street, a heightened sense of expectation takes hold of him. The slow going, owing to the snow, only adds to this feeling. Marissa's house is down at the end of the block, the second house from the last. Marissa, he knows, is waiting for him, expecting him, counting the minutes probably, and with a sense of anxiety born of not knowing exactly where he is, of having to trust that his journey to her is going according to plan—slowed by snow, to be sure, but free from any malevolent whim of fate. He called her from his grandmother's house at about nine-thirty to tell her he was on his way. *I just got in myself*, she said. *The roads are treacherous, Alan. Please be careful.* The drive from Fort Lee to Hoboken proved manageable for him, but it took easily twice as long as it normally would have. Now he pulls up the sleeve of his coat and under the light of a streetlamp checks the time. Nearly eleven. He can imagine that Marissa might be frantic by now, the way his mother often was when Mike was late getting home from work.

Finally he comes to Marissa's house and makes his way up the unshoveled steps to her front door. He rings, and seconds later enters through the buzzing door. As he begins to climb the stairs to her second-floor apartment he hears her door open and looks up as she emerges onto the landing, radiant in the illumination of a forty-watt bulb.

"Alan, I was frantic with worry," she calls out to him.

In the next moment they're in each other's arms, their lips and seemingly every part of them locked together with the intoxicating force of their unfailing response to each other even as the stiffening in Alan's slacks urges him—and them—into the interior of her apartment and toward her bedroom. Inside they move, like partners in a three-legged race—barely making it onto the bed before Alan, his coat tossed onto the floor and his slacks halfway down his legs, feels her take hold of him and guide him into her.

Minutes later they're still in each other's arms, still half clothed, talking quietly now, enjoying that other bond they share, the one that supersedes human sexuality and approaches a level of intimacy he didn't think possible—a sense of belonging together that continues to surprise him no less thoroughly than Marissa's physical beauty continues to surprise him.

Now he feels himself hardening again and begins to nuzzle Marissa's neck.

"Uh, uh," she says, having none of it. "It's Christmas Eve, we got presents to open."

She sits up in bed and pulls up her jeans and begins to fasten her bra and generally pull herself together. Alan, though, remains on his back, looking up at her in wonder and self-renewing delight.

"C'mon you," she says, standing now. "Don't you want your present?"

"I could do with a replay of the recent past," he says, not troubling himself with whether Marissa did or didn't get the pun. Then he stands as well and does up his clothes. "But I thought we were going to open presents tomorrow morning?"

"You can open your big present tomorrow," Marissa says. "But we always opened one present apiece on Christmas Eve when I was growing up."

They move from the bedroom toward the living room now, and Alan says, "You got me two presents? I only got you one."

"That don't matter," she says.

They enter the living room and settle themselves on the floor in front of the small tree they picked out a few days ago. Eyeing two presents that sit under the tree—one the size of a hardbound book and the other smaller, evidently more intimate—Alan remembers the necklace he bought for Marissa and goes back into the bedroom to fetch it from his coat pocket.

"Where'd you disappear to?" she says seconds later as he reenters the living room, but then she sees the tiny gift-wrapped box in his hand. "I hope you didn't spend too much," she says, a mix of delight and concern dancing in her eyes.

Alan merely smiles and places the box under the tree with the other presents.

"It's that big one over there," Marissa says, pointing to the book-size gift.

He takes the gift in his hands and notices that there's some give on either side of it. This, apparently, is no ordinary book. Or maybe not a book at all.

Making no attempt to hide his excitement, he tears off the wrapping paper. He can see immediately that what he holds in his hands is in fact a book and that it's leather-bound with some decorative gilding along the perimeter of the cover. But there's no print of any kind, neither on the cover nor on the spine. He glances over at Marissa and she meets his unasked question with an unarticulated answer: *Go on and open the book, Alan.* Alan opens it and sees nothing but equally spaced horizontal lines. He leafs through the pages as if words might magically appear before his eyes, but this doesn't happen.

"A diary?" he says, more confused than disappointed by the present.

"Not a diary," Marissa says, "a blank book."

"Thanks, Marissa. It was very—"

"You don't like it," she says. "That's okay, right now you think it's just a blank book, 'and what do I want with a blank book?' you're probably saying to yourself. But it don't always have to be blank."

"You want me to keep a journal?"

"It's up to you what you do with it, Alan, but I'll tell you why I got it for you. You're always saying how you're frustrated writing that scientific stuff you have to write for your job. And you're always reading stories and novels. So why don't you write a story or a novel or a play or something?"

"I've written plays," Alan says.

"You have? Why didn't you tell me?"

"It never came up," he says.

"Do you still write them?"

"No, it's been years since I've written a play."

"What about stories?" she says. "I bet you could write some good stories if you put your mind to it. Maybe someday you could write a story about me. You know, a Jersey girl who's afraid that if she got engaged to a guy he'd drop dead on her."

"And who's unbelievably gorgeous," Alan adds.

"You could throw that in," she says, blushing.

Alan looks down at the book and thumbs through it again. "Maybe you're right," he says. "Maybe it would be a good idea for me to write something creative for a change." Then he adds, "But what if it isn't any good?"

"Are you kidding me? I see that stuff you write for your job. I can tell good writing from bad, and you're a good writer."

Alan shrugs her off. "But when it comes to creative writing . . . I don't know, I never really did any except for those few plays in college."

"Whatever you put your mind to, Alan, I know you can do it. You may not believe in yourself right now, but I believe in you."

Marissa's words trigger in him a sense of déjà vu. Where has he heard them before, or words to that effect? Not from his ex-wife, certainly, and God knows not from Mike. . . . And then he realizes it was from his mother. *Whatever you put your mind to, Alan, you can do.* How old was he when she first said those words to him? Seven? Nine? And why were the other words, the denigrating words courtesy of Mike, the ones Alan latched on to, that he believed as gospel? A wave of regret passes over him as he remembers that his mother is no longer in the world, no longer able to occupy herself with the primary focus of her life: his well-being.

"What's wrong, Alan?" he hears Marissa say. "You look sad all of a sudden."

"I'm fine," he says, bouncing back with a jaunty smile.

Marissa gives him a skeptical look, then rises from the floor and takes him by the hand. "Come," she says. "I got another surprise for you."

She leads Alan into the kitchen and he takes a seat at the far end of the table, opposite the refrigerator.

"No, Alan," she says, directing him to the other side of the table. "You sit over there with your back to the refrigerator. I don't trust you."

"You don't trust me to do what?"

"I don't trust you not to look. Now you go over to that chair and close your eyes and don't turn your head."

"Yes ma'am," he says, liking this game she's playing. "How's this?" he says now, sitting in the chair that was assigned to him and with his head down on the table like a first grader at nap time.

"That's good," Marissa says. "Now just stay like that while I get this . . ."

A moment later Alan becomes aware that Marissa is standing over him and that she's placed something on the table.

"Okay," she says. "You can open your eyes."

Alan opens his eyes. "Ice box cake!" he says. "But how did you know?"

"Your cousin Loretta told me. She said your mother used to make it all the time for you when you were a little boy, that it was your favorite."

"That's true, but how did she know this?"

"I don't know," Marissa says, "she just did. I guess she's just the kinda person that remembers things."

Alan studies the rectangular casserole dish that Marissa placed in the center of the table. Ice box cake—layers of chilled vanilla and chocolate pudding sandwiched between a Graham cracker crust and topped with shredded coconut—was indeed his favorite dessert as a child, surpassing even the occasional carton of ice cream Mike would bring home from the corner drug store.

"Thanks," Alan says looking up at Marissa, whose delight in his own delight is the greatest gift he could imagine. He becomes aware of an increasingly recurrent feeling he's loath to put a name to.

"How can I turn down a piece of ice box cake?" he says to escape the feeling.

Marissa moves to a cabinet and retrieves a plate, which she sets down before him. Then, after she doles out a piece of cake onto his plate, she sits down across from him.

"Aren't you having any?" he says when he notices there's no plate on her side of the table.

"I'm gonna pass," she says. "I gained two pounds since Thanksgiving."

Alan gives her a once-over. "I hadn't noticed," he says.

"Sure you did. You're just too polite to say anything."

"No, I swear. I hadn't noticed."

Marissa seems to dismiss his protestations as mere gallantry and then eyes the casserole dish. "Well, maybe I can have a little piece," she says.

He watches as she returns to the cabinet and then back to the table with a plate for herself.

"Go on, Alan," she says. "Take a bite."

"I'm waiting for you."

Marissa takes what she describes as a sliver from the casserole dish and together they begin to eat.

"This is delicious," she says. "I can understand why it was your favorite."

When they've had their fill of ice box cake (Marissa had *two* slivers—amounting, Alan noted, to one regular-size piece), she begins to heat up the coffee she made for herself when she returned from the Tedescos.

"You want tea, Alan?"

"Tea's good."

Marissa gets the tea and coffee together and then sits back down at the table opposite him. "So how was the party?" she says. "You had a good time at your grandmother's?"

"That would be overstating the case. Let's just say I survived the evening."

"How about your father? Is he any better?"

"He's the same. I get the feeling he's not going to make much improvement beyond this. But something strange did happen. I don't know, maybe it's not a big deal, but Dolly—you know, my stepmother—and her daughter, Vera . . . . . It turns out they're going down to Florida for a vacation."

"A vacation? Without your father?"

"That's the way I look at it too. Dolly tried to justify it

by saying what a hard year she's had—first with the mela-
noma scare and now with my father's stroke—but it seems
to me you don't go off on a vacation when your husband is
just out of the hospital and in obvious need of someone to
look after him."

"That *is* strange," Marissa says. "But who's gonna take
care a him when she's away? Your aunt Fiona?"

"No, he'll be going to a nursing home. It's probably a
good solution, if Dolly's hell-bent on going. At least he'll
have good care for the couple of weeks they're away.

"But I don't know," he continues. "It seems inappropriate under the circumstances. Maybe she's right, though.
Maybe she needs to rejuvenate herself before she can really
be there for my father the way he'll need her to be."

Marissa peers down into her coffee cup and then takes
a sip. Alan expects her to comment on his comment, but
she remains silent.

"And how about you?" he says. "You had a good time at
the Tedescos?"

"I always have a good time when I'm there. I should
see more a them like I used to—they're only in Ridgefield,
that's not so far."

This was one of the pleasant turns-of-events Alan
learned about as he got to know Marissa better. After he
learned of the tragic loss of her parents and her two fiancés, he assumed she was alone in the world. So he was surprised, and quite happy, to find out that Lucille and Eddie
Tedesco, the parents of Marissa's first fiancé, Robbie, had
all but officially adopted her after Robbie's death. And that

with their five surviving children, two of whom were close to Marissa's age, they were able to provide her with what amounted to a surrogate family.

"A penny for your thoughts."

Alan looks up. "You can't spring for a dollar?"

"Very funny. But tell me. What were you thinking about just now?"

"Nothing," he says. "I was just daydreaming. You know me—if I'm not thinking, I'm daydreaming."

Marissa smiles and intertwines her fingers into his. They remain silent for several moments, but their days of feeling awkward in the face of silence have long-since passed.

"More tea?" Marissa says now.

"No, I'm fine." Alan looks up at the clock. It's well past midnight. "Maybe we should think about going to bed," he says.

"Just let me finish up this cup a coffee."

Alan, who's always been a light sleeper, envies Marissa's ability to fall asleep on a dime, despite whatever quantity of caffeine she might have consumed. He watches now as she takes a sip of coffee and swishes it around on her tongue as if she's at a wine-tasting.

"I forgot to ask, Alan. How was the Christmas party last week?"

"The company party? It was okay."

"Just okay?"

Alan shrugs and says nothing.

"Alright, be that way," Marissa says. "I'm gonna go in

and wash up, it's getting late." She stands and disappears around a corner and into the bathroom.

Since Marissa is slave to a somewhat lavish and time-consuming bedtime ritual, Alan knows there's no point in getting undressed quite yet. So he remains at the kitchen table and wonders why women seem to require detailed accountings of life's most mundane events—for instance, unremarkable company Christmas parties like the one he attended last week. If something noteworthy happened at the party—say, if one of the proofreaders got roaring drunk and made a pass at the company president, who happens to be a woman—Alan might very well have volunteered this information to Marissa. But nothing happened.

Of course, that isn't exactly true. On a personal level, Alan felt awkward in Rick's presence for the few minutes they tried to sustain a conversation. Now that he thinks about it, he would like to be able to tell Marissa about Rick's sudden and unexpected promotion to marketing manager, and how the promotion led to iciness between him and Rick. But Alan simply can't risk going into it with her. Such a discussion might lead to a recounting of the period just after Stephanie's death, when Rick provided tremendous emotional support for him. And Stephanie, Alan decided early on, is off limits to Marissa. Initially he decided to stay mum about her because he feared that Marissa might convey the story to Loretta, with predictable results. But he's learned in the last month that Marissa is entirely trustworthy. He would trust her with his darkest secret, so why not this one? It's a question he's tried to keep tucked away in a corner of his mind, but one which increasingly demands his attention. The ironic thing is that he knows at least part of the answer: telling Marissa about Stephanie would be tantamount to making a commitment to her. Why this is so—and in what *way* it's so—he couldn't say. Perhaps he's afraid that in telling Marissa about Stephanie he would be unable to keep his emotions reined in, and who knows what road his unchecked emotions might lead him down? His patina of invulnerability, or at least a seeming lack of vulnerability, would be destroyed. He would appear as if naked before her, which would imply a need, if not an urge, to effect an emotional consummation that, together, they managed to keep at bay despite the many forces pulling them together. As it is, Marissa has never seen him cry, nor has he seen her cry, not really—and God knows she must have cried extensively with all she went through. And that was the way they tailored their unwritten script. Negative emotion—anger or profound sadness—has remained unexpressed between them. Alan, for his part, allows himself to get only so close to Marissa before he pulls back, and he's certain it's the same for her. In fact, a barrier arose between them almost at the moment they met. It was as if they were each saying to themselves: *Here is a person I can't allow to really touch my life; the risk is too great.* And so, when it became clear to each of them that they were dealing with something more complicated than a simple fling, they fell into a highly circumscribed "arrangement." They would not be a "couple" in the traditional sense. Alan's family (except for Loretta) was off limits to Marissa. Marissa's surrogate family (the Tedescos) was off limits to Alan. They would never know each other's friends. They would never be seen in public together in a location that was likely to be frequented by people either of them knew. Theirs would be a backstreet affair. It played into Marissa's fear of getting too close to a man again, and it played into Alan's fear of finding himself seriously involved with a woman who, in his eyes and despite his tremendous admiration for her as a person, not to mention the rest of it, is from the wrong side of the tracks—or, to be more precise, the wrong side of the river.

Yes, the whole thing is sad, he has to admit. Then again, sadness isn't exactly a rare commodity in life. Marissa has suffered her share, certainly. And now Mike and Uncle Vini and Aunt Yolanda too: each betrayed by their body. And, of course, Stephanie. Probably the saddest thing of all, when a child dies.

Alan listens for an indication that Marissa might be on her way out of the bathroom. Certain she isn't, he pulls out his wallet and slips his one photograph of Stephanie from behind his driver's license. He studies the photograph and notices, for the first time, a resemblance between Stephanie and Marissa. You can see it in the set of their cheekbones and in the fullness of their lips. And the eyes—the same deep-brown eyes. It's a wonder he never noticed it! If he and Marissa were to have a child together, a daughter . . . But he doesn't allow himself to complete the thought.

He waits another minute, then takes a few steps toward the bathroom. "Are you okay in there, Marissa?" he calls out.

From the other side of the bathroom door he hears

her say something about tweezing her eyebrows. Alan has known Marissa for two months now, and he still can't figure out why she chooses bedtime to tweeze her eyebrows or file her nails or engage in some other form of cosmetic enhancement. This is a small price to pay, though, for what he knows will follow once she finally emerges from the bathroom and into her bedroom.

He drifts into the living room and plants himself in front of Marissa's one bookcase. He's already familiar with its contents—various romance novels and some back issues of *Reader's Digest*—but now he peruses the shelves in the hope that he might stumble onto something more interesting. His eye comes to rest on a thick leather-bound book with gilding, but no type, on its spine. In confusion he thinks for a moment that this must be the blank book Marissa just gave him, but then he glances over and sees it resting under the Christmas tree where he left it. He removes the other book from the bookcase and begins to thumb through it. Almost immediately he realizes it's a diary—*Marissa's* diary. His impulse is to put it back in place (he's always believed that someone's private thoughts should remain private), but he spots the date December 3, 1968. Something about that date seems meaningful to him, and then he remembers what it is: Marissa's parents were killed sometime toward the middle of the school year in 1968. Unable to resist temptation, he reads the short entry that follows.

We buried my parents today. I didn't think I'd be able to get through it but Robbie was there for me to lean on. He said that I would be okay, that he knew I was strong. I don't know if I am or not but I'll do my best. But the best thing that Robbie said was that someday, God willing, I'd be a mother, and that every time I looked at my children I'd see a little bit of my parents in them. Not a resemblance which there wouldn't be because I'm adopted but just because they're my parents. I'm not sure how to explain it but I know what I mean. And when Robbie said this it reminded me that alls I ever wanted to be was a mother, that that's always been my biggest wish, so it was good that Robbie said this. I'm so lucky to have him.

Alan puts the book back. He tries to remember if Marissa has ever mentioned to him that her fondest wish is to become a mother. Then it comes to him: when they first met, at Loretta's son's birthday party, she said something about wanting to be a mother.

Inevitably he thinks of his own mother and, inevitably again, of her death. He was twenty-one at the time, which was young for such a loss, but Marissa was only seventeen and she lost *both* her parents. He doesn't want to imagine what she must have gone through. And then the rape, and Robbie's death, and her *other* fiancé's death. And, on top of that, whatever it was that had evidently been so horrendous she chose not to reveal it to him. It occurs to him that he might sneak another look at her diary and perhaps come across an account of the elusive event, but no, he isn't about to stoop to that level, despite his curiosity.

Alan puts the diary back in place on the bookshelf and begins to wander aimlessly around the living room. Then his mind drifts to the blank book Marissa gave him, and all at once he sees this gift in a new light. She didn't merely give him the book to do with as he pleased. She also suggested that "someday" he might want to write a story about her. "Someday," as in: *someday when I'm no more than a memory to you.* The implication was transparent. Marissa, inadvertently or not, was letting him know that she considered their relationship doomed—that despite the affinity they share, despite their intense animal attraction to each other and their obvious need for each other, they will inevitably part company sooner or later.

Alan already knows this, of course, but somehow her telling him has made all the difference. From this point forward, what he's consistently tried to ignore will demand center stage.

But what to do about it? For now, he can do nothing. It's Christmas Eve, and it would be not only inappropriate but cruel of him to give Marissa any sign that over the next days and weeks he'll be considering a means to extricate himself from their affair. Besides, in a few minutes she'll be lying in his arms in bed, and sleep will be the last thing on their minds. Is he supposed to deny himself the pleasure that awaits him?

He takes a few steps toward the bathroom and says, "Marissa, will you be in there much longer?"

"Just another ten minutes is all."

Alan knows that "ten minutes" means at least another twenty.

Shaking his head over what he considers to be Marissa's unique, if not downright strange, bedtime ritual, he wanders back into the living room and once again to the bookcase. He removes Marissa's diary from it and opens it to somewhere in the middle, although he doesn't intend to read anything. As it turns out, though, the first words of the entry on that page—*I was in New York this morning*—pique his curiosity, since Marissa mentioned to him, without saying why, that at some point she stopped going into the city.

Once again unable to resist temptation, Alan reads the first few sentences in the entry. Something about them seems troubling to him so he reads further. And then his heart stops. Furiously he reads the remainder of the entry. Aware now that his heart is beating with the rapidity of a little bird's, he reads the entry again. And then a third time.

How can this have happened!? he says to himself. But yet, there it is: spelled out in black, cursive letters on a few white, ruled pages.

He closes the diary and puts it back on the shelf. Feeling almost light-headed, he takes a few steps to the living room sofa and sinks into it. His mind is a jumble, his thoughts racing willy-nilly and with no indication that they might settle down anytime soon. Then, with a sense of having uncovered a lost object that had remained hidden in plain sight, he realizes that this incident—the one Marissa so painfully described in her diary—had to have been the incident she was so traumatized by she kept it from him, even though she'd confided to him the other tragic events in her life.

But this realization is irrelevant. What matters now is that this new information about her past makes it that-much-more urgent that he break it off with her as soon as he possibly can.

A few minutes later they're lying in bed together. Marissa is in Alan's arms, her head resting on his chest as he plays absently with her hair, but in a distracted fashion that doesn't escape her attention.

"Are you okay, Alan?" she says. "You look upset."

"No, I'm just . . . I'm just tired."

"Tired? I think I got something that'll wake you up."

Marissa kisses him on the mouth now and moves her hand down his chest and down and down until it reaches its destination. But Alan, for the first time in their brief history together, is not stirred.

"I'm sorry, Marissa," he says. "I'm just too tired."

Though probably hurt by this, Marissa says she understands and then rolls over and is soon asleep. But Alan lies awake for a long time, alternating waves of astonishment at the revelation in Marissa's diary with bouts of the anger it engendered in him—even as something tells him that his anger is irrational—and all of this against the backdrop of his certainty that ending their relationship will be no simple task for him.

20

It's Thursday morning and people are just drifting into the office. Alan sits at his desk, a container of coffee and a corn muffin sitting amid a few scattered folders and errant sheets of paper. A moment later, one of the secretaries—a pretty good-looking one—passes through his office on her way to who knows where. It occurs to Alan that he might want to ask her out, if only as a way to help get his mind off Marissa.

But maybe that wouldn't be a good idea. Once he frees himself of Marissa, it might make more sense to declare a moratorium on the whole male-female thing for a while. He needs to stop seeing women as either potential mates or irrelevancies. He needs to widen, not narrow, his horizons. A moratorium would give him a chance to concentrate on other aspects of his life. His job situation, for one.

He hears a sound and turns his head to see that Jerome, his new office mate, has entered the room.

"What's up?" Alan says, and Jerome waves vaguely at him.

It's not that Jerome is unfriendly, exactly, but since he's far more science geek than writer, he's often lost in thought—probably a matter of his mind dazzling itself with one far-flung scientific insight after another. Actually, Alan prefers Jerome's relative taciturnity to his occasional and completely unpredictable forays into verbalizing these insights. On such occasions Alan can only mumble *uh huhs* and try to effect a look of comprehension, when all he comprehends is that he'd like Jerome to fall through the floor. Jerome, sad to say, is not Rick. And Rick, even sadder to say, is not his old self now that he's head honcho. And saddest of all, Rick and Alan are no longer what they used to be to each other. No longer office mates. No longer equals. No longer friends, try as they might to keep up the charade.

It would not be hyperbole to say that Rick's unexpected promotion to marketing manager, about three months ago, caused an intense reaction in Alan. Even though he hadn't coveted the position Rick landed, Rick's promotion triggered in Alan a cascade of emotions—envy, outrage, humiliation, to name a few—which, though he knew to be irrational, he simply couldn't squelch. And although he did his best to control these emotions in the face of all the hoopla surrounding the promotion, it was depressing to think that a non-talent like Rick had been able to take a step up in the world while he—Alan—was on the fast track to nowhere.

He takes the last bite of his muffin and drains his coffee

cup, then tosses the paper plate and Styrofoam cup into the trash. He moves a couple of folders to one side of the desk and opens a third.

"*Further Advances in Geriatric Physiology,*" he reads aloud. "J. R. Schmidt, PhD." Alan leafs through Schmidt's notes but soon lets them fall to the desk unread.

He turns his head and looks across at Jerome, whose desk and typewriter stand are crammed into the opposite corner of the office. (Moving the desks was one of Rick's first innovations as marketing manager, although he himself had wasted countless hours every week sitting across from Alan, running his mouth off.) It's barely nine a.m. and Jerome is already banging away at his IBM Selectric, apparently convinced that the little brochure he's working on will advance the cause of science and thereby, if only indirectly, cure mankind's ills. But Jerome is young. Couldn't be more than twenty-two or twenty-three, Alan guesses. Wait till he's a little older. Then he'll realize that idealistic notions are just that: notions. What you need in life, Alan sees now, is substance. A life chasing rainbows and waiting for ships to come in is essentially self-delusional. But a life getting one's shit together: that makes sense, especially when you've just turned thirty. So he's decided it's time to get his proverbial ducks in a row and proceed from there. First on his agenda, of course, is to end it with Marissa—which, as he predicted, is proving to be a daunting task despite her "transgression," if that's what you'd call it. But he's determined to get this matter resolved. Then there's finding a new job. And once he has a new job—and especially if it comes with enough of a raise—he can start thinking about moving out of his shoebox of an apartment. He can see himself in a one-bedroom, maybe on the Upper West Side, maybe West End Avenue. Maybe a new wardrobe to go with his new apartment. And maybe a new woman in his life to go with the rest of it.

Unbidden, the image of Brooke comes into his mind. If things had turned out the way they were supposed to, there would be no need to think of new women, nor would there be a Marissa to wrest himself free of. There would be he and Brooke—the way it was supposed to be from the beginning. Her decision to move to Seattle was understandable. She'd lost her daughter, she needed to make a fresh start. Maybe someday he'll get that letter: *Dear Alan, Things aren't really working out in Seattle. I miss New York and I miss you.* Maybe someday.

The phone rings and a minute later he's in Rick's office, sitting across from the man himself.

"So," Rick says leaning back in his swivel chair. "How are things going?"

"Things?" Alan says. "You mean in the job?"

"I mean in general. But how about the job? Any complaints?"

Alan can think of a litany of things he could complain about, but he says, "No, things are going well enough."

Rick leans toward him now. "And what about Jerome? He's been here a few weeks now. How do you think he's working out?"

"How do *I* think he's working out? You mean as a copy-writer?"

"As a copywriter, but also as someone to share an office with."

"Well," Alan says, "he doesn't say much, but he seems to be on top of things. But shouldn't you be telling me? You're the boss, after all."

Rick's smile seems to deflect Alan's remark. Then he says, "Do you ever look at his copy?"

"I've read a few things. It's no worse than Grace's or Binky's."

Alan has become aware that Rick is thrumming his fingers on the desktop. He seems a little agitated, which is unlike him.

"Here's the thing," Rick says finally. "The boys upstairs are making noises about the quality of the copy that's been coming out of the marketing department. Not yours, mind you, but the other three, especially Binky's. They're blaming the copy for the recent decline in sales. I don't know if you knew it, but sales have been down a little since I took over. These things go in cycles, as I'm sure you know, and three months isn't enough time to begin pointing fingers, but . . .

"Anyway," he continues, "they have the *big* boss to answer to, so they're looking for a scapegoat."

"And you're the scapegoat," Alan says.

"Me? By association, maybe, but not directly. They're blaming the copy, but I don't write the copy."

No, but you're supposed to edit it, Alan says to himself.

"Anyway," Rick goes on, "I had this idea. You probably can imagine what my day is like, running in one direction and another, trying to stay on top of every little detail. I don't have the time to devote to editing the copy the way it needs to be edited. And frankly, editing's not my strong suit anyway. So I got this idea, Alan, and I think you'll agree it makes a lot of sense. We could make you copy chief—in addition to your other duties, of course. You're a great writer, everybody knows that, and I think with you in charge of the editing we could really turn the copy department around."

Alan takes a moment to consider what he's just heard. Then he says, "What do you mean you *could* make me copy chief? Are we talking promotion here or not?"

Rick lets out a single *tsk*. "Promotion?" he says. "That was my original idea, yes. But when I proposed it to them they gave me a song and dance about budget constraints, etcetera, etcetera. But they thought it was a great idea, in theory. They admire your work, you know."

Alan waits for Rick to spit out exactly what's on his mind, then realizes that Rick is waiting for him to connect the dots.

"Let me get this straight," Alan says. "Are you suggesting that I take over the duties of copy chief without an official promotion and without a raise?"

"It would only be for a little while, Alan. Just until we can show them what a difference it would make with you editing the copy. And then I'm sure they'll be able to squeeze out a few extra bucks from one place or another."

"You're sure of this," Alan says, again making no attempt to hide his sarcasm.

Rick leans back in his chair again—a transparent attempt to regain the power in the negotiation. "You've got to look at the big picture," he says. "In the short run you might think it's insulting or demeaning for you to have to take on more responsibility without a raise, but you'll be getting the experience of being a copy chief. You can put that on your resume when the time comes for you to look for another job—which I hope isn't while I'm still here. And in my letter of reference I'll say you were actually copy chief, that you actually had the title. Who'd know the difference?"

Alan is too amused by all this to feel the anger he knows is probably justified. What's more, for the first time since Rick has taken over as marketing manager, Alan feels that he—not Rick—is the one with the power. In a way it's sad to watch his old friend squirm, clearly fearing for his job. But there's a kind of poetic justice here, so why not enjoy it for a while before he says *Sure, Rick, what the hell. It'll make the day go faster.*

"Of course," he hears Rick say now, "there are plenty of kids fresh out of college who'd jump at a chance like this. And these BFA programs, from what I hear, are turning out one crackerjack writer after another."

For the briefest moment Alan questions what he just

heard, but then it becomes all too clear: *Toe the line, man, or you can kiss your job goodbye.* He closes his eyes in an attempt to control his anger, and when he opens them to see Rick's smug face smiling across at him, he knows he's lost the battle.

"Sure, Rick," he says, "why not? You've got me over a barrel, so why the hell not?"

"I'm glad you see it that way, Alan," Rick says getting to his feet. "It'll turn out for the best, you'll see, and you'll really be helping the company."

Like he could give a shit about the company!

Rick reaches across the desk now and extends a hand to Alan. And Alan—the new, more mature Alan, the one who's no longer in his twenties—shakes Rick's hand and turns up the corners of his mouth, the closest he can come to a smile. Then he turns and heads back to his tiny office, licked for the time being but knowing that in the end—that is, when he gives his notice—he'll have the last laugh.

21

Pinecrest Gardens is a clean and seemingly well-run facility. It's also the nursing home where Mike is staying until Dolly and Vera get back from Florida. Except Dolly and Vera won't be coming back. And Mike won't be returning home. And it's Alan's job to break the news to him.

On the Sunday after Rick strong-armed him into toeing the party line, Alan drives out Route 80 for what will be his second visit to Mike at the nursing home. As he turns into the entrance and begins to drive down the long, wooded path that leads to the main building, Alan wonders how he's going to be able to pull this off. For the whole of his trip from Manhattan he was rehearsing in his mind exactly what he's going to say, but now that he's only minutes away from having to say it his mind goes blank.

He pulls into the parking lot and parks some distance from the building, as if the extra thirty or forty yards he'll have to walk will give him time to garner the courage he's going to need. Inside he turns left down a long corridor and then, though he's certain Mike is in room twenty-three, seeks confirmation from the first nurse he sees.

"That's right, twenty-three," the woman says, and Alan wishes he could take her along for moral support.

He enters Mike's room—Dolly, in her magnanimity, has arranged for a private room—and spots Mike dozing in a chair that sits beneath a window at the far end of the room.

As Alan approaches him, Mike gives a snort and is suddenly awake. He glances around, woozy from sleep. "Alan, you're here," he says. "How come you're late?"

"I'm not late," Alan says, his voice sounding weak to him the way he supposes it will sound when he starts to spell out to Mike exactly what he can expect from the rest of his life. "I said I'd be here by two o'clock." He looks at his watch. "It's two o'clock."

"But I thought you were coming twelve thirty, you said."

"No, I said two, but it doesn't matter. I'm here now."

Mike seems to accept this explanation, and Alan finds a chair and pulls it around to the window side of the room. Facing Mike now, but at a distance he finds non-threatening, he says nothing.

"So how you been doing?" Mike says. "I thought you might call this week, I ain't heard from you since, when was it, Monday night?"

Alan is aware that, if he wanted to, he could use Mike's remark as entrée into what he has to say. Instead, not yet feeling up to the task, he says, "I've been kind of busy, Dad. But you look pretty good. Your face doesn't seem to be drooping quite as much as it was the last time I saw you."

Mike doesn't respond to this, and for a moment Alan wonders if he might have dropped dead like that guy on the Dick Cavett Show a few years back.

"What's that?" Mike says as if coming to.

"I said your face isn't drooping the way it was, and your speech seems a little better too. It's less slurred than it was."

Mike seems to think about this and then shrugs. "What-aya gonna do?" he says.

Alan doesn't quite know what Mike was referring to with this remark—the drooping face and slurred speech or life in general? Probably life in general, he decides.

"But how about you?" Mike says. "How's the job going?"

"Actually, I have an interview coming up."

"You're looking for a new job?"

"It's about time, don't you think? I've been at Spaniel for a few years now and it doesn't seem to be going anywhere."

Mike shifts himself in his chair, and Alan can tell it was an effort for him to do so.

"But I thought your friend is boss now. What's his name, Dick?"

"Rick."

"Rick. Didn't they make him boss?"

"He's my immediate supervisor, yes."

"So maybe you shouldn't be so quick to be looking

somewheres else. It's good to have friends in high places, you know."

Alan tries to think of a way to change the subject, and then he thinks of one: he could tell Mike what he's come here to tell him.

"By the way," Mike says. "Aunt Fiona called—Wednesday, I think it was. Did she tell you Ralph and Glenda are going to France in a few days?"

"I hadn't heard that," Alan says.

"They're going there for a month. On vacation. But it's like that when you're the boss. You can make your own hours."

"What about the children?" Alan says, an unexpected afterthought to a bit of news he has no interest in.

"What about them?"

"They're not taking them out of school for a month, are they?"

"No, the mother-in-law's gonna stay with them. Glenda's mother, I forget her name. Plus they got that live-in nanny."

Alan knows he's supposed to say something about how impressive it is to be able to take a month-long vacation, live-in nanny or not, but he remains silent.

"And he hired an interpreter for when they're over there," Mike says.

"What, no bodyguard?"

Mike seems not to have heard Alan's remark. "Those two think nothing a getting on a plane," he says. "They're always going all over, but who can blame them they got the money. If you got it spend it, is what I say."

"How's the food here?" Alan says, although he's asked this question a number of times since Mike landed in the nursing home a couple of weeks ago.

"Can't complain," Mike says. "It ain't home cooking, though. I could go for a plate a Dolly's lasagna right now. You ever have her lasagna?"

"Several times," Alan says.

"She makes good lasagna. When are they supposed to be back, the two a them? It was this Wednesday coming, right? Or was it Saturday?"

Here's the opening Alan has been waiting for. Only a coward would let it slip through his fingers.

"That's the thing, Dad," he says. "Vera called the other night."

"Vera? She called? How come?"

"Well," Alan begins, but nothing follows.

"Is everything okay down there? Is Dolly sick or something?"

Sick of you, he'd like to say.

"No, everything's fine. Except . . . Look Dad, there's no easy way to say this so I'm just going to say it. Dolly's filing for divorce."

Alan waits for a response from Mike, but at first all he gets is a look of confusion. Then he sees Mike's face begin to crumple—into what, he can only guess. Disbelief? Outrage? Humiliation? Anger?

"Divorce?"

The word has escaped Mike's lips as if through a microscopically small cylinder, and it hangs in the air just as Mike's life seems to hang in the balance of Alan's response. Alan is aware that his response will either rock Mike's world or restore it to normality. Because Mike, Alan can tell, is waiting for him to say *Sorry Dad, you misunderstood me. I didn't say Dolly's filing for divorce, I said she's filing her nails.* Mike is waiting for anything at all that might negate what he's just heard. Or so it seems to Alan, who, after all, is neither a mind reader nor someone who's in the habit of telling people their life will never be the same.

But now Mike says, "I can't believe it," and Alan knows that this means he can. The worst is over. The bomb has been dropped and the debris is massive, but there were no casualties.

"But . . . why?" Mike says, maybe for the first time in his life looking to Alan for an answer of any kind.

"Vera says they're filing on grounds of mental cruelty."

"Mental cruelty!? What's she talking about, mental cruelty? I don't . . ." Mike lets his voice trail off into some kind of oblivion.

"I can only go by what Vera told me," Alan says now, "and that's second-hand information. Something about how you're always yelling at her mother and making her scrub the kitchen floor even though both her knees are arthritic. . . . I don't know," he adds by way of summing things up. "Since I never lived with the two of you, I couldn't say exactly what Dolly's gripe is."

If he wanted to—if he were a sadist, perhaps, or if he wanted to get back at Mike for past transgressions—he could tell him the whole story. For instance, the part about how Dolly can no longer stand to live with a man who doesn't seem to be bothered by the loss of his ability to control his bowels. (*He sits around in dirty diapers all day long, Alan, and it stinks to high heaven,* Vera said. *But it don't faze him in the slightest. And my mother's supposed to live with that? Could* you *live with that?*) And then there's the part about how Dolly is disgusted, absolutely disgusted, by Mike's refusal to follow the doctors' instructions and do the exercises they say he has to do if he wants to regain a degree of his former functioning. (*Cause there's a time limit on these things, the doctors say. If you don't do the exercises, then after a certain period a time you can't get it back, the way you were. But your father don't seem to care. As long as he's got my mother waiting on him hand and foot, then as far as he's concerned everything's hunky-dory.*)

Alan could tell Mike these things, but there are a few things he could mention to Dolly and Vera as well, if he thought it would make a difference. He could tell them, for one thing, that when you take a vow to stay with a person for better or worse, you don't bail out at the first hint of trouble. Nobody knows better than he—Alan—that Mike Agnalini is no picnic to live with, but the man has had a stroke, and not a minor one. He's impaired. He's suffering. And for his wife to pack her bags and go off to Florida with her old maid of a daughter and then to put her house up for sale so that she can finance some condominium on the

Gulf Coast and then file for divorce is nothing short of abandonment. It's beyond sleazy. In Vera's words, it stinks to high heaven.

Alan is surprised by his own anger. But his anger is justified, he supposes. After all, Mike is family, and when a family member faces a crisis, the whole family pulls together. This may be a cliché, but he wouldn't want to be a member of a family that doesn't operate in this fashion.

"I'm sorry this happened to you, Dad. It's not fair."

Alan has long-since passed the age when he would actually believe such a statement. There's no "fair" or "unfair" in life. Just life. But this is the sentiment Mike needs to hear. He needs to be told that it was unfair when his wife was taken away from him in the prime of their life together. And that it was unfair for him to have a stroke. And that it was unfair that he got saddled with Dolly, a woman who's proven to be so lacking in character. The illusion of unfairness will help him deal with this upheaval in his life. Illusions can be quite useful at times.

"But what's gonna happen to me now?"

Alan looks across at Mike and realizes that his question was not rhetorical. Mike wants to know what will come next for him, and it falls to Alan, in his new and nebulous role, to come up with an answer.

"We'll have to take it one day at a time," he says to Mike. "The first thing is, we have to decide whether you're going to contest the divorce."

Mike seems to have fallen into a state of catatonia at this remark, as if the idea of making a decision of such monumental importance to his future has all but paralyzed him. He says nothing, but his eyes seem to search Alan's for some kind of guidance.

"It's your decision ultimately, Dad, but from the way Vera explained it to me there's nothing here to contest. There's no community property—you have your house and Dolly still has hers, you have your car and she has hers. . . . There's furniture you bought together since you've been married, but Dolly, according to Vera, says you can have everything, for the most part. The only thing there is to contest is the fact that she's divorcing you, but that's not something that can be contested legally. Not if she can justify her claim of mental cruelty."

"And how's she gonna do that? I'm no different than any other husband. Sure, I yell sometimes. Sure I ask her to make me a sangwich or get me a can a soda. But what husband don't ask his wife to do things for him? Is that mental cruelty? You tell me."

"It doesn't matter what I think," Alan says. "Besides, the more important question is, Do you want to be with a woman who no longer wants to be with you?"

Mike closes his eyes in response to this question, and Alan knows the answer: except for the paperwork, the marriage of Mike Agnalini and Dolly La Forgia Agnalini has been dissolved.

Mike looks up now. "But how am I gonna manage on my own?" he says. "Since the stroke there's a lot a things I can't do like I used to. Maybe Aunt Fiona could come and help out."

Alan was afraid of this; Mike seems to think he'll be able to return home.

"You know, Dad," he says, "without somebody there round the clock I don't think you'd be able to move back home."

"But what about Aunt Fiona? She only lives next door, and she's got time on her hands."

Again Alan is faced with the dilemma of what to tell Mike and what to leave out. This time he opts for a closer approximation of full disclosure. "I talked to Aunt Fiona yesterday," he says, "and I'm afraid she made it clear she wouldn't be able to give you the kind of help you'll need."

Mike seems outraged by the news that his sister has refused to take care of him—almost as outraged as he was to learn that his wife is divorcing him. "But Fiona's my sister," he says. "She's gonna turn her back on me too?"

"It's not a matter of turning her back," Alan says, "it's a matter of degree. She simply can't give you the degree of help you'll need. She's older than you, remember, and she has her own health problems."

Mike seems to consider this explanation, and then, reluctantly, seems to accept it. "But where am I gonna live?" he says. "How can I live in that house with no one to help me? I could hire a full-time nurse, but how am I gonna afford that?"

Is it denial or sheer stupidity, Alan wonders, that keeps Mike from seeing the obvious?

"Look, Dad," he says, "we have to be realistic. Under

the circumstances the only possibility is for you to stay in the nursing home. Or, at least, *a* nursing home."

Immediately Alan wants to knock himself upside the head for letting that last part slip out.

"Whataya mean *a* nursing home?" Mike says. "I don't follow what you're saying."

Trapped, Alan tells himself there might be an advantage to getting it all out in the open; it would save Mike from some unpleasant surprises down the road. "The thing is," Alan says, "I talked to the business office here on Friday, and it turns out you'd need another six-thousand dollars a year to be able to stay here. I'm basing this on what you told me about your Social Security checks. They said they'd give you a grace period of a couple of months, but if you can't come up with the money—at least for the first year—you'd have to move to a public nursing home."

"Public . . . You mean like that place in Paterson we went to that time when Aunt Christine broke her hip?"

"Right," Alan says. "I remember that. That was a public facility."

Mike glances around the room as if it's filled with potential eavesdroppers. "But that place was full a coloreds," he says, his voice lowered accordingly. "You're telling me I'm gonna have to spend the rest a my life with coloreds?"

It would be ironic indeed, Alan thinks to himself, if Mike had to spend his remaining days flanked by the primary object of his bigotry. But now he says, "Actually, Dad, there might be a way around it. You're not going to be able to stay in the house anyway, so you could sell it and that would finance maybe five or six years at Pinecrest. And then we could see where we stand at that point."

Mike, however, has already begun to shake his head. "No way," he says. "That house is your inheritance, Alan. It's all I got to leave you if something happens to me. There's no way I'm gonna sell the house, so get that through your head."

Alan didn't imagine his idea would fly—they've talked before about the importance to Mike that he leave Alan with as big an inheritance as possible—but he had to throw it out there. And this brings him to his second suggestion: Ralph. Having spent a lifetime playing second fiddle to Ralph in Mike's eyes, he would prefer not to have to provide Ralph an opportunity to come off as the hero. But it's a small step from golden boy to hero, so what does Alan really have to lose? Besides, he's long-since accepted defeat on this particular front.

"I'll tell you what, Dad," he says. "I'll give Ralph a call tonight. An extra six-thousand a year would be nothing to him."

Again Mike shakes his head. "I don't wanna start with that," he says. "I got my pride, you know."

"You don't think Ralph owes you? You practically raised him."

"Right, I practically raised him. But I also taught him you gotta make your own way in this world. That you can't go relying on other people. And then I gotta be asking him for money like I was a little kid? . . ."

"Let me handle it, Dad. I won't make it sound like you're begging. Just let me talk to him, I don't think he'll turn us down."

Mike pauses, apparently thinking it over, and then reluctantly—or perhaps with a show of reluctance—agrees to Alan's suggestion.

Taking advantage of what he sees as a kind of denouement, Alan looks pointedly at his watch. "I've got some stuff to take care of back in Manhattan today," he says. "I really should be going."

"Sure," Mike says. "You go, you got a life a your own."

Alan stands now and thinks about putting a hand on Mike's shoulder, but it's just not him. "I'll call you tonight," he says. "Try not to worry. It'll all work out."

A minute later he's in the parking lot leaning on his car. For some reason he's not ready to get back in the car and back onto Route 80. This whole thing with Dolly has been a shock not only to Mike but to Alan as well. He thinks about how Mike, in the coming days and weeks, will uncover layer upon layer of indignities and ironies and further causes for outrage. The initial news of Dolly's plan to divorce him amounted to a first strike but not yet an all-out assault. The assault will be slow and insidious, and the pain of it will linger indifferently until either time or death takes care of it once and for all. As for Alan, he'll bear witness to it all and do what he can to make Mike's life a little easier, a little less depressing. What, besides this, can he do?

22

When Alan called Ralph that night, he learned from Ralph's wife that he was away on business and wouldn't be back till Saturday. So the question of whether Ralph will come through for Mike has remained unanswered all week. But it's Friday now and, as Mike said, Alan has a life of his own.

With a lighter-than-usual step, he approaches a coffee shop on East Fifty-eighth Street, down the block from Baines & Taylor, where he's just had what he considers to have been a successful first interview.

He stops just inside the entrance of the coffee shop and surveys the interior. On his left is a typical lunch counter but on his right is a partitioned-off dining area which gives the place an air of being somewhat upscale, or at least of shooting for this type of ambiance. He opts for one of the small tables-for-two that line the dining-area side of the partition and settles into a chair that faces out into the room. Seated to his right, he notices, is a ruddy-looking man who, perhaps a hundred years ago, might have been considered a giant, and Alan finds himself moving his chair imperceptibly away from the man's table. He glances at his menu now and decides on the fried fish platter. Then he notices that the giant has stood up and begun to make his way around the partition to the cash register.

"What can I get you today?"

Alan looks up to see a too-thin blonde—pushing forty, he guesses, and sporting a hint of a cigarette cough—standing over him and tapping her order pad with a pencil. She takes his order and goes about her business, then returns a minute later with a basket of rolls.

He breaks off a piece of one of the rolls and takes a bite. Then he happens to turn his head slightly in the direction of the table the giant has vacated, and out of the corner of his eye he sees, just beyond it, a young woman who appears to be engrossed in a paperback book, even as her coffee and what seems to be a cruller sit ignored on the table before her. He looks directly over at the woman, and his eyes focus on the bush of black, frizzy hair that sits regally atop her head.

The woman seems to sense she's being looked at, and she turns her head in Alan's direction and meets his gaze. He gives her a cautious smile, which she acknowledges with a look of mild curiosity. Then she takes a sip of coffee and returns to whatever she's reading.

Alan hesitates and then, emboldened by his successful job interview, says, "I'm sorry, but I can't help wondering what you're reading."

The woman throws the same curious look in his direction, then holds up the book for him to see.

Since there's a table separating them—albeit a small one—Alan has to lean sideways to make out the cover. "*As a Man Grows Older*," he reads aloud. "You're reading Italo Svevo, I can't believe it! *Nobody* reads Italo Svevo!"

"Evidently some people do."

"You're not going to believe this," Alan says, aware that he's attracted the attention of some of his fellow diners, "but I did my master's thesis on him. 'Self-loathing in the Novels of Italo Svevo.'"

The woman's lips take on the shape of a fledgling smile. "You expect me to believe this?" she says.

"Why not?"

"Self-loathing? It's too strong a concept, it has no plasticity to it. They'd never let you write a paper like that."

"But they did," Alan says. "And it applies. In Svevo's first novel, for example, the protagonist kills himself. Sounds like self-loathing to me."

The woman seems to realize she's been recruited into conversation, and it seems to Alan she's on the brink of nipping the whole thing in the bud and turning back to her book. She doesn't do this, however. Instead she says, "What's the title of his first novel?"

"*A Life.*"

"He didn't come up with very good titles, did he."

"They probably sound better in Italian," Alan says.

In the next moment he catches the waitress's eye and,

with a degree of assertiveness uncommon to him, asks her to move his table settings to the table on his right—the one recently vacated by the giant.

"I'll have the bus boy clean that off for you, sir," she says, obviously annoyed by the imposition.

Alan looks back at the woman with the bushy hair and sees that she's gone back to her book. A few moments later an uncommonly short bus boy—perhaps Vietnamese or Taiwanese—shows up and clears off the table next to Alan's and then moves his bread basket and table settings over to it.

Alan moves to the new table and waits for the woman to acknowledge in some way that he's now several feet closer to her than he was just moments ago. Finally she turns her head and gives him an inscrutable look, then resumes reading.

Now that he's seen her up close, he's struck by her eyes. He's seen eyes like this before but can't think where. If he had to, he would describe them as ethereal, kind of glassy and liquid and of indeterminate color—somewhere between agate blue and wheat yellow. Was it on an Alaskan Malamute that he's seen such eyes? A Samoyed?

"I hope I'm not bothering you," he says to her, "but I don't usually meet women who read anything more ambitious than Jacqueline Susann. I suppose that makes me an opportunist."

The woman looks up from her book. "An opportunist? In what way?"

"What I mean is, at the risk of being a pest I wanted to take this opportunity to talk to someone I'm sure I'd enjoy talking to."

"It's a free country," she says, but this time she doesn't go back to her book.

Alan, meanwhile, thinks he might have detected a hint of a European accent in her voice. "Are you European?" he says.

"I grew up in Europe," the woman says. "First in Vienna and later in Copenhagen. And then we moved to the States when I was thirteen. But I don't think of myself as European or American," she adds. "I think of myself as a Jew."

He wonders why she might have volunteered this information. Maybe she assumes he's a fellow tribesman and her comment was a way of cementing a certain bond she sensed between them. Or maybe it was a veiled attempt to get him to back off.

"I'm not a Jew myself," he says, "but if I had any best friends I'm sure some of them would be Jewish."

The woman smiles. "You're an interesting sort, and if I had more time I'm sure I'd enjoy talking with you further, but I have to get back to work." She picks up her check and gives Alan a half smile of farewell.

"You're leaving so soon?" he says, remembering a line a college friend of his used to use. "But I don't even know your name and I haven't even asked you to marry me yet." At these words he glances at her left hand and notices that the ring finger is bare. "Surely you could give me your phone number—ideally not a bogus one."

The woman stands now but doesn't move away from her table. "I'm living with someone," she says.

Alan is taken down a peg by this, but says, "Living with someone as in, 'In the first blush of new romance,' or living with someone as in, 'This is getting old and I'm not sure how much more of it I can take'?"

"I'm living with someone," she repeats, and then steps away from the table and begins to walk toward the cash register.

Liking what he sees from behind, he calls out to her. "My name is Alan, by the way."

To his surprise she turns back toward him and, with the most open smile he's seen from her yet, she says, "My name is Zoriah."

Zoriah!

Alan watches the woman—Zoriah!—pay her bill and disappear from his life forever. A few years ago he might have thrown a ten at the cashier and raced out onto the street to further accost this European-American Jewess with the mysterious eyes and the mysterious name, and to hell with the fact that she's living with someone. But no longer. Too many wasted hours chasing unlikely dreams.

The waitress, in the midst of a sudden attack of tubercular coughing, places Alan's lunch before him and he looks down at it but with little interest now. Who is this woman Zoriah? he asks himself. Why has she come into his life? Obviously not as a potential replacement for Marissa, for even if she was unattached there didn't seem to be enough chemistry between them to get them through more than a date or two (which would make the act of running out onto the street after her that-much-more ludicrous). But he's been thinking a lot lately about symbols and grand schemes and the architecture of a person's life. When a "presence" appears in your life from out of nowhere, you'd best pay attention. And even if it's a matter of arbitrarily attaching meaning to an otherwise insignificant event, the very act of fabricating meaning can itself be instructive. What, then, he wonders, can he take from the fact that Zoriah touched his life for a moment? The answer comes to him almost immediately: she's the prototype of what he's been looking for in a woman—intelligent, edgy, different, good-looking . . . She's a reminder that such women are out there—needles in haystacks, perhaps, but out there nonetheless—and that it behooves him to put himself in a position to field them when he comes across them and maybe to seek them out. To actively tinker with his life to allow for the possibility of positive change. *That's* the ticket, he tells himself. And he's been doing it, he supposes. The job interview is proof. New job, new people, new women . . . It all adds up to the possibility of a new life.

But first the obstacle of obstacles: Marissa. Despite his feelings for her and despite the pain of being away from her, even for as short a period as three or four days, he simply has no choice but to bite the bullet and end it before it consumes him. But he's been over this a million times; the benefits of breaking it off with her are no more transparent now than they were after their first date. But the difficulty of it . . . The difficulty grows with each kiss, with each touch, with each thought of her. Marissa has begun to infiltrate his blood, to take hold of him from the inside out. Because of her he's lost sight of himself, seeing himself now as no more than ancillary to whatever force it is that propels them one to the other. And what's more, his initial reaction to what he learned from that snippet of her diary—a reaction that he saw as highly motivating when it came to the idea of ending their relationship—that reaction has grown increasingly milder over the weeks, making it correspondingly more difficult for him to muster the courage he knows he'll need to end it once and for all. But isn't it another example of fate's handiwork, he argues to himself, that Zoriah came into his life on a Friday, just hours before he'll be going out to Hoboken? The timing is inspired and the inspiration undeniable; together the timing and inspiration should surely be enough to provide the impetus he's lacked to this point. No, it won't be easy to tell Marissa it's over between them, especially right before Valentine's Day, but he would be a fool—no, a coward—not to run with the opening he's been given.

He takes a few bites of lunch but leaves most of it untouched, then checks his watch. One-forty-five. Marissa gets off at five-thirty on Fridays, which means he has to get through nearly three hours before he can go out there. He could go back to the office, of course, but it would be pointless to do so since it would be next to impossible to concentrate. And besides, Rick lets everyone leave at four on Fridays anyway.

Alan leaves a couple of dollars on the table, then pays

his check and goes out onto the street. At a pay phone he leaves a message with Rick's secretary. "Please tell Rick that something came up and I'm going to have to take the rest of the afternoon off. And tell him I hope it's not a problem." And it won't be a problem, Alan knows; ever since he's taken over as unofficial copy chief, the powers-that-be have expressed their happiness with the work that's been coming out of the copy department, and Rick, accordingly, has been treating him like the Second Coming.

He walks over to Fifty-seventh Street and after crossing Fifth Avenue enters Central Park. He begins to amble down the path that leads to the zoo but then stops short. If he's going to think of his life in symbolic terms, he realizes, it might not be a good idea to spend time perusing captive animals. What he needs is to spend the afternoon occupied with a neutral activity, something that will take his mind off what he's about to do. He could take in a movie, for instance, or go to a museum. And then when it's getting to be time, he'll make his way to the Port Authority bus terminal and try to gear himself up for what's to come.

He exits the park and walks west on Fifty-seventh Street. At the corner of Fifty-seventh and Avenue of the Americas, still undecided about how to spend the afternoon, he pauses to look west as far as the eye can see. The day is rather gray and the visibility poor, but he imagines that he can see, at the foot of West Fifty-seventh, the West Side Highway and beyond it the river and across it New Jersey itself, looking much as it might have looked to those first Dutch settlers, those perpetrators of a riotous, boundless dream. Time passes with lightning speed and renders everything in its path meaningless in the end. And so the act of a young man getting on a bus so that he can break a young woman's heart is, in the long run, inconsequential. But that's in the long run.

Part VI

23

He did it, he should be proud of himself! Alan Agnalini, not known for taking life by the horns, actually went out to Hoboken and took a wrecking ball to Marissa's heart, difficult as it was for him. Now he's free to get on with his life.

Except he can't. Life without Marissa is only marginally livable—if that. More than a month has passed since the breakup, but the deep funk he was thrown into only deepens. The best he can do to counter this is to grasp at straws, seeking anything that might distract him. Even something as boring as visiting Mike can provide a degree of respite. So it's with a certain sense of relief that, on yet another Sunday, he walks down the hall to Mike's room and enters.

Mike is sitting up in a chair watching TV, but when he sees Alan he reaches for the remote control and silences the Ipana toothpaste spokesman in mid-pitch.

"How was the drive?" Mike says by way of greeting.

"Uneventful," Alan says. He takes a chair and moves it

around the bed to the window side of the room and sits down.

A fledgling lull ensues, which Mike breaks when he says, "You remember your cousin Jimmy? Jimmy Palmieri? You know, Aunt Marie's son, the oldest one?"

"How could I forget Jimmy Palmieri? He lived down the block from us."

"Right," Mike says. "Anyways, Aunt Yolanda called the other day and said that his son—the one who just turned three, she said—that the doctors ran some tests and they're saying he's retarded."

"I'm sorry to hear that," Alan says.

In the next moment, and obviously as a delayed reaction to the word "retarded," he has a vision of Marissa's half-retarded cousin from Delaware, storming into her room and pinning her to the bed. . . . He shakes off the vision, but this is the way it's been going with him. Every piece of news he learns, every woman he passes on the street, every sound he hears—like the sound of a garbage truck backing up, which reminds him of his cousin Dominic, the garbage man, who used to live in Hoboken—everything reminds him of Marissa. It's as if the world is conspiring to torment him with the memory of her. This, he knows, is not the case. The conspiracy is self-inflicted. A conspiracy of his mind and his emotions and his senses coming together to drag him down as he drags himself through another day, waiting for the proverbial light at the end of the tunnel. But the only tunnel he can think about is the one named after Lincoln, and the fact of its existence is just one more thorn in the side of his resolve. It would be so easy to just get in his car or get on a bus and allow the Lincoln Tunnel to possibly restore to him the life he had when Marissa was its focal point. If he can tough it out, though, then surely the day will come when he has no further need of tunnels. People get over these things, he reminds himself. What would he do, for instance, if Marissa, like so many before her, were to die? He would get on with his life, because he would have no choice. He would put one foot in front of the other, and in time he would once again be the person he'd been—a person with aspirations, a person who understands that self-betrayal, in whatever form, is the ultimate act of cowardice. And he would be stronger for having gone through what he went through. This is a positive message, isn't it? So why does he feel so rotten?

"You tired today, Alan?"

He looks back at Mike and quickly reorients himself. "No, I was just daydreaming. Sorry."

"Got a lot on your mind, huh?"

Alan doesn't answer, but he supposes the look on his face—probably one of consternation—is answer enough.

"Anyways, the little boy is retarded like I said. It's a shame, but what can you do?"

"Not much," Alan says.

Silence prevails for a time and then Mike, as if he realizes he's forgotten to turn off the oven, says, "Oh, did I tell you? Dolly's house is up for sale."

"I told you that a couple of weeks ago, Dad."

Mike appears not to have remembered this but says,

"Right, I remember you said something about that. But I don't get it," he adds. "We coulda sold that house a year ago like I kept telling her, but . . ."

Alan can see that Mike has had an epiphany, which no doubt accounts for the sudden death of whatever he was in the process of saying. The content of the epiphany is obvious to Alan, moreover, and now he listens as Mike tells him what he already knows.

"*Now* I see what she did, that rat. She held on to the house cause she was thinking in the back a her mind that if the marriage didn't work out, or if I dropped dead which she was probably waiting for to happen anyway, then she'd get all the money from the house herself."

Mike opens his mouth as if to add to what he's just said but ends up adding nothing. Alan, for his part, has always seen the wisdom in Dolly's holding on to the house, but pointing this out to Mike has never been an option.

They remain silent for an extended moment. Finally Mike says, "I meant to tell you, Alan. You know Florence down the block? Mrs. Guziolano? She's gonna be coming in once a week or so to clean our house. Aunt Fiona says she likes to keep busy now that her husband died. And she refuses to take any money."

"That's nice of her," Alan says. "She's not exactly rolling in dough."

"Some people are like that. They like to help people out. My cousin from Brooklyn was like that. Rosalie—I don't think you ever met her."

Mike is overtaken by a coughing fit. After it's subsided

he says, "But Aunt Fiona says everybody's worried who the new neighbors might be, once Dolly's house is sold. They're worried they might be hippies or something. Or coloreds, maybe. They got plenty a coloreds in Paterson, and spics too, and who's to say they won't start buying out where we are."

"You have enough to worry about, Dad."

"Cause it's your inheritance too, Alan. If the property values go down, then your inheritance goes right with it."

"And I have enough to worry about, myself."

"You say that now," Mike points out, "but you don't know how you're gonna feel five, ten years from now. I still say you're gonna end up in that house before it's all said and done."

Alan has no stomach for this turn in the conversation, but he's at a loss as to how to redirect it. This proves of no consequence, however, for now he hears Mike say, "Which reminds me. You still seeing that girl from Hoboken—what's her name, Marsha?"

"Marissa," Alan says, his stomach taking a turn of its own.

"Loretta says she's very pretty but you never talk about her. How come?"

Alan could fill several legal pads with all the reasons he's chosen not to mention Marissa to Mike. It's bad enough his cousin Loretta has taken it upon herself to broadcast his—Alan's—love life to the entire family, but that doesn't mean he has to give the gossip more legs than it already has.

"I'd prefer not to talk about her, Dad. We broke up, but I'd like to leave it at that."

Mike shrugs, and silence again takes hold of the room. Fortunately, if only in the interest of father-son unity in the abstract, the silence is not long-lasting.

"So what about that job you're up for?" Mike says. "You hear about that yet?"

"I didn't get it."

Mike seems to take this news in stride. After a moment he says, "You can't win 'em all."

Alan waits for Mike to add something to his comment but nothing follows, and although relieved that he's evidently not to be grilled about what might have gone wrong in the interviewing process, Alan is slightly crestfallen at the very same realization.

"But I still say you should hang on to what you got, Alan. You got that friend—what's his name, Vic?"

"Rick."

"Rick. He must be a smart cookie to be promoted like he was, and if he's your friend like you say, then he'll be looking out for you. You never know, there could be a job opening coming up soon in the company and he goes and puts your name in for it, and just like that you get a promotion too."

"Stranger things have happened," Alan says.

"See what I mean?" Mike says, obviously missing the sarcasm in Alan's comment. "You gotta take advantage of your friends. That's what they're there for."

Alan glances at his watch. Perhaps a horde of his relatives will show up unexpectedly and then he can make an escape, citing room-occupancy laws.

"You should talk to your cousin about getting you a job if you're gonna still be looking."

"My cousin? Who, Loretta?"

"Not Loretta," Mike says. "Ralph. Who did you think?"

"I thought Loretta."

"No—Ralph. He's got connections."

"Ralph's in real estate, Dad. I'm in publishing. I don't know how much help he could be. Besides, I can find my own job."

"Suit yourself," Mike says with another of his patented shrugs.

Alan eyes a copy of *TV Guide* on Mike's night table. It isn't Dostoevsky, but any reading material at this point would provide a welcome diversion.

"Speaking a Ralph," Mike says now, "did you hear? They bought up this big parcel a land in Bayonne—right across from the bridge to Staten Island. They're gonna be putting up a shopping mall there."

Alan says nothing to this, but then remembers that Mike's statement started as a question. "No, I hadn't heard that," he says.

"He'll be making out like a bandit on that deal. But it don't surprise me none, he was always a go-getter from the time before he went to school even. Did I ever tell you about the time he had that lemonade stand in front a the house? Four years old he was."

"Right, I've heard that story," Alan says, remembering that by Ralph's own admission he was seven at the time.

"You had jobs a your own when you was a kid, but with Ralph . . . I don't know, he always had a nose for money. Some people are like that, they just got that knack for making money."

Alan, who clearly lacks the knack, looks across at the *TV Guide* with renewed longing.

"You know something," Mikes says as if he's been goosed, "maybe they're back by now."

"Who?"

"Ralph and Glenda. Maybe they're back."

"I'm going to be calling him tonight, Dad. Even if they're back they might be jet lagged or something. I'll talk to him tonight and I'll let you know what he says either tonight if it's not too late or first thing tomorrow."

Mike's face expresses some displeasure with this plan. "I still don't understand how it was you didn't get to talk to him before they left on vacation," he says.

"I already told you, Dad. Glenda must have forgotten to tell him that I'd called. And when I called again, Glenda's mother said they'd already left for France. But they'll be home soon. I'll call him tonight and then we'll know where we stand."

Mike grudgingly seems to accept this explanation. A few more seconds tick off the clock. Then he says, "What time you got?"

Alan looks at his watch. "Twenty of three."

"Twenty a three? That's late already. They're probably back by now I bet. Why don't you call him, Alan?"

Tacking a new tack, Alan says, "Don't they make you pay for long distance calls here?"

"Sure they make you pay. But it's only to Westchester— that can't cost that much. Besides, I'm gonna end up owing so much money, what the hell difference is a long distance call gonna make?"

Alan eyes the phone, which sits on the night table next to Mike's bed. Deciding there's no hope of winning this argument, he steps to the phone and picks up the receiver and begins to dial.

"You know his number by heart, Alan?"

"I'm good with numbers. It's the secret to my success." He sits down on the bed and waits. After a few rings some-one picks up.

"Glenda, is that you? . . . No, I wasn't sure if you'd be back yet. . . . No, I hadn't heard that about France. . . . You know, if you want I can call back later if you need to sleep or anything. . . . That's okay, I know you had a lot on your mind. . . . No, that's okay. . . . Sure, I can hold on. . . ."

Alan looks across at Mike and can't help feeling a stab of empathy for the man; at some point Alan might find his own life hanging on the whim of a rich nephew/surrogate son.

"Yes—Ralph. How are you doing? . . . Right, Glenda said it wasn't what you expected. . . . Me? Can't com-plain. . . . Right, I was trying to reach you before you left.... Well, here's the deal. I'm sure you've heard from your mother that Dolly has filed for divorce.... I know, it's unbelievable. .... I never really liked her either. But anyway, the situation is this: for my father to be able to stay at the nursing home he's in now, we would need an extra six-thousand dollars or so a year. .... No, it's private. .... No, they don't take Medicaid, I've checked .... Right. .... Right. .... No, we'd like to avoid a public facility if we can.... That was the first thing I suggested, but he won't hear of it. .... Assets? No, nothing other than the house and the car. .... It's less than two years old. .... Right, a '75 Olds Cutlass. I don't know how much we could get for it. .... You could do that? ... That's really great of you, Ralph.... He's right here, I could put him on the line. .... No, I understand. You go get some rest, I'll call you tomorrow and leave the phone number of the nursing home with your secretary.... I'll tell him. .... Thanks again, Ralph. You go get—"

Somewhat miffed at having been cut off in mid-sentence, Alan hangs up the phone. He looks across at Mike, whose face, though noticeably more relaxed than Alan has seen it since he broke the news about Dolly, still betrays a degree of anxiety, as if Mike isn't certain he heard what he just heard.

"Good news," Alan says. "Ralph says to tell you he'll be happy to pay for whatever you need. He says it's the least he can do."

"You see that?" Mike says. "I knew he wouldn't let me down."

"I'm really happy for you, Dad. I'm sure that takes a load off your mind."

"But this has gotta stay private between the three of us, you know."

Fat chance, Alan thinks to himself, remembering his aunt Fiona's penchant for meddling in her son's life.

"I won't say a word," he says.

"Good, cause I don't want nobody knowing my private business."

His mission accomplished, even though he didn't intend to undertake it quite so soon or in Mike's presence, Alan thinks this might be a good time to politely make his exit and make his way back to Manhattan. He stands now. "I should be getting back, Dad," he says moving toward the door. "But that's great news. I think you'll be happy here once you get used to it."

Mike, however, seems oblivious to Alan's intention to leave. "But did he say when he's coming out to visit me?"

"Who, Ralph?"

"Yeah—Ralph. Did he say if he's gonna be coming out here soon, he ain't been out here yet."

"No, he didn't say anything, but they just got back today. I'm sure that once they get settled they'll be coming out here."

"I'm glad," Mike says, then adds, "But when you get back to New York, Alan, why don't you give him another call? You know, to remind him he should come out and visit me."

Soon Alan is on Route 80, headed back to the city. It occurs to him that a few miles down the road he could hop on the Jersey Turnpike and in no time he'd be in Hoboken. He can see himself camped out in the park down the block from Marissa's house. *She emerges from her house and begins to walk toward the park, but then stops short. He can feel her eyes upon his. In the next moment they run toward each other and fly into each other's arms. Minutes later they enter her bedroom and soon reenter that magical world . . .*

But this would not be a good thing, he reminds himself. If he can just get past the exit to the turnpike he'll be okay. Not wanting to tempt fate, he switches on his left turn signal and checks the side-view mirror, then slips over into the next lane.

24

"So, Alan. You look troubled today. What's up?"

He looks across at Rhonda.

"I . . ." he begins, but his mind shuts down. And this doesn't surprise him. There's so much to say, so many feelings to contend with, that he has no idea where to begin. Finally he hears himself utter a single word. "Marissa."

"Are you seeing her again?" Rhonda asks. "You haven't mentioned her in a while."

"I'm not seeing her again but in a way I am, because I can't get her out of my mind. I've been trying not to mention her in our sessions, but that's not getting me anywhere. In a weird way it's as if I'm possessed by the memory of her, so there's no point in trying to pretend otherwise.

"But something specific happened," he goes on, "and it's really bothering me. I was at the nursing home Sunday, visiting my father. And something he said reminded me of Marissa. And I guess that was the final straw, because when

I left later on I realized that this isn't a problem I can handle. I'm haunted by her and I don't know what to do about it. Everything reminds me of her. Everywhere I go, everyone I meet, every song I hear on the radio . . ."

Rhonda says nothing at first. Then she says, "You're going through a form of grieving, Alan. You've suffered a tremendous loss. But one way or the other you're going to have to find a way to deal with this. My guess is that you've thought of trying to get back with her, am I wrong?"

"No, you're right. I keep thinking I should go back to her, but I don't even know if she'd take me back. But I think I might be making a terrible mistake if I tried to get back with her. Except every day it gets harder and harder not to pick up the phone and call her. I tell myself that if I can just hold out for a few more days, a few more weeks, then things might start to ease up, that I might start to get over her. But this doesn't happen. I'm in worse shape now than I was the day after I broke up with her. Far worse shape."

"Yet you still haven't admitted to yourself that you're in love with her."

"Actually," he says, "I've given up trying to convince myself that I'm not in love with her. I'm more in love with her now than I ever was, and it's obvious to me that I've been in love with her all along. But that just makes the whole thing harder to deal with."

Rhonda jots something in her notebook. Then she says, "The whole thing? What do mean by the whole thing?"

And here Alan is faced with a dilemma. Does he confine his remarks to his confusion about whether he should or shouldn't try to get back with Marissa, or does he unburden himself completely? After a few seconds, as if he's been prodded by some other-worldly force, he says, "Something unbelievable happened. I haven't told a soul about it.

"It was Christmas Eve and Marissa was in the bathroom getting ready for bed. I kind of accidentally stumbled across her diary on the bookshelf, and I couldn't help reading some of it. Actually I only read two entries, but the second entry . . ." He takes a deep breath and continues. "I couldn't believe what I was reading. I don't know if you remember this, but a couple of days after Stephanie died, Brooke described the car crash to me. She said that a young woman was crossing the street in a hurry, trying to beat the light, and that their cabdriver, who was turning into the crosswalk, had to stop short. And that's what caused the car in back of them to plow into them."

"Yes, I remember your mentioning that," Rhonda says. "But what does this—Wait. Are you saying that Marissa was the one who was running across the street to beat the light?"

"It's unbelievable, but it was right there in her diary. And the entry was dated the same day as the accident: June 7, 1975."

Again Rhonda jots something in her notebook, but it seems to Alan that she's just buying time to regain her professional objectivity.

"And when you read this, Alan, how did it make you feel?"

"I'm not proud of this," he says, "but my first reaction—after the disbelief, that is—was anger. But I knew, even as I was feeling it, that there was something irrational about my anger. It took me a few days, but I finally realized that it had to do with my ego. If the little girl who died in that car crash had been a total stranger to me, just some anonymous person, I never would've felt anger at learning that Marissa, almost certainly, caused the accident. On the contrary, I would've felt compassion for her. She made an innocent mistake dashing across the street the way she did, and she was obviously suffering for it. Her diary entry was painful for me to read, and not just because suddenly, from out the blue, I was faced again with the reality of that accident. The fact is, Marissa blamed herself totally, and she was convinced she would be going to hell because of this. The word 'remorse' doesn't begin to cover it."

After a moment he adds, "If there's a saving grace, it's that Marissa had only limited information about the accident. She heard the two cars collide and heard a woman shouting 'Stephanie!, Stephanie!' And then she looked into the back of the cab and saw the woman bending over a little girl, who seemed to be unresponsive. But that was the extent of what she knew because she ran away. She wrote in her diary that when she got back to Hoboken she immediately drove out to see Lucille Tedesco—if you recall, her kind of surrogate mother—and made her swear not to tell her if she read in the paper or heard on the news that the little girl in the accident had died. So I assume that Marissa made it a point not to read the paper or listen to the news for a while. My guess is she has no idea whether the child lived or died.

"Anyway, I realized that anger on my part made no sense. If anything, after those first couple of days I began to feel increasing concern for Marissa and for how this tragedy, on top of all the others, had added to the burden she's been living with all these years. So, as you can see, this knowledge that Marissa was, let's say, instrumental in the accident that killed Stephanie—this just complicates everything. If I try to get back with her, do I tell her I know about this? Do I open up that can of worms, or do I live with the secret? It seems neither one of these things is a good option."

"No," Rhonda says, "life doesn't always provide us with good options. Sometimes it's a matter of choosing the lesser of two evils."

Alan says nothing in response. Finally Rhonda says, "The way I see it, Alan, there's only one choice that makes sense in this situation. If you decide to go back to her, you've got to tell her that you know about this incident, and here's why. A lie, even if it's just a lie of omission, will almost always cause problems in a relationship, sometimes irrevocable problems.

"I don't generally mention this to my patients, but I started out as a marriage counselor. And in those ten, nearly ten, years, I encountered, I would say, hundreds of couples whose marriages were severely threatened, and often destroyed, by a lie or, as I said, a lie of omission. A relationship can't thrive, not long-term, unless it's based on honesty. If one or both parties suspect dishonesty, in any form or to any degree, then that suspicion will inevitably fester and begin to undermine the relationship. So my advice, Alan, is if you're going to give it another go with Marissa, you need to come clean. About everything."

Again Alan is mute. Finally he says, "But it would kill

her. How can I tell her: one, that the little girl she might
have killed is in fact dead? And then, on top of that, that
the little girl was my daughter? I don't see how I could put
her in a position where she'd have to deal with information
like this. I don't know if she could handle it. I mean, how
could she?"

Alan puts his head in his hands—an instinctive gesture,
he supposes, but one he doubts will do him any good.

Then he hears Rhonda say, "You're right, Alan. It
wouldn't be easy for her to process this information. But
you're forgetting what a strong woman Marissa is. Many
people faced with the tragedies she's had to deal with
would just wilt, and maybe never recover. But Marissa
has always found her way back. Sure, it was never easy for
her. Sure, I'm certain she had to deal with periods of deep
despair and who knows what else, but she always bounced
back. You have to believe that she would have the strength
to handle this new information, especially if you make it
clear to her that you know she never meant to hurt anyone
by doing what she did."

Alan remains silent, but Rhonda's words have reached
him. How many times has he told her what an incredibly
strong woman Marissa is? If nothing else, it would be hyp-
ocritical of him to withhold information from her because
he feels she wouldn't be able to handle it.

"I'm going to repeat myself here," Rhonda says,
"because I can't state this too firmly: if you're going to
reestablish a relationship with Marissa—if you expect it to

work this time—then you, and I mean you plural, need to make honesty the cornerstone of that relationship."

When he doesn't respond, Rhonda goes on. "You have to admit, Alan, that honesty was sorely lacking in your relationship with her from the start. We've gone over this before, so I don't have to tell you that your whole relationship with Marissa was based on lies and half-truths. From day one, neither one of you was honest about your motives. Marissa agreed to go out with you, we can safely assume, because in her mind you weren't a threat. Someone who, because you're so different from her, she'd be free to fool around with for a while without having to worry about the marriage issue. And you, as you've admitted, went out with her as a kind of experiment—almost as a lark—simply because she's so beautiful. Fine, that's okay for a first date and maybe for a brief fling. But when things started to get more serious, neither one of you would own up to your feelings. Instead you fabricated ground rules, almost as if you were carrying on an extra-marital affair. That's dishonest. You never sat down, the two of you, and said, 'There's something more here than we thought there would be, and maybe we should talk about redefining our relationship'. You didn't do this. You just went on until one of you took the initiative to end it, while neither of you had ever taken the initiative to change it or even to define it. Again, that's dishonest. Dishonest to yourselves and dishonest to each other."

Alan has no answer for this. Everything Rhonda just

said is true. Their relationship was based on a series of lies. Lies and half-truths—those were her words, weren't they?

"And the ironic thing," Rhonda adds, "is that you're both honest people. I know for a fact that you are, Alan, and from what you've said about Marissa I'm sure she's honest as well. And yet you couldn't be honest with each other. And look at the result. So that's why I'm saying that now—if you're really serious about giving this another shot, and assuming she is as well—then you need to be honest with each other. Given what you now know about Marissa's role in the accident, you need to let her know that you know. Like it or not, this is the situation, and putting all your cards on the table is crucial if you're going to have any chance at a successful relationship."

As he leaves Rhonda's building and emerges onto the street, Alan feels more conflicted than ever. Yes, he agrees with Rhonda that if he's going to get back with Marissa it will have to be on a new foundation. But *should* he get back with her? He loves her, he admits that now. And he doubts he'll ever find another love that comes close to this one. But would he be giving up too much of himself to have a life with her? Would their different backgrounds erode, and ultimately destroy, their relationship? Would it destroy *him*? Or would a life with Marissa finally reveal to him who he truly is?

25

If Alan thought that opening up to Rhonda would some-how make it easier for him to deal with the absence of Marissa in his life, he was sadly mistaken. On the contrary, a torrent of emotions has overtaken him in the past couple of weeks, and his only strategy to counter it has been to stay as busy as possible. His primary way of doing this has been to go into work early and to leave even later than usual. And so, on this particular night (it's well past five), he finds him-self in his office, finishing up his revision of a brochure on electromagnetic fields.

Not that he's having much success keeping his mind on electromagnetic fields. Loretta's phone call to him last night has his head spinning. Why did she have to call him to announce that Marissa had abruptly quit her job at the hair salon? This was a question that Alan, as tactfully as possible, posed to his cousin, but all he got for an answer was *I don't know. I just thought you should know.* Well-inten-

tioned or not, Loretta's phone call has served only to rein-
force the difficulty he's been having in keeping his mind on
anything other than Marissa and what they had together.
Still, he's determined to get past this.

In a few minutes he'll leave the office, but then what?
He doesn't feel like going home to a TV dinner, or going
straight home at all. Maybe he should just walk home and
stop at a coffee shop somewhere for dinner.

He turns back to the brochure, figuring another ten
minutes will be enough to finish the revision, but then he
senses something—not a sound, exactly, but more like
a change in the atmosphere. He swivels around from his
typewriter and there, standing in the doorway, is Brooke.

She smiles at him and seems to take some delight in
his obvious surprise. "I *knew* you'd be working late. Some
things never change, right Alan?"

"Brooke!" he says, aware that he's risen to his feet. "I
can't believe it, I never thought I'd see you again!"

Brooke has taken a few steps into the office and Alan
a few steps toward her, so that they stand face to face now,
though not at a distance that would imply any intimacy
between them.

"How've you been, Alan?"

"I'm okay," he says. "And you look like you're okay. But
why are you in the city? You have a concert here?"

"Do you mind if I sit?" Brooke takes the chair at
Jerome's desk and turns it around to face Alan, who does
the same with his chair. "Seattle has a lot going for it," she
says, "but it's not New York. I knew in the back of my mind

that I would be making a mistake by moving out there, but it was one of those things where your mind's telling you one thing but your heart's telling you something else. It was good to get away from the city for a while, but then I started missing it."

"You've moved back?" Alan says.

Brooke gives him a mock-suspicious look. "A couple of weeks ago. You're disappointed?"

"Not at all," he says. "I'm . . ." But what, precisely, is he? How does he feel about this turn of events? How does it impact his situation, his life?

"I'm just surprised," he says. "You said you might be back in the city someday, but . . . I don't know, I guess I shouldn't be surprised."

"I liked it out there, but I know I've made the right decision, coming back."

After a beat, Alan says, "So where are you living?"

"Chelsea. Twenty-second, toward Ninth Avenue. I have a one-bedroom in a brownstone. The neighbors seem nice. . . ."

Alan says nothing and Brooke seems to scrutinize him for a moment. For his part, he's disconcerted to note that Brooke, though no less attractive than she was the last time he saw her, is not a stunningly good-looking woman. Not by Marissa standards, at any rate. Immediately he feels guilty, and incredibly shallow, for reducing Brooke to a physical object.

As if to atone for this, he says, "But where are my manners? Can I buy you dinner? To celebrate your return?"

A little while later they enter a restaurant on East Thirty-ninth Street and settle across from each other in a corner booth. They engage in small talk until after the waiter has taken their orders. Then Brooke says, "Another reason I'm back here is that I'm going back to school. I've applied to Juilliard and I don't think I'll have any trouble getting in. I'll be getting a master's in musicology."

"Musicology?" Alan says. "*That's* a switch."

Brooke takes a sip of water and gives him what appears to be a brave smile. "After Stephanie died," she says, "I began to think of giving back in some way. It's hard to explain. I love to perform, but somehow it doesn't seem like enough. I guess I need a more direct connection with people."

Alan nods his head in response to this last part about needing a more direct connection with people, but he remains focused on the fact that Brooke mentioned Stephanie's death at all. He's pleased to see that she's dealt with the tragedy to the point where she can at least say their daughter's name without having to fend off a resurgence of grief. He's especially impressed by the courage she's shown—and shown from the very beginning—in dealing with Stephanie's death, yet he feels it would be inappropriate in some way for him to say this to her.

"I think that's a great idea," he says instead, referring to her plans. "So you're thinking about teaching in a university?"

Again Brooke seems to scrutinize him, as if she perceives something different about him, something she didn't expect to see. "That's the plan," she says.

The waiter arrives with their entrees, and Brooke focuses on the task of eating. Not out of inordinate hunger, it seems to Alan, but perhaps as a source of distraction. Their conversation throughout dinner and into dessert skirts around the edges, remaining essentially meaningless. No further mention of Stephanie, no allusion to their night of lovemaking nor to Alan's assertion to Brooke, two weeks later, that he could see himself falling in love with her. In fact, Brooke seems to have little interest in his life since they last saw each other, and Alan is not sure she would welcome anything beyond cursory questions about hers. Finally his mind starts to wander. Soon, despite his best efforts not to do so, he begins to think about Marissa.

Brooke takes a sip of coffee now and says, "You're in love, Alan, am I right?"

The question stuns him. Is it that obvious? Evidently so, and this would explain why Brooke has seemed so remote throughout dinner; she must have figured out early on that he was involved with someone.

"Yes," he says. "I'm in love. I denied it for a long time, but then . . . Then I stopped denying it."

"You gave in to your feelings," Brooke says.

"Yes. To my feelings."

Brooke waits a second before she says, "And it ended badly."

Alan looks across at her, searching for some motive in this line of inquiry. "It didn't end well," he says. "I'm coping with it, though. Doing what I can, anyway."

Brooke takes a bite of her apple strudel and then

another sip of coffee. She glances openly at her watch. Several seconds go by, then several more.

"She's not the kind of woman I thought I'd fall in love with," Alan begins tentatively. "She's . . . Well, she's not like you and me, she's kind of . . ."

Finally it becomes clear that Brooke has no intention of responding to what he just said. She has no interest in playing the role of sympathetic ear. He'd like to ask her how she knew he's just gone through a breakup, but to do so would further insult her. If insult her is what he's done, simply by being in the emotional state he's in.

Suddenly he realizes what should have been obvious to him all along: Brooke appeared in his office tonight because she was hoping they could pick up where they left off after their night in bed together. How could he have missed this? The question, though, is irrelevant. What's relevant is that in the absence of a romantic relationship between them, nothing is left for him and Brooke. Friendship is no longer a possibility, not after their lovemaking. At least not in the context of his feelings for Marissa.

Alan takes a sip of coffee and glances at his own watch. A few moments later the waiter comes by and asks them if they want more coffee. Almost in unison they say no.

"Just the check please," Alan adds.

As they wait for the check, they exchange idle remarks about the weather, Alan aware of Brooke's need to keep her pride intact. He couldn't have imagined a scenario in which he would reject her overtures, but here he is—living one.

Out on the street a cab pulls up and Alan holds the back

door open for Brooke. "I'm glad you're back in the city," he says. "And good luck with grad school."

"Thanks, Alan. You take care of yourself."

The cab pulls away and he watches it move up the block toward Fifth Avenue. Then he turns and begins to walk slowly toward the river. No cab for him tonight. Not with his need to walk off the last two hours of his life, if such a thing is possible.

It's not until Alan nears his neighborhood that a thought occurs to him which, once again, he can't believe he didn't think of earlier: Brooke knows he's in love with someone, but she has no idea that the woman he's in love with is the same woman whose impulsive act set off the chain reaction that led to her daughter's death. News she could certainly do without.

26

The next afternoon Alan sits alone in his office. It's about ten after four and everyone else from the copy department has left to begin their weekend. But Alan sits, and he asks himself the same question he's been asking himself all day: where do I go from here? And he gets the same answer: who knows? Not only has he lost Marissa and Rick—now he's lost Brooke. Again! Why couldn't she have waited another six months, or a year or two, before she moved back to the city? Or why couldn't she have moved back before his feelings for Marissa got out of control? Why did she have to come back when he's emotionally unavailable to her? He knows that these are ridiculous questions—he figured out long ago that he's not the center of the world—but still, what impeccably bad timing! And how ironic is it that after years of dreaming of a life with Brooke, he's otherwise-involved when he finally gets a legitimate shot at perhaps getting his wish?

He feels a stab of self-pity in response to this thought, and a reflexive yearning for consolation. Not that consolation is what he needs right now. What he needs is to pull himself together. To think rationally about his problems, objectively about them. To mount an unbiased assessment of them, and then to act in accordance with reality rather than with the self-indulgent claptrap his mind all-too-often spits back at him.

His self-directed advice uplifts him to an extent, but then, as if in punishment for experiencing a moment of relative relief, a tremendous wave of depression hits him. Not washes over him, but hits him—and with the imagined force of a six-car pileup. How did his life turn out like this? This is not what he, as a child, envisioned for himself. He has no friends, no money, no sex life, no love life . . .

And especially no love life. None. He gave that away. How could he have done this? How could he have thrown away what he had with Marissa, when it was so much more than sex and so much more than anything he'd ever had with a woman? Because of his assumptions? For instance, his assumption that once she gets past her fear of getting too close to a guy she's going to need someone from her own world—someone with the same background and the same interests. And his assumption that he too is going to need someone from his own world. But he had that with his marriage, and how did *that* work out? Assumptions, any right-minded person will tell you, are nothing more than predictions based on past experience. And sometimes they can lead you down a path you wish you hadn't taken.

No, breaking up with her, at least for the reasons he did, was an ill-thought-out act. And now he's suffering the consequences. Because now it's not just about his longing to touch her, his longing to smell her hair, to bury his head in her breasts, to make love to her as if it's the last time anyone in the world will ever make love . . . It's about his need to talk to her. And to have her listen to him and understand him—even the parts he doesn't understand himself. And it's about his need to hear what she has to say about the matter. And to feel unique and appreciated and special— the way she made him feel from that very first date, even when everything seemed to be going so badly. The need, simply, is to be with her. He *needs* to be with her. He *needs* to be back with her. He needs her. That's what it comes down to. He needs her.

A month and a half ago he convinced himself that this need was insignificant or that it could be satisfied by someone else, but a month and a half ago he didn't understand it—not its nature, not its depth, not its relevance to the essential part of him, the part he thinks of as *I* and *me*. A month and a half ago he was a jackass, and now he's willing to make a jackass of himself or worse if only he can get back with her.

Maybe she's moved on with her life. Maybe the idea of going back to what they had is a dream that would prove unattainable for any number of reasons. But this is a moot point. Because he can't stay away any longer. Staying away from her is not working, not to the tiniest degree. To hell with the future and to hell with common sense and to hell with his idea of the "kind" of woman he allegedly needs— his so-called prototype. The woman he needs—the real, actual woman he needs—is Marissa.

He looks at the clock. Almost four-twenty-five. Marissa gets off at five-thirty on Fridays, which means if he leaves the office right now and races over to the bus terminal he should be able to make it out to Hoboken with a few minutes to spare. And then? And then when she sees him she'll react however she reacts. Maybe she'll tell him to take a hike. Maybe she'll kick him in the groin or cut him dead. But even if that turns out to be the case it's a step up from where he is now, because then, at least, the possibility of getting back with her will have been removed and he'll have no choice but to get on with his life to the extent that he can. But as long as there's a chance he might get back with her he's useless to himself and to everyone else. He must—he simply must—know where he stands with her.

Alan turns off his desk lamp and grabs his jacket. Emerging from his building a minute later, he turns and then breaks into a fast jog as he heads west on Fortieth Street. In less than five minutes he reaches Eighth Avenue and crosses it to the bus terminal. Inside he jogs to the main escalator and then goes up another escalator to the platform.

There's an empty seat on one of the benches, but he opts to lean against the side of the building. He notices a driver in a nearby stall sitting behind the wheel, reading a newspaper. To the drivers who make this run every day, the next trip out to Jersey is more of the same, but to Alan it's monumental—scary and exhilarating all at once.

He looks up and sees that the bus to Hoboken has swung around a corner and is pulling up to the waiting passengers, who form an impromptu line. For some reason, though, Alan hangs back. It seems to him that every cell in his body is urging him to take his place on line, but something paralyzes him. He can feel his mind flagging beneath the weight of a multitude of fragmentary, indefinable thoughts. And then suddenly, as has happened so many times before, the accident that took Stephanie's life appears as if before his eyes: Marissa dashing across the street to beat the light, the cab turning into the intersection but then stopping short, the sound of a car rear-ending it, Brooke's cries of *Stephanie!, Stephanie!*, Marissa fleeing in panic . . . The scene vanishes. And Alan, after he glances at the bus and the boarding passengers, vanishes as well.

After walking the streets for a few hours, he arrives back at his apartment. He takes off his jacket and goes through the mail, then wanders into the front room and switches on a lamp. Standing now at the bookcase, he lets his eyes move from one book to another without really seeing anything. Then he notices a spine with no writing on it, and he realizes it's the blank book Marissa gave him for Christmas. He takes the book from the shelf and opens it, although there's nothing to look at but lines. He hasn't thought about the book for months, but now he can hear Marissa saying

Maybe someday you'll write a story about me. You know, a Jersey girl who's afraid that if she got engaged to a guy he'd drop dead on her.

He stands at the bookcase for some time, thumbing through the blank pages. Then he imagines himself sitting down at the kitchen counter. In his mind he opens the book and begins to write. *I was at a child's birthday party in Jersey City. That's when I saw . . .*

But he knows he won't do this. To fictionalize her, or even to make her the subject of a verbatim account, would be a form of letting go. And he's not ready to let go.

He takes a step toward one of the room's two windows but returns to the bookcase. He runs a finger up and down the spine of the blank book as if he's touching Marissa's face. Then he turns from the bookcase and stares out into the empty room.

Part VII

27

Alan has just finished dinner and he's sitting on the couch watching the Jerry Lewis Labor Day Telethon. Since it's early on, the second or third hour of the Sunday night preceding Labor Day, a well-rested Jerry is doing his classic shtick—mugging for the camera, insulting imaginary audience members, and so on. If asked, Alan would have to admit that this doesn't make for riveting television, but it's relaxing. And why not relax? He's had a pretty full weekend, first with his date on Saturday night (nothing of consequence, but a date nonetheless) and then with his brunch at Rick and Sally's today. On the whole, things aren't going badly. About five months out from his bus-platform realization that he simply could not, and would not, tell Marissa that her actions led to the death of a child—five months out and things are starting to get back on an even keel. The ache is still there whenever he thinks of her (he wouldn't expect otherwise), and in his more somber moments it overtakes him with a sudden vengeance. Increasingly, though, he's been able to keep it at a safe distance. This is a positive development, as was his official promotion to copy chief, with its attendant raise. Although a few months old by now, the promotion hasn't ceased to be a source of optimism for him. A promotion, after all, is evidence that good things can happen. Life upended can right itself. And the related but unexpected reconciliation between him and Rick is further proof of this. This part is especially gratifying—being back in the fold, as it were. Being able to spend time with Rick and Sally and little Emily, the way it was for him in the old days. All of it is cause for optimism, so why not enjoy Jerry and his kids, and Charo, and The Flying Wallendas? Life is too short to deprive yourself of such diversions.

The phone rings. Alan turns off the TV and moves to the kitchen and picks up. "Hello?"

"Alan, it's Loretta. You know, your cousin."

Although annoyed, and knowing he's about to hear some dirt about Marissa, Alan does his best to sound pleased that his cousin has called.

"Loretta," he says. "Nice to hear from you."

"That's kind a you to say, Alan, and I don't mean to bother you, but there's something you need to know."

"About Marissa, right?"

"Right. Remember, Alan, when back—I think it was April—when I called to tell you that Marissa had quit her job, just up and walked out?"

"I remember it like it was yesterday," he says, hoping

he'd done a good enough job camouflaging the sarcasm in his remark.

"Well, just the other day I heard through the grapevine that she had moved outa Hoboken altogether. Sold her house and everything. And they're saying she moved just a couple days after she quit the job. Plus nobody knows where she moved to."

"And you called to tell me she's a missing person?"

"No. Well, I guess you could say she's missing. Or at least *half* missing."

Baffled, Alan says nothing, knowing that his cousin will eventually get to the point.

"I know it's confusing, Alan," she says, "but here's the thing. I don't know if you knew this, but I always get my hair done in the shop in Hoboken where I work. But a while ago I heard there's this fantastic beautician that moved to Jersey from somewheres, and that she worked at a shop up in Cliffside Park. That's a hike for me, but I figured, 'Lemme give her a try.' So I drove up there yesterday afternoon, and you're not gonna believe, Alan, what happened."

"Let me guess. You ran into Marissa."

"How did you know?" Loretta says. "That's right. Just as I was sitting down to get my hair done who should I see walking out from the back room than Marissa. I know she saw me but I could tell she was trying to make pretend that she didn't. And then the next thing I know she walks up to one a the other hairdressers, who I guess was the boss, and then she gets her bag and walks outa the shop. She musta said she was feeling sick or something. But here's the thing, Alan. She's pregnant. From the looks a her I'd say she's about seven months along, maybe a little more than that."

For Alan this conversation has suddenly taken on relevance. "Seven months, you said?"

"That's my best guess, Alan. I'd say seven months, maybe a little more."

He does a quick mental calculation. Seven months would take them back to the beginning of February, right before the breakup. Although he was plotting the breakup at the time, trying to figure out just how to go about it, he allowed his physical passion for Marissa to remain unchecked. Could it be, though, that she was stepping out on him? He highly doubts this. No, the baby is his, there's no question.

"So that's what I mean, Alan," he hears his cousin say. "It ain't my business, but I know you broke up with her right before Valentine's Day, cause she come into the shop on that Monday following—which was Valentine's Day, which probably made it even worse for her—and told me about it. We weren't real close friends or nothing, but I could tell she needed to get it off her chest. But she made me swear I wouldn't let you know how upset she was. So I'm guessing that this baby is yours, and that's why I called. Cause this is the kinda thing a man should know about, when a woman's carrying his baby."

"Absolutely," Alan says, but he's too distracted to say much beyond that. "I . . . ," he begins, but his train of thought gets derailed.

"And you're sure it was Marissa?" he says now. "Everybody's got a double, they say. Maybe it was just some pregnant lady who looked a lot like her."

"It was Marissa, I'd stake my life on it. Her face was a little fuller, but you'd expect that with someone in her condition."

Alan thanks Loretta for the information, this time genuinely grateful that she called. He hangs up but not before getting the name and phone number of the beauty salon where all this took place.

He steps back into the front room. What is he to make of this new development? From Jerry Lewis one minute to the all-but-certainty that he's once again—or soon going to be—a father. He feels his body revving up as if preparing itself for sudden movement, even as thoughts swirl around in his head and seem to render him incapable of any movement at all. Again the question *What do I make of this?* takes precedence over his other thoughts. But it's a vague question at best. You don't "make" anything of something you haven't had time to process. The better question would be *What do I do now?* And it's a better question because it implies its own answer: you track her down, confront her, find out what's what, and take it from there.

Absently he moves toward one of the two windows that line the back wall of the front room and looks out onto the backyard of the building opposite, registering nothing. Suddenly it hits him: Marissa quit her job abruptly because she didn't want Loretta to know she was pregnant. Which means she didn't want him—Alan—to know that she was pregnant with his child. But why? Did she think he'd encourage her to have an abortion or to give the baby up for adoption? Did she think he would deny paternity, or be a cavalier, distant father to the child? Did she think that telling him she was pregnant with his child would rope him into a marriage he didn't want? Not that it matters. What matters is that he has to challenge this decision of hers. To willfully deny him access to his child? This isn't something he can brush aside.

The next day, Labor Day, seems interminably long to Alan but he gets through it. Back in the office on Tuesday morning, even before he's had his coffee and corn muffin, he makes the call.

"Hair Today," he hears a nasal female voice say. "Priscilla speaking."

Alan gives a bogus name and says he's calling to make an appointment for his wife, who's at the dentist. "She said she'd like to see someone named Marissa. And the latest appointment she has today, if possible."

And he's in luck; Marissa's five-thirty appointment canceled, so he grabs it.

He struggles through the rest of the day, trying to keep his mind off what he's about to do, and trying to keep his excitement at the thought of seeing Marissa from getting the better of him. At around four-forty he leaves the office, and then, about a half hour later, he arrives at a bus stop on Anderson Avenue, the main drag in Cliffside Park. After a second he spots the salon, across Anderson and a few doors north of the corner. Making sure that Marissa won't see him if she happens to look out the window onto the street, he walks a few blocks north and then crosses to the salon side. His guess is that she'll hang around for about twenty or twenty-five minutes before she concludes that her five-thirty client is a no-show. Then, since this was to be her last appointment of the day, she'll leave the salon (and presumably through the front door, since North Jersey streets generally don't have alleys in back of them). Alan decides that at around five-forty he'll begin to walk back in the direction of the salon and keep an eye out for the moment she walks out onto the street.

As it turns out, Marissa doesn't appear on the street until past six, but when she does, Alan pounces. Jogging in her direction from about half a block away, he shouts, "Marissa, Marissa! Wait up!" He sees her turn in his direction and look around in confusion, but finally their eyes meet and almost immediately she turns and begins to walk rapidly in the opposite direction from where Alan is coming.

Just a couple of doors down from the salon he catches up to her. "Marissa," he says, placing a hand on her shoulder. She turns toward him, and once again he's struck by her physical beauty, almost to the point where he forgets why he's come out to Jersey to see her.

"Alan!" she says, obviously distressed to see him. "What are you doing here!? Why did you come here!?"

Almost instinctively Alan glances down at her belly. "We need to talk," he says.

"There's nothing to talk about," she says and begins to turn away, but Alan places a hand on her shoulder again.

In the meantime he's become aware that passersby are beginning to look in their direction. "Is there a coffee shop near here?" he says in a half-whisper. "Somewhere where we can sit down and talk?"

Marissa begins to say something but nothing comes out. Instead she looks Alan directly in the eyes as if appraising a piece of antique furniture. Finally she says, "Loretta told you she saw me."

"You thought she wouldn't tell me?" he says. "Yes, that's why I'm here. You know why I'm here," he adds, reflexively glancing down again at her belly.

Marissa pauses for another moment and then says, "Okay, I'll give you ten minutes. But just ten. I gotta get home to get dinner on the table for my husband."

Alan's mouth opens in shock, but then it occurs to him that finding a husband would be a predictable next step for Marissa given this development in her life. "You're married?" he says.

In response to this, Marissa holds up her left hand to display a rather gaudy diamond and a perhaps-too-wide gold band on her ring finger. "That's what I said," she says. "My husband don't like it if dinner's not on the table when he gets home."

Alan forms a mental image of this husband of hers: a beer-bellied greaser type with a pack of "smokes" rolled up in a sleeve of his T-shirt. Almost simultaneously the thoughts *What has Marissa gone and gotten herself into?* and *My child is going to have* this *as his father? Or* her *father?—*

these thoughts flood his brain and leave a moment of near-panic in their wake.

"Follow me," he hears Marissa say now.

He follows her as she walks back to the salon and then enters it. Immediately he's overcome by the fumes of God-knows-what hair chemicals, which leads him to wonder if working in a beauty salon might not pose some long-term health risks. "This is . . . This is my friend Alan," he hears Marissa say to another of the stylists, probably her boss. "Would it be okay if we could go into the stockroom for a few minutes? There's something important we need to discuss, the two of us."

"Sure, take as long as you need," the woman says, though she's obviously confused by the request.

Alan follows Marissa down a narrow hall and then into a small kitchen. "Could you take two a those chairs, Alan, into that room over there?" she says, pointing to an open doorway off the kitchen. He does as requested and then waits for Marissa to sit before he does. The room is tiny, even smaller than the room in Loretta's basement where they met. But back then they weren't surrounded by stacks of boxes of hair products. Alan feels momentarily trapped, as if the elevator he's riding in has come to a sudden, jolting stop mid-floor.

"I know why you're here, Alan," she says. "And I'm not gonna deny that this baby is yours. But it's yours only cause you're the one that got me pregnant. I got a husband now and he's gonna be my baby's father. I won't have my child

having two fathers—going back and forth and not knowing what's what."

Marissa has said these words with the utmost conviction, and Alan can see that he's not going to have an easy
time convincing her that he should have some kind of presence in their child's life.

"But Marissa," he says now, "this child is my flesh and
blood, you just admitted it. You can't deny me my own
child."

Marissa averts her eyes and says nothing to this. Since
spotting her on the street a few minutes ago, Alan has been
struggling to keep at bay any feelings he still has for her. But
seeing her now, sitting there, not only beautiful but beautifully childlike in the way she keeps her eyes from meeting
his, the way she seems to be making an effort to keep her
body's vibrations contained, separate from his—it's simply
too much for him. There's no question that he stills loves
her. And he can feel her love for him, and he'd bet anything
that the self-righteous anger she's displayed to this point in
their brief meeting has existed in part to hide that love not
only from him but from herself.

She turns her gaze back to him now. "I don't know
if I can legally keep you from my baby, but I'm asking
you . . . No, I'm telling you that this is the way it has to be.
This baby is *my* baby. I'm carrying her—or him—inside a
me. This baby is part a my own body. And that gives *me*
certain rights. I don't mean legal rights but . . . You know
what I mean."

And Alan knows what she means. And what she feels.

He's always been able to read between the lines with Marissa, to empathize with her. He hates the thought of hurting her in any way, but hurting himself to save her from pain or anguish—surely that's not the answer.

"We don't always get what we want in life," he says now. "I understand exactly where you're coming from. You want your child to have a normal life. Normal, as you see it, and maybe normal as it *should* be. But life doesn't really care about what *should* be. Sometimes you have to make certain compromises in—"

"Don't lecture me!" she snaps at him. "Do you think this is easy for me? You think it's easy for me to say to my baby's father that he can't be a part a her life? I know this is causing you pain, Alan," she adds, softening now, "but I have to put my baby first. Please, if you ever loved me . . ."

And there it is. For the first time, one of them has used the word "love" with regard to their past relationship. It's as if her simple plea—*if you ever loved me*—has given them, both separately and jointly, permission to redefine their relationship retroactively.

But Alan, perhaps out of an instinctive need to maintain a status quo he both chose and now finds himself stuck with, chooses not to go through the door Marissa has opened for him.

"Whatever we meant to each other," he says, "whatever it might have been—it's not relevant here. What's relevant is that this child is my flesh and blood. My flesh and blood," he repeats, feeling for the first time the full impact of those words, the reality they imply.

Marissa says nothing. Again she looks away, but this time she seems to be considering something. Finally she says, "Wait here."

She slips from the room, and for a few moments Alan strains to make out some words she's exchanging with a woman out front, evidently the one she spoke with a few minutes ago. Then he hears her reenter the kitchen and drop a coin into a pay phone he recalls seeing as they passed through the kitchen into the stockroom.

"Bobby?" he hears her say a few moments later. Alan listens as Marissa tells her husband that something came up at work and she won't be home in time to get his dinner on the table. She adds something about a TV dinner and then says, "I'll make it up to you." This likely suggestion of apology-via-sex angers Alan for a moment, as if he still claimed sole access to Marissa's body and her affections.

"Sorry," Marissa says as she returns to the stockroom and sits back down. After a few moments, during which she seems to be fortifying herself for something, she says, "After you hear what I gotta say, you're not gonna want nothing more to do with me—*or* my baby."

He can't imagine a situation in which that would be the case, but the last thing he wants to do is to make light of whatever this is about. He says nothing.

"You remember, Alan," she says, "that time when I told you all the bad things that happened to me? You know, my parents dying, and the rape, and Robbie dying? And then I said there were two more bad things?"

"I remember," Alan says. How could I possibly forget? he doesn't add.

"Well, I accidentally said there were two more things, which there are, but I only meant to say one more thing."

"You told me about your other fiancé," Alan says. "The one who fell off the building."

"You remember!" Marissa says, apparently surprised by this. "Anyways, the thing I didn't wanna say then I gotta say now.

"I told you once, near the beginning when we were going out, that it was a long time since I was in New York. Well, there was a time I used to go there every week. I would go every Saturday morning to do my clothes shopping. Early, before the stores got too crowded. So there was this one time, it was in June, not this last June and not the one before but the one before that. 1975 it was. I was crossing the street and just as I stepped off the curb the light turned red, but I kept crossing the street cause I figured I could make it across before the cars started turning into the crosswalk. But what happened is that when I was about halfway across the street I heard this pop—that's what it sounded like, a pop—and when I looked up I saw this taxicab that was turning into the crosswalk, except it wasn't moving, it was stopped. And then I heard this woman shout, 'Stephanie!, Stephanie!' And that's when I realized that a car had hit the taxicab from behind. I looked into the back seat of the cab then, and I saw the mother, she was a young woman, and I could barely make out a little girl and she didn't seem to be moving. And then I panicked, Alan, cause I knew I caused the accident by trying to run across the street against the light. But I panicked and ran away, so I didn't know how bad the little girl was hurt, or if she died maybe. But I knew that whatever happened it was my fault and I was gonna go to hell if that little girl died or was crippled for life or something.

"Anyways, once I could start thinking straight about what happened I drove out to Lucille Tedesco's—you know, Robbie's mother—and I told her what happened and I made her swear that if she heard on the news or read in the papers about the accident, that she wouldn't tell me, cause I didn't wanna know about the accident, which they mighta reported if the little girl died in it. But I kept hearing in my head that mother calling out her little daughter's name. And then I had to wait till later in the day, but as soon as I could I drove straight to church and made a confession, and I musta been in that confessional it seems like forever cause I couldn't stop crying. And then finally I went home, but what happened is that the next morning, as I was getting ready for church, without thinking I turned on the radio cause it looked like it might rain. And that's when I heard the announcer talking about the accident with the cab and all. And then he said that the little girl died."

Marissa falls silent. Her story has come to an end, but for Alan, the part of it he didn't already know—namely, that Marissa has known about Stephanie's death all along—makes him feel like he's been hauled into an alley and beaten to within an inch of his life. It's another piece of unbelievable news that life has blindly and indifferently seen fit to bestow upon him. And the irony of it is almost laughable. He decided not to seek a reconciliation with Marissa to spare her the knowledge that her impulsive act caused the death of a child. Except she already knew this! His decision to spare her unspeakable pain turns out not only to have been unnecessary but to have been a self-inflicted wound. He's certain that together they would have gotten past the fact that it was *his* daughter who died in the accident; it was knowledge of the death itself—*that* was what he wanted to protect her from.

And so this is the reality Alan is left with: Marissa is a married woman with a child on the way. She's moved on, whereas he feels stuck in a no-man's land between what might have been and what will never be.

"So that's the thing I never wanted to tell you," he hears Marissa say. "Or never wanted to tell no one. I killed that little girl, and I know God's gonna punish me for this. And now that you know, I can't believe you'd wanna have someone like me in your life, even if it means giving up your own baby."

Alan reflects on these last few words. Certainly he can understand why the idea that you might have been responsible for someone's death is something you'd want to keep to yourself, but he can't understand why Marissa seems to think that his knowing about this incident would change his mind about laying claim, to the extent that he could, to the child she's carrying.

"That's a terrible story," he says now, doing his best to

sound as if news of this incident has come as a total shock to him. "But you're not going to hell, Marissa. That's nonsense. And it doesn't mean that I want nothing to do with you. This changes nothing. The child you're carrying is still mine, and nothing you might have done in the past will change that."

"But I killed that little girl, I'm a murderer. I—"

"Marissa, please. I understand this is upsetting to you, that it's a heavy burden to carry around. But murderer!? That's just . . . You're not a murderer. You're just someone who did something you probably shouldn't have done. And besides"—and here he knows he's about to spout orthodoxy he rejected years ago. "Besides, you've atoned for your sin, if that's what it was. You made your confession. The slate has been wiped clean."

Marissa's face relaxes a bit at this thought.

Alan gets to his feet now and takes a step toward the kitchen. "But I'm not going to force the issue right now," he says looking down at her. "I need a little more time to think this through, but I know where you work. You'll be hearing from me again before too long."

Marissa looks up at him, and he seems to detect a rueful half-smile on her lips. That's when her strategy becomes clear to him: she told him about the accident in an attempt to drive him away for good. But if that didn't work she knew she would be quitting her job soon and he would have a hard time tracking her down, and maybe after a while he would just give up trying. Alan looks hard at her. She's a beautiful woman, no doubt, but she's not unwilling to resort to subterfuge to get her way. Then again, wouldn't a mother bear resort to subterfuge—or whatever was in her arsenal—to protect her cubs?

He turns to leave the stockroom but turns back.

"There's something I've been wondering, Marissa. Why didn't you tell me you were pregnant?"

Marissa closes her eyes, and after a moment he sees a few tears escape from them. Then she looks up at him.

"You *know* why, Alan. Cause if you knew I was pregnant you woulda wanted to marry me. You know, to do the right thing. But it wouldna been the right thing for us. It woulda never worked out between us. We had something special, Alan, something I'll never forget. But we both know we're better off apart."

Marissa gets to her feet. "You have to go now," she says. "This is too hard on me."

Alan takes the bus back to Manhattan, but instead of taking public transportation back to his apartment he takes a cab to Eighty-seventh Street and First Avenue, where he last parked his car. Soon he's crossing the George Washington Bridge and then heading west on Route 4. After another fifteen minutes or so he takes the exit for his hometown of Morehead.

Five minutes later he turns onto Carter Street and parks directly across from his house. With Mike permanently in the nursing home, Ralph rented out the Agnalini half of the duplex to an unmarried middle-aged man who's rumored to have a thing for adolescent boys, though Aunt Fiona has told Mike that she's seen no indication of this. Besides, she said, she's more concerned about the black family who moved into Dolly's old house. And the one who recently moved in down the block.

Not wanting his aunt Fiona to spot him, Alan puts the car back in drive and proceeds down the block. At the corner he makes a right and then a quick left. After one more block he arrives at the south entrance to Herrick Park— the three-blocks-long former vacant lot in which he spent much of his childhood and adolescent leisure hours, especially once Ralph made it clear that he had better things to do than to spend time with his little "brother."

Alan gets out of the car and walks slowly down the short path that leads to the park proper. The sky is cloudless with only a crescent moon for illumination, so Alan is certain no neighbors will see him wandering around the park after hours. His intention, though, isn't to wander so much as it's just to be there—to revisit his childhood in some small, imperfect way in the hope that doing so will provide him with some answers.

He walks farther into the park and halts about twenty yards from a chain-link fence which borders the entire three-blocks length of the park. Beyond the fence is a set of high hedges and beyond that a two-story factory. The Catholic school kids in his neighborhood (which meant just about everyone) used to blithely throw rocks through the factory windows and then confess that particular sin on Saturday afternoons, only to resume the practice once they'd gone to Mass on Sunday and received Holy Communion.

He wonders where those kids are now: Ralph Sonelli and Jimmy Muzia. Jimmy Dogan and Timmy Flynn. Bobby Santono, Dennis Viamonte . . . Of course, they're no longer kids; like Alan, they're grown men. Has any of them had a woman appear from out of the blue and say *You have a five-year-old daughter and I want you to be a father to her?* Has any had a pregnant woman say *Yes, the baby is yours but you'll never be part of its life?* Not likely on either count. No, each of them has his own story, maybe more troubling than Alan's, maybe less so. But the point is, in each case it's his story alone. And maybe that's the ultimate gift—that you get to live your own story, to have your own life.

Alan looks up at the sky and focuses on the warm breeze that buffets his face. Then he takes a deep breath as if to breathe in the very essence of life, although he knows that in his case, as it is with many other people, such a thing is not possible. Besides, communing with nature is not going to erase what he's feeling right now. Marissa was right: they never would have made it together, not long-term. This is something he knew from the beginning but lost sight of. At some point, probably shortly before his impulsive decision to go out to Hoboken and see if they could start over, Alan's certainty that they could never survive a life together for any meaningful length of time—this certainty found its way into the deep recesses of his subconscious. And without access to it, and despite his efforts to get over Marissa, he would sometimes find himself indulging in fantasies of a future life with her. But it wasn't about a life with her, ten or twenty or thirty years down the road. It was about a life with her as they are now—a young woman and a young man. Time doesn't stand still, though, and Marissa's pronouncement, back in the beauty salon, that it never could have worked for them—these words jolted Alan back to reality. So here he is, facing a simple fact that he has no choice but to accept: what he had with Marissa is in the past.

Fine, but that doesn't solve the other problem. Marissa wants to keep him from his child. That's what he has to deal with now. Except, he supposes, he's already dealt with it to an extent. On the drive out to Morehead, in addition to dealing with the resurrected certainty that the idea of a life with Marissa was a fool's errand, he asked himself whether pursuing some kind of shared-custody arrangement might not be another fool's errand. He can see now that this was a rhetorical question. Even if he could manage to secure such an arrangement, the tension between Marissa and him would be undeniable and unending. No child should be caught in the middle of something like this. Better to accept defeat and let Marissa raise her child as she sees fit.

On the other hand, he reminds himself, this is *his child* she's carrying. His flesh and blood, as he told her back in the beauty salon. He's already lost a child, and even though he never knew that child the loss was devastating for him. Now he has a second chance at fatherhood. And he knows he's grown to the point where he's ready—more than ready—to take on the responsibility.

And yet, even putting aside the certainty of difficulties with Marissa that would arise from his having a role in her baby's life, and even putting aside the negative effect this tension would have on the child's development—even dismissing these things as nothing more than life's tendency to be less than perfect—something tells him that demanding a role in the child's life would be wrong in some way. But in what way? Is fatherhood less important—or, at least, significantly less important—than motherhood? Doesn't a father—

And there, as if delivered to him from some unknown place, is his answer. The word "motherhood" has triggered the memory of Marissa's admission to him, on the afternoon they met, that her primary ambition in life was to be a mother. *Alls I ever wanted to be was a mother.* Those were her exact words. Why did he bury them deep in his subconscious? And months later, when he accidentally came across her diary and couldn't help reading some of it, didn't he read those exact words, or something like them? How could he have forgotten the fondest wish of the woman who unquestionably is the love of his life? But that's a question for another time. What's staring him in the face right now is the certainty that as a final gesture of love for this woman, he must give her what she wants: her child, to be raised her way, in conjunction with the man she chose to be her husband. *If you ever loved me . . .* That was her plea back in the beauty salon. *If you ever loved me, Alan, let me have my child.* How can he do otherwise?

So history has repeated itself, but with a twist: first the child he never met, now the child he'll never meet.

He looks up at the factory again and then to the vast expanse of sky above it. No skywriting appears there to explain why a person's life plays out the way it does. A younger Alan might have stood there for some time, pondering the inexplicable. The older version turns and heads back to his car.